NORMAL PEOPLE

Sally Rooney was born in 1991 and lives in Dublin. Her work has appeared in the *New Yorker*, *Granta*, *The White Review*, *The Dublin Review* and *The Stinging Fly*. Her debut novel, *Conversations with Friends*, was a *Sunday Times*, *Observer* and *Telegraph* Book of the Year and was shortlisted for the Dylan Thomas Prize, the Desmond Elliott Prize and the Rathbones Folio Prize. Rooney is the winner of the *Sunday Times*/PFD Young Writer of the Year Award.

by the same author

CONVERSATIONS WITH FRIENDS

SALLY ROONEY

Normal People

FABER & FABER

First published in the UK in 2018
by Faber & Faber Ltd
Bloomsbury House
74–77 Great Russell Street
London WC1B 3DA

This export edition published in 2018

Typeset by Typo•glyphix
Printed and bound by CPI Group (UK) Ltd, Croydon CR0 4YY

A CIP record for this book
is available from the British Library

ISBN 978-0-571-34729-2

It is one of the secrets in that change of mental poise which has been fitly named conversion, that to many among us neither heaven nor earth has any revelation till some personality touches theirs with a peculiar influence, subduing them into receptiveness.

George Eliot, *Daniel Deronda*

January 2011

Marianne answers the door when Connell rings the bell. She's still wearing her school uniform, but she's taken off the sweater, so it's just the blouse and skirt, and she has no shoes on, only tights.

Oh, hey, he says.

Come on in.

She turns and walks down the hall. He follows her, closing the door behind him. Down a few steps in the kitchen, his mother Lorraine is peeling off a pair of rubber gloves. Marianne hops onto the countertop and picks up an open jar of chocolate spread, in which she has left a teaspoon.

Marianne was telling me you got your mock results today, Lorraine says.

We got English back, he says. They come back separately. Do you want to head on?

Lorraine folds the rubber gloves up neatly and replaces them below the sink. Then she starts unclipping her hair. To Connell this seems like something she could accomplish in the car.

And I hear you did very well, she says.

He was top of the class, says Marianne.

Right, Connell says. Marianne did pretty good too. Can we go?

Lorraine pauses in the untying of her apron.

I didn't realise we were in a rush, she says.

He puts his hands in his pockets and suppresses an irritable sigh, but suppresses it with an audible intake of breath, so that it still sounds like a sigh.

I just have to pop up and take a load out of the dryer, says Lorraine. And then we'll be off. Okay?

He says nothing, merely hanging his head while Lorraine leaves the room.

Do you want some of this? Marianne says.

She's holding out the jar of chocolate spread. He presses his hands down slightly further into his pockets, as if trying to store his entire body in his pockets all at once.

No, thanks, he says.

Did you get your French results today?

Yesterday.

He puts his back against the fridge and watches her lick the spoon. In school he and Marianne affect not to know each other. People know that Marianne lives in the white mansion with the driveway and that Connell's mother is a cleaner, but no one knows of the special relationship between these facts.

I got an A1, he says. What did you get in German?

An A1, she says. Are you bragging?

You're going to get six hundred, are you?

She shrugs. You probably will, she says.

Well, you're smarter than me.

Don't feel bad. I'm smarter than everyone.

Marianne is grinning now. She exercises an open contempt for people in school. She has no friends and spends her lunchtimes alone reading novels. A lot of people really hate her. Her father died when she was thirteen and Connell has heard she has a mental illness now or something. It's true she is the smartest person in school. He dreads being left alone with her like this, but he also finds himself fantasising about things he could say to impress her.

You're not top of the class in English, he points out.

She licks her teeth, unconcerned.

Maybe you should give me grinds, Connell, she says.

He feels his ears get hot. She's probably just being glib and not suggestive, but if she is being suggestive it's only to degrade him by association, since she is considered an object of disgust. She wears ugly thick-soled flat shoes and doesn't put make-up on her face. People have said she doesn't shave her legs or anything. Connell once heard that she spilled chocolate ice cream on herself in the school lunchroom, and she went to the girls' bathrooms and took her blouse off to wash it in the sink. That's a popular story about her, everyone has heard it. If she wanted, she could make a big show of saying hello to Connell in school. See you this afternoon, she could say, in front of everyone. Undoubtedly it would put him in an awkward position, which is the kind of thing she usually seems to enjoy. But she has never done it.

What were you talking to Miss Neary about today? says Marianne.

Oh. Nothing. I don't know. Exams.

Marianne twists the spoon around inside the jar.

Does she fancy you or something? Marianne says.

Connell watches her moving the spoon. His ears still feel very hot.

Why do you say that? he says.

God, you're not having an affair with her, are you?

Obviously not. Do you think it's funny joking about that?

Sorry, says Marianne.

She has a focused expression, like she's looking through his eyes into the back of his head.

You're right, it's not funny, she says. I'm sorry.

He nods, looks around the room for a bit, digs the toe of his shoe into a groove between the tiles.

Sometimes I feel like she does act kind of weird around me, he says. But I wouldn't say that to people or anything.

Even in class I think she's very flirtatious towards you.

Do you really think that?

Marianne nods. He rubs at his neck. Miss Neary teaches Economics. His supposed feelings for her are widely discussed in school. Some people are even saying that he tried to add her on Facebook, which he didn't and would never do. Actually he doesn't do or say anything to her, he just sits there quietly while she does and says things to him. She keeps him back after class sometimes to talk about his life direction, and once she actually touched the knot of his school tie. He can't tell people about the way she acts because they'll think he's trying to brag about it. In class he feels too embarrassed and annoyed to concentrate on the lesson, he just sits there staring at the textbook until the bar graphs start to blur.

People are always going on at me that I fancy her or whatever, he says. But I actually don't, at all. I mean, you don't think I'm playing into it when she acts like that, do you?

Not that I've seen.

He wipes his palms down on his school shirt unthinkingly. Everyone is so convinced of his attraction to Miss Neary that sometimes he starts to doubt his own instincts about it. What if, at some level above or below his own perception, he does actually desire her? He doesn't even really know what desire is supposed to feel like. Any time he has had sex in real life, he has found it so stressful as to be largely unpleasant, leading him to suspect that there's something wrong with him, that he's unable to be intimate with women, that he's somehow developmentally impaired. He lies there afterwards and thinks: I hated that so much that I feel sick. Is that just the way he is? Is the nausea he feels when Miss Neary leans over his desk actually his way of experiencing a sexual thrill? How would he know?

I could go to Mr Lyons for you if you want, says Marianne. I won't say you told me anything, I'll just say I noticed it myself.

Jesus, no. Definitely not. Don't say anything about it to anyone, okay?

Okay, alright.

He looks at her to confirm she's being serious, and then nods.

It's not your fault she acts like that with you, says Marianne. You're not doing anything wrong.

Quietly he says: Why does everyone else think I fancy her, then?

Maybe because you blush a lot when she talks to you. But you know, you blush at everything, you just have that complexion.

He gives a short, unhappy laugh. Thanks, he says.

Well, you do.

Yeah, I'm aware.

You're blushing now actually, says Marianne.

5

He closes his eyes, pushes his tongue against the roof of his mouth. He can hear Marianne laughing.

Why do you have to be so harsh on people? he says.

I'm not being harsh. I don't care if you're blushing, I won't tell anyone.

Just because you won't tell people doesn't mean you can say whatever you want.

Okay, she says. Sorry.

He turns and looks out the window at the garden. Really the garden is more like 'grounds'. It includes a tennis court and a large stone statue in the shape of a woman. He looks out at the 'grounds' and moves his face close to the cool breath of the glass. When people tell that story about Marianne washing her blouse in the sink, they act like it's just funny, but Connell thinks the real purpose of the story is something else. Marianne has never been with anyone in school, no one has ever seen her undressed, no one even knows if she likes boys or girls, she won't tell anyone. People resent that about her, and Connell thinks that's why they tell the story, as a way of gawking at something they're not allowed to see.

I don't want to get into a fight with you, she says.

We're not fighting.

I know you probably hate me, but you're the only person who actually talks to me.

I never said I hated you, he says.

That gets her attention, and she looks up. Confused, he continues looking away from her, but in the corner of his eye he still sees her watching. When he talks to Marianne he has a sense of total privacy between them. He could tell her anything about himself, even weird things, and she would never repeat them, he knows that. Being alone with her is like opening a door away from normal life and then closing it behind him. He's not frightened of her, actually she's a pretty relaxed person, but he fears being around her, because of the confusing way he finds himself behaving, the things he says that he would never ordinarily say.

A few weeks ago when he was waiting for Lorraine in the hall, Marianne came downstairs in a bathrobe. It was just a plain white bathrobe, tied in the normal way. Her hair was wet, and her skin had that glistening look like she had just been applying face cream. When she saw Connell, she hesitated on the stairs and said: I didn't know you were here, sorry. Maybe she seemed flustered, but not really badly or anything. Then she went back up to her room. After she left he stood there in the hall waiting. He knew she was probably getting dressed in her room, and whatever clothes she was wearing when she came back down would be the clothes she had chosen to put on after she saw him in the hall. Anyway Lorraine was ready to go before Marianne reappeared so he never did get to see what clothes she had put on. It wasn't like he deeply cared to know. He certainly didn't tell anyone in school about it, that he had seen her in a bathrobe, or that she looked flustered, it wasn't anyone's business to know.

Well, I like you, Marianne says.

For a few seconds he says nothing, and the intensity of the privacy between them is very severe, pressing in on him with an almost physical pressure on his face and body. Then Lorraine comes back into the kitchen, tying her scarf around her neck. She does a little knock on the door even though it's already open.

Good to go? she says.

Yeah, says Connell.

Thanks for everything, Lorraine, says Marianne. See you next week.

Connell is already heading out the kitchen door when his mother says: You can say goodbye, can't you? He turns to look over his shoulder but finds he cannot actually look Marianne in the eye, so he addresses himself to the floor instead. Right, bye, he says. He doesn't wait to hear her reply.

In the car his mother puts on her seatbelt and shakes her head. You could be a bit nicer to her, she says. She doesn't exactly have an easy time of it in school.

He puts the keys in the ignition, glances in the rear-view. I'm nice to her, he says.

She's actually a very sensitive person, says Lorraine.

Can we talk about something else?

Lorraine makes a face. He stares out the windshield and pretends not to see.

Three Weeks Later

(FEBRUARY 2011)

She sits at her dressing table looking at her face in the mirror. Her face lacks definition around the cheeks and jaw. It's a face like a piece of technology, and her two eyes are cursors blinking. Or it's reminiscent of the moon reflected in something, wobbly and oblique. It expresses everything all at once, which is the same as expressing nothing. To wear make-up for this occasion would be, she concludes, embarrassing. Without breaking eye contact with herself, she dips her finger in an open pot of clear lip balm and applies it.

Downstairs, when she takes her coat off the hook, her brother Alan comes out from the living room.

Where are you going? he says.

Out.

Where's out?

She puts her arms through the sleeves of her coat and adjusts the collar. She's beginning to feel nervous now and hopes her silence is communicating insolence rather than uncertainty.

Just out for a walk, she says.

Alan moves to stand in front of the door.

Well, I know you're not going out to meet friends, he says. Because you don't have any friends, do you?

No, I don't.

She smiles now, a placid smile, hoping that this gesture of

submission will placate him and he'll move away from the door. Instead he says: What are you doing that for?

What? she says.

This weird smile you're doing.

He mimics her face, contorted into an ugly grin, teeth bared. Though he's grinning, the force and extremity of this impersonation make him look angry.

Are you happy that you don't have friends? he says.

No.

Still smiling, she takes two small steps backwards, and then turns and walks towards the kitchen, where there's a patio door onto the garden. Alan walks after her. He grabs her by the upper arm and tugs her back from the door. She feels her jaw tighten. His fingers compress her arm through her jacket.

If you go crying to Mam about this, says Alan.

No, says Marianne, no. I'm just going out for a walk now. Thank you.

He releases her and she slips out through the patio door, closing it behind her. Outside the air feels very cold and her teeth start to chatter. She walks around the side of the house, down the driveway and out into the street. Her arm is throbbing where he grabbed it. She takes her phone from a pocket and composes a text, repeatedly hitting the wrong key, deleting and retyping. Finally she sends it: On my way. Before she puts the phone back, she receives a reply: cool see you soon.

At the end of last term, the school soccer team reached the final of some competition and everyone in the year had to take the last three classes off to go and watch them. Marianne had never seen them play before. She had no interest in sport and suffered anxiety related to physical education. In the bus on the way to the match she just listened to her headphones, no one spoke to her. Out the window: black cattle, green meadows, white houses with brown roof tiles. The football team were all together at the top of the bus, drinking water and slapping each other on the shoulders to raise morale. Marianne had the sense that her real life was happening somewhere very far away, happening without her, and she didn't know if she would ever find out where it was and become part of it. She had that feeling in school often, but it wasn't accompanied by any specific images of what the real life might look or feel like. All she knew was that when it started, she wouldn't need to imagine it anymore.

It stayed dry for the match. They had been brought there for the purpose of standing at the sidelines and cheering. Marianne was near the goalposts, with Karen and some of the other girls. Everyone other than Marianne seemed to know the school chants off by heart somehow, with lyrics she had never heard before. By half-time it was still nil-all, and Miss Keaney handed around boxes of juice and energy bars. For the second half, the ends changed around, and the school forwards were playing near where Marianne was standing. Connell Waldron was the centre forward. She could see him standing there in his football kit, the shiny white shorts, the school jersey with number nine on the back. He had very good posture, more so than any of the other players. His figure was like a long elegant line drawn with a brush. When the ball moved towards their end of the pitch he tended to run around and maybe throw one of his hands in the air, and then he went back to standing still. It was pleasurable to watch him, and she didn't think he knew or cared where she was standing. After school some day she could tell him she had been watching him, and he'd laugh at her and call her weird.

At seventy minutes Aidan Kennedy brought the ball up the left side of the pitch and crossed it over to Connell, who took a shot from the corner of the penalty area, over the heads of the defenders, and it spun into the back of the net. Everyone screamed, even Marianne, and Karen threw her arm around Marianne's waist and squeezed it. They were cheering together, they had seen something magical which dissolved the ordinary social relations between them. Miss Keaney was whistling and stamping her feet. On the pitch Connell and Aidan embraced like reunited brothers. Connell was so beautiful. It occurred to Marianne how much she wanted to see him having sex with someone; it didn't have to be her, it could be anybody. It would be beautiful just to watch him. She knew these were the kind of thoughts that made her different from other people in school, and weirder.

Marianne's classmates all seem to like school so much and find it normal. To dress in the same uniform every day, to comply at all times with arbitrary rules, to be scrutinised and monitored for misbehaviour, this is normal to them. They have no sense of the school as an oppressive environment. Marianne had a row with the History teacher, Mr Kerrigan, last year because he caught her looking out a window during class, and no one in the class took her side. It seemed so obviously insane to her then that she should have to dress up in a costume every morning and be herded around a huge building all day, and that she wasn't even allowed to move her eyes where she wanted, even her eye movements fell under the jurisdiction of school rules. You're not learning if you're staring out the window daydreaming, Mr Kerrigan said. Marianne, who had lost her temper by then, snapped back: Don't delude yourself, I have nothing to learn from you.

Connell said recently that he remembered that incident, and that at the time he'd felt she was being harsh on Mr Kerrigan, who was actually one of the more reasonable teachers. But I see what you're saying, Connell added. About feeling a bit imprisoned in the school, I do see that. He should have let you look out the window, I would agree there. You weren't doing any harm.

After their conversation in the kitchen, when she told him she liked him, Connell started coming over to her house more often. He would arrive early to pick his mother up from work and hang around in the living room not saying much, or stand by the fireplace with his hands in his pockets. Marianne never asked why he came over. They talked a little bit, or she talked and he nodded. He told her she should try reading *The Communist Manifesto*, he thought she would like it, and he offered to write down the title for her so she wouldn't forget. I know what *The Communist Manifesto* is called, she said. He shrugged, okay. After a moment he added, smiling: You're trying to act superior, but like, you haven't even read it. She had to laugh then, and he laughed because she did. They couldn't look at each other when they were laughing, they had to look into corners of the room, or at their feet.

Connell seemed to understand how she felt about school; he said he liked hearing her opinions. You hear enough of them in class, she said. Matter-of-factly he replied: You act different in

13

class, you're not really like that. He seemed to think Marianne had access to a range of different identities, between which she slipped effortlessly. This surprised her, because she usually felt confined inside one single personality, which was always the same regardless of what she did or said. She had tried to be different in the past, as a kind of experiment, but it had never worked. If she was different with Connell, the difference was not happening inside herself, in her personhood, but in between them, in the dynamic. Sometimes she made him laugh, but other days he was taciturn, inscrutable, and after he left she would feel high, nervous, at once energetic and terribly drained.

He followed her into the study last week while she was looking for a copy of *The Fire Next Time* to lend him. He stood there inspecting the bookshelves, with his top shirt button undone and school tie loosened. She found the book and handed it to him, and he sat down on the window seat looking at the back cover. She sat beside him and asked him if his friends Eric and Rob knew that he read so much outside school.

They wouldn't be interested in that stuff, he said.

You mean they're not interested in the world around them.

Connell made the face he always made when she criticised his friends, an inexpressive frown. Not in the same way, he said. They have their own interests. I don't think they'd be reading books about racism and all that.

Right, they're too busy bragging about who they're having sex with, she said.

He paused for a second, like his ears had pricked up at this remark but he didn't know exactly how to respond. Yeah, they do a bit of that, he said. I'm not defending it, I know they can be annoying.

Doesn't it bother you?

He paused again. Most of it wouldn't, he said. They do some stuff that goes a bit over the line and that would annoy me obviously. But at the end of the day they're my friends, you know. It's different for you.

She looked at him, but he was examining the spine of the book.

Why is it different? she said.

He shrugged, bending the book cover back and forth. She felt frustrated. Her face and hands were hot. He kept on looking at the book although he'd certainly read all the text on the back by then. She was attuned to the presence of his body in a microscopic way, as if the ordinary motion of his breathing was powerful enough to make her ill.

You know you were saying the other day that you like me, he said. In the kitchen you said it, when we were talking about school.

Yeah.

Did you mean like as a friend, or what?

She stared down into her lap. She was wearing a corduroy skirt and in the light from the window she could see it was flecked with pieces of lint.

No, not just as a friend, she said.

Oh, okay. I was wondering.

He sat there, nodding to himself.

I'm kind of confused about what I feel, he added. I think it would be awkward in school if anything happened with us.

No one would have to know.

He looked up at her, directly, with total attention. She knew he was going to kiss her, and he did. His lips were soft. His tongue moved into her mouth slightly. Then it was over and he was drawing away. He seemed to remember he was holding the book, and began to look at it again.

That was nice, she said.

He nodded, swallowed, glanced down at the book once more. His attitude was so sheepish, as if it had been rude of her even to make reference to the kiss, that Marianne started to laugh. He looked flustered then.

Alright, he said. What are you laughing for?

Nothing.

You're acting like you've never kissed anyone before.

Well, I haven't, she said.

He put his hand over his face. She laughed again, she couldn't stop herself, and then he was laughing too. His ears were very red and he was shaking his head. After a few seconds he stood up, holding the book in his hand.

Don't go telling people in school about this, okay? he said.

Like I would talk to anyone in school.

He left the room. Weakly she crumpled off the seat, down onto the floor, with her legs stretched out in front of her like a rag doll. While she sat there she felt as if Connell had been visiting her house only to test her, and she had passed the test, and the kiss was a communication that said: You passed. She thought of the way he'd laughed when she said she'd never kissed anyone before. For another person to laugh that way might have been cruel, but it wasn't like that with him. They'd been laughing together, at a shared situation they'd found themselves in, though how to describe the situation or what was funny about it Marianne didn't know exactly.

The next morning before German class she sat watching her

classmates shove each other off the storage heaters, shrieking and giggling. When the lesson began they listened quietly to an audio tape of a German woman speaking about a party she had missed. *Es tut mir sehr leid.* In the afternoon it started snowing, thick grey flakes that fluttered past the windows and melted on the gravel. Everything looked and felt sensuous: the stale smell of classrooms, the tinny intercom bell that sounded between lessons, the dark austere trees that stood like apparitions around the basketball court. The slow routine work of copying out notes in different-coloured pens on fresh blue-and-white lined paper. Connell, as usual, did not speak to Marianne in school or even look at her. She watched him across classrooms as he conjugated verbs, chewing on the end of his pen. On the other side of the cafeteria at lunchtime, smiling about something with his friends. Their secret weighed inside her body pleasurably, pressing down on her pelvic bone when she moved.

She didn't see him after school that day, or the next. On Thursday afternoon his mother was working again and he arrived early to pick her up. Marianne had to answer the door because no one else was home. He had changed out of his school uniform, he was wearing black jeans and a sweatshirt. When she saw him she had an instinct to run away and hide her face. Lorraine's in the kitchen, she said. Then she turned and went upstairs to her room and closed the door. She lay face down on the bed breathing into the pillow. Who was this person Connell anyway? She felt she knew him very intimately, but what reason did she have to feel that? Just because he had kissed her once, with no explanation, and then warned her not to tell anyone? After a minute or two she heard a knock on her bedroom door and she sat up. Come in, she said. He opened the door and, giving her an enquiring look as if to see whether he was welcome, entered the room and closed the door behind him.

Are you pissed off with me? he said.

No. Why would I be?

He shrugged. Idly he wandered over to the bed and sat down. She was sitting cross-legged, holding her ankles. They sat there in silence for a few moments. Then he got onto the bed with her. He touched her leg and she lay back against the pillow. Boldly she asked if he was going to kiss her again. He said: What do you think? This struck her as a highly cryptic and sophisticated thing to say. Anyway he did start to kiss her. She told him that it was nice and he just said nothing. She felt she would do anything to make him like her, to make him say out loud that he liked her. He put his hand under her school blouse. In his ear, she said: Can we take our clothes off? He had his hand inside her bra. Definitely not, he said. This is stupid anyway, Lorraine is right downstairs. He called his mother by her first name like that. Marianne said: She never comes up here. He shook his head and said: No, we should stop. He sat up and looked down at her.

You were tempted for a second there, she said.

Not really.

I tempted you.

He was shaking his head, smiling. You're such a strange person, he said.

Now she's standing in his driveway, where his car is parked. He texted her the address, it's number 33: a terraced house with pebble-dash walls, net curtains, a tiny concrete yard. She can see a light switched on in the upstairs window. It's hard to believe he really lives in there, a house she has never been inside or even seen before. She's wearing a black sweater, grey skirt, cheap black underwear. Her legs are shaved meticulously, her underarms are smooth and chalky with deodorant, and her nose is running a little. She rings the doorbell and hears his footsteps coming down the stairs. He opens the door. Before he lets her in he looks over her shoulder, to make sure that no one has seen her arrive.

One Month Later

(MARCH 2011)

They're talking about their college applications. Marianne is lying with the bedsheet pulled carelessly over her body, and Connell's sitting up with her MacBook in his lap. She's already applied for History and Politics in Trinity. He's put down Law in Galway, but now he thinks that he might change it, because, as Marianne has pointed out, he has no interest in Law. He can't even visually imagine himself as a lawyer, wearing a tie and so on, possibly helping to convict people of crimes. He just put it down because he couldn't think of anything else.

You should study English, says Marianne.

Do you think I should, or are you joking?

I think you should. It's the only subject you really enjoy in school. And you spend all your free time reading.

He looks at the laptop blankly, and then at the thin yellow bedsheet draped over her body, which casts a lilac triangle of shadow on her breast.

Not all my free time, he says.

She smiles. Plus the class will be full of girls, she says, so you'll be a total stud.

Yeah. I'm not sure about the job prospects, though.

Oh, who cares? The economy's fucked anyway.

The laptop screen has gone black now and he taps the trackpad to light it up again. The college applications webpage stares back at him.

After the first time they had sex, Marianne stayed the night in his house. He had never been with a girl who was a virgin before. In total he had only had sex a small number of times, and always with girls who went on to tell the whole school about it afterwards. He'd had to hear his actions repeated back to him later in the locker room: his errors, and, so much worse, his excruciating attempts at tenderness, performed in gigantic pantomime. With Marianne it was different, because everything was between them only, even awkward or difficult things. He could do or say anything he wanted with her and no one would ever find out. It gave him a vertiginous, light-headed feeling to think about it. When he touched her that night she was so wet, and she rolled her eyes back into her head and said: God, yes. And she was allowed to say it, no one would know. He was afraid he would come then just from touching her like that.

In the hallway the next morning he kissed her goodbye and her mouth tasted alkaline, like toothpaste. Thanks, she said. Then she left, before he understood what he was being thanked for. He put the bedsheets in the washing machine and took fresh linen from the hot press. He was thinking about what a secretive, independent-minded person Marianne was, that she could come over to his house and let him have sex with her, and she felt no need to tell anyone about it. She just let things happen, like nothing meant anything to her.

Lorraine got home that afternoon. Before she'd even put her keys on the table she said: Is that the washing machine? Connell nodded. She crouched down and looked through the round glass window into the drum, where his sheets were tossing around in the froth.

I'm not going to ask, she said.

What?

She started to fill the kettle, while he leaned against the countertop.

Why your bedclothes are in the wash, she said. I'm not asking.

He rolled his eyes just for something to do with his face. You think the worst of everything, he said.

She laughed, fixing the kettle into its cradle and hitting the switch. Excuse me, she said. I must be the most permissive mother of anyone in your school. As long as you're using protection, you can do what you want.

He said nothing. The kettle started to warm up and she took a clean mug down from the press.

Well? she said. Is that a yes?

Yes what? Obviously I didn't have unprotected sex with anyone while you were gone. Jesus.

So go on, what's her name?

He left the room then but he could hear his mother laughing as he went up the stairs. His life is always giving her amusement.

In school on Monday he had to avoid looking at Marianne or interacting with her in any way. He carried the secret around like something large and hot, like an overfull tray of hot drinks that he had to carry everywhere and never spill. She just acted the same as always, like it never happened, reading her book at the lockers as usual, getting into pointless arguments. At lunch-time on Tuesday, Rob started asking questions about Connell's mother working in Marianne's house, and Connell just ate his lunch and tried not to make any facial expressions.

Would you ever go in there yourself? Rob said. Into the mansion.

Connell jogged his bag of chips in his hand and then peered into it. I've been in there a few times, yeah, he said.

What's it like inside?

He shrugged. I don't know, he said. Big, obviously.

What's she like in her natural habitat? Rob said.

I don't know.

I'd say she thinks of you as her butler, does she?

Connell wiped his mouth with the back of his hand. It felt greasy. His chips were too salty and he had a headache.

I doubt it, Connell said.

But your mam is her housemaid, isn't she?

Well, she's just a cleaner. She's only there like twice a week, I don't think they interact much.

Does Marianne not have a little bell she would ring to get her attention, no? Rob said.

Connell said nothing. He didn't understand the situation with Marianne at that point. After he talked to Rob he told himself it was over, he'd just had sex with her once to see what it was like, and he wouldn't see her again. Even as he was saying all this to himself, however, he could hear another part of his brain, in a different voice, saying: Yes you will. It was a part of his consciousness he had never really known before, this inexplicable drive to act on perverse and secret desires. He found himself fantasising about her in class that afternoon, at the back of Maths, or when they were supposed to be playing rounders. He would think of her small wet mouth and suddenly run out of breath, and have to struggle to fill his lungs.

That afternoon he went to her house after school. All the way over in the car he kept the radio on very loud so he didn't have to think about what he was doing. When they went upstairs he didn't say anything, he let her talk. That's so good, she kept saying. That feels so good. Her body was all soft and white like flour dough. He seemed to fit perfectly inside her. Physically it just felt right, and he understood why people did insane things for sexual reasons then. In fact he understood a lot of things about the adult world that had previously seemed mysterious. But why Marianne? It wasn't like she was so attractive. Some people thought she was the ugliest girl in school. What kind of person would want to do this with her? And yet he was there, whatever kind of person he was, doing it. She asked him if it felt good and he pretended he didn't hear her. She was on her hands and knees so he couldn't see her facial expression or read into it what she was thinking. After a few seconds she said in a much smaller voice: Am I doing something wrong? He closed his eyes.

No, he said. I like it.

Her breath sounded ragged then. He pulled her hips back against his body and then released her slightly. She made a noise like she was choking. He did it again and she told him she was going to come. That's good, he said. He said this like nothing could be more ordinary to him. His decision to drive to Marianne's house that afternoon suddenly seemed very correct and intelligent, maybe the only intelligent thing he had ever done in his life.

After they were finished he asked her what he should do with the condom. Without lifting her face off the pillow she said: You can just leave it on the floor. Her face was pink and damp. He did what she said and then lay on his back looking up at the light fixtures. I like you so much, Marianne said. Connell felt a pleasurable sorrow come over him, which brought him close to tears. Moments of emotional pain arrived like this, meaningless or at least indecipherable. Marianne lived a drastically free life, he could see that. He was trapped by various considerations. He cared what people thought of him. He even cared what Marianne thought, that was obvious now.

Multiple times he has tried writing his thoughts about Marianne down on paper in an effort to make sense of them. He's moved by a desire to describe in words exactly how she looks and speaks. Her hair and clothing. The copy of *Swann's Way* she reads at lunchtime in the school cafeteria, with a dark French painting on the cover and a mint-coloured spine. Her long fingers turning the pages. She's not leading the same kind of life as other people. She acts so worldly at times, making him feel ignorant, but then she can be so naive. He wants to understand how her mind works. If he silently decides not to say something when they're talking, Marianne will ask 'what?' within one or two seconds. This 'what?' question seems to him to contain so much: not just the forensic attentiveness to his silences that allows her to ask in the first place, but a desire for total communication, a sense that anything unsaid is an unwelcome interruption between them. He writes these things down, long run-on sentences with too many dependent clauses, sometimes connected with breathless semicolons, as if he wants to recreate a precise copy of Marianne in print, as if he can preserve her completely for future review. Then he turns a new page in the notebook so he doesn't have to look at what he's done.

What are you thinking about? says Marianne now.

She's tucking her hair behind her ear.

College, he says.

You should apply for English in Trinity.

He stares at the webpage again. Lately he's consumed by a sense that he is in fact two separate people, and soon he will have to choose which person to be on a full-time basis, and leave the other person behind. He has a life in Carricklea, he has friends. If he went to college in Galway he could stay with the same social group, really, and live the life he has always planned on, getting a good degree, having a nice girlfriend. People would say he had done well for himself. On the other hand, he could go to Trinity like Marianne. Life would be different then. He would start going to dinner parties and having conversations about the Greek bailout. He could fuck some weird-looking girls who turn out to be bisexual. I've read *The Golden Notebook*, he could tell them. It's true, he has read it. After that he would never come back to Carricklea, he would go somewhere else, London, or Barcelona. People would not necessarily think he had done well; some people might think he had gone very bad, while others would forget about him entirely. What would Lorraine think? She would want him to be happy, and not care what others said. But the old Connell, the one all his friends know: that person would be dead in a way, or worse, buried alive, and screaming under the earth.

Then we'd both be in Dublin, he says. I bet you'd pretend you didn't know me if we bumped into each other.

Marianne says nothing at first. The longer she stays silent the more nervous he feels, like maybe she really would pretend not to know him, and the idea of being beneath her notice gives him a panicked feeling, not only about Marianne personally but about his future, about what's possible for him.

Then she says: I would never pretend not to know you, Connell.

The silence becomes very intense after that. For a few seconds he lies still. Of course, he pretends not to know Marianne in school, but he didn't mean to bring that up. That's just the way it has to be. If people found out what he has been doing with Marianne, in secret, while ignoring her every day in school, his life would be over. He would walk down the hallway and people's eyes would follow him, like he was a serial killer, or worse. His friends don't think of him as a deviant person, a person who could say to Marianne Sheridan, in broad daylight, completely sober: Is it okay if I come in your mouth? With his friends he acts normal. He and Marianne have their own private life in his room where no one can bother them, so there's no reason to mix up the separate worlds. Still, he can tell he has lost his footing in their discussion and left an opening for this subject to arise, though he didn't want it to, and now he has to say something.

Would you not? he says.

No.

Alright, I'll put down English in Trinity, then.

Really? she says.

Yeah. I don't care that much about getting a job anyway.

She gives him a little smile, like she feels she has won the argument. He likes to give her that feeling. For a moment it seems possible to keep both worlds, both versions of his life, and to move in between them just like moving through a door.

He can have the respect of someone like Marianne and also be well liked in school, he can form secret opinions and preferences, no conflict has to arise, he never has to choose one thing over another. With only a little subterfuge he can live two entirely separate existences, never confronting the ultimate question of what to do with himself or what kind of person he is. This thought is so consoling that for a few seconds he avoids meeting Marianne's eye, wanting to sustain the belief for just a little longer. He knows that when he looks at her, he won't be able to believe it anymore.

Six Weeks Later

(APRIL 2011)

They have her name on a list. She shows the bouncer her ID. When she gets inside, the interior is low-lit, cavernous, vaguely purple, with long bars on either side and steps down to a dance floor. It smells of stale alcohol and the flat tinny ring of dry ice. Some of the other girls from the fundraising committee are sitting around a table already, looking at lists. Hi, Marianne says. They turn around and look at her.

Hello, says Lisa. Don't you scrub up well?

You look gorgeous, says Karen.

Rachel Moran says nothing. Everyone knows that Rachel is the most popular girl in school, but no one is allowed to say this. Instead everyone has to pretend not to notice that their social lives are arranged hierarchically, with certain people at the top, some jostling at mid-level, and others lower down. Marianne sometimes sees herself at the very bottom of the ladder, but at other times she pictures herself off the ladder completely, not affected by its mechanics, since she does not actually desire popularity or do anything to make it belong to her. From her vantage point it is not obvious what rewards the ladder provides, even to those who really are at the top. She rubs her upper arm and says: Thanks. Would anyone like a drink? I'm going to the bar anyway.

I thought you didn't drink alcohol, says Rachel.

I'll have a bottle of West Coast Cooler, Karen says. If you're sure.

Wine is the only alcoholic beverage Marianne has ever tried, but when she goes to the bar she decides to order a gin and tonic. The barman looks frankly at her breasts while she's talking. Marianne had no idea men really did such things outside of films and TV, and the experience gives her a little thrill of femininity. She's wearing a filmy black dress that clings to her body. The place is still almost empty now, though the event has technically started. Back at the table Karen thanks her extravagantly for the drink. I'll get you back, she says. Don't worry about it, says Marianne, waving her hand.

Eventually people start arriving. The music comes on, a pounding Destiny's Child remix, and Rachel gives Marianne the book of raffle tickets and explains the pricing system. Marianne was voted onto the Debs fundraising committee presumably as some kind of joke, but she has to help organise the events anyway. Ticket book in hand, she continues to hover beside the other girls. She's used to observing these people from a distance, almost scientifically, but tonight, having to make conversation and smile politely, she's no longer an observer but an intruder, and an awkward one. She sells some tickets, dispensing change from the pouch in her purse, she buys more drinks, she glances at the door and looks away in disappointment.

The lads are fairly late, says Lisa.

Of all the possible lads, Marianne knows who is specified: Rob, with whom Lisa has an on-again off-again relationship, and his friends Eric, Jack Hynes and Connell Waldron. Their lateness has not escaped Marianne's notice.

If they don't show up I will actually murder Connell, says Rachel. He told me yesterday they were definitely coming.

Marianne says nothing. Rachel often talks about Connell this way, alluding to private conversations that have happened between them, as if they are special confidants. Connell ignores this behaviour, but he also ignores the hints Marianne drops about it when they're alone together.

They're probably still pre-drinking in Rob's, says Lisa.

They'll be absolutely binned by the time they get here, says Karen.

Marianne takes her phone from her bag and writes Connell a text message: Lively discussion here on the subject of your absence. Are you planning to come at all? Within thirty seconds he replies: yeah jack just got sick everywhere so we had to put him in a taxi etc. on our way soon though. how are you getting on socialising with people. Marianne writes back: I'm the new popular girl in school now. Everyone's carrying me around the dance floor chanting my name. She puts her phone back in her bag. Nothing would feel more exhilarating to her at this moment than to say: They'll be on their way shortly. How much terrifying and bewildering status would accrue to her in this one moment, how destabilising it would be, how destructive.

Although Carricklea is the only place Marianne has ever lived, it's not a town she knows particularly well. She doesn't go drinking in the pubs on Main Street, and before tonight she had never been to the town's only nightclub. She has never visited the Knocklyon housing estate. She doesn't know the name of the river that runs brown and bedraggled past the

Centra and behind the church car park, snagging thin plastic bags in its current, or where the river goes next. Who would tell her? The only time she leaves the house is to go to school, and the enforced Mass trip on Sundays, and to Connell's house when no one is home. She knows how long it takes to get to Sligo town – twenty minutes – but the locations of other nearby towns, and their sizes in relation to Carricklea, are a mystery to her. Coolaney, Skreen, Ballysadare, she's pretty sure these are all in the vicinity of Carricklea, and the names ring bells for her in a vague way, but she doesn't know where they are. She's never been inside the sports centre. She's never gone drinking in the abandoned hat factory, though she has been driven past it in the car.

Likewise, it's impossible for her to know which families in town are considered good families and which aren't. It's the kind of thing she would like to know, just to be able to reject it the more completely. She's from a good family and Connell is from a bad one, that much she does know. The Waldrons are notorious in Carricklea. One of Lorraine's brothers was in prison once, Marianne doesn't know for what, and another one got into a motorcycle crash off the roundabout a few years ago and almost died. And of course, Lorraine got pregnant at seventeen and left school to have the baby. Nonetheless Connell is considered quite a catch these days. He's studious, he plays centre forward in football, he's good-looking, he doesn't get into fights. Everybody likes him. He's quiet. Even Marianne's mother will say approvingly: That boy is nothing like a Waldron. Marianne's mother is a solicitor. Her father was a solicitor too.

Last week, Connell mentioned something called 'the ghost'.

Marianne had never heard of it before, she had to ask him what it was. His eyebrows shot up. The ghost, he said. The ghost estate, Mountain View. It's like, right behind the school. Marianne had been vaguely aware of some construction on the land behind the school, but she didn't know there was a housing estate there now, or that no one lived in it. People go drinking there, Connell added. Oh, said Marianne. She asked what it was like. He said he wished he could show her, but there were always people around. He often makes blithe remarks about things he 'wishes'. I wish you didn't have to go, he says when she's leaving, or: I wish you could stay the night. If he really wished for any of those things, Marianne knows, then they would happen. Connell always gets what he wants, and then feels sorry for himself when what he wants doesn't make him happy.

Anyway, he did end up taking her to see the ghost estate. They drove there in his car one afternoon and he went out first to make sure no one was around before she followed him. The houses were huge, with bare concrete facades and overgrown front lawns. Some of the empty window holes were covered over in plastic sheeting, which whipped around loudly in the wind. It was raining and she had left her jacket in the car. She crossed her arms, squinting up at the wet slate roofs.

Do you want to look inside? Connell said.

The front door of number 23 was unlocked. It was quieter in the house, and darker. The place was filthy. With the toe of her shoe Marianne prodded at an empty cider bottle. There were cigarette butts all over the floor and someone had dragged a mattress into the otherwise bare living room. The mattress was stained badly with damp and what looked like blood.

Pretty sordid, Marianne said aloud. Connell was quiet, just looking around.

Do you hang out here much? she said.

He gave a kind of shrug. Not much, he said. Used to a bit, not much anymore.

Please tell me you've never had sex on that mattress.

He smiled absently. No, he said. Is that what you think I get up to at the weekend, is it?

Kind of.

He didn't say anything then, which made her feel even worse. He kicked a crushed can of Dutch Gold aimlessly and sent it skidding towards the French doors.

This is probably three times the size of my house, he said. Would you say?

She felt foolish for not realising what he had been thinking about. Probably, she said. I haven't seen upstairs, obviously.

Four bedrooms.

Jesus.

Just lying empty, no one living in it, he said. Why don't they give them away if they can't sell them? I'm not being thick with you, I'm genuinely asking.

She shrugged. She didn't actually understand why.

It's something to do with capitalism, she said.

Yeah. Everything is, that's the problem, isn't it?

She nodded. He looked over at her, as if coming out of a dream. Are you cold? he said. You look like you're freezing.

She smiled, rubbed at her nose. He unzipped his black puffer jacket and put it over her shoulders. They were standing very close. She would have lain on the ground and let him walk over her body if he wanted, he knew that.

When I go out at the weekend or whatever, he said, I don't go after other girls or anything.

Marianne smiled and said: No, I guess they come after you.

He grinned, he looked down at his shoes. You have a very funny idea of me, he said.

She closed her fingers around his school tie. It was the first time in her life she could say shocking things and use bad language, so she did it a lot. If I wanted you to fuck me here, she said, would you do it?

His expression didn't change but his hands moved around under her jumper to show he was listening. After a few seconds he said: Yeah. If you wanted to, yeah. You're always making me do such weird things.

What does that mean? she said. I can't make you do anything.

Yeah, you can. Do you think there's any other person I would do this type of thing with? Seriously, do you think anyone else could make me sneak around after school and all this?

What do you want me to do? Leave you alone?

He looked at her, seemingly taken aback by this turn in the discussion. Shaking his head, he said: If you did that . . .

She looked at him but he didn't say anything else.

If I did that, what? she said.

I don't know. You mean, if you just didn't want to see each other anymore? I would feel surprised honestly, because you seem like you enjoy it.

And what if I met someone else who liked me more?

He laughed. She turned away crossly, pulling out of his grasp, wrapping her arms around her chest. He said hey, but she didn't turn around. She was facing the disgusting mattress with the rust-coloured stains all over it. Gently he came up behind her and lifted her hair to kiss the back of her neck.

Sorry for laughing, he said. You're making me insecure, talking about not wanting to hang out with me anymore. I thought you liked me.

She shut her eyes. I do like you, she said.

Well, if you met someone else you liked more, I'd be pissed off, okay? Since you ask about it. I wouldn't be happy. Alright?

Your friend Eric called me flat-chested today in front of everyone.

Connell paused. She felt his breathing. I didn't hear that, he said.

You were in the bathroom or somewhere. He said I looked like an ironing board.

Fuck's sake, he's such a prick. Is that why you're in a bad mood?

She shrugged. Connell put his arms around her belly.

He's only trying to get on your nerves, he said. If he thought he had the slightest chance with you, he would be talking very differently. He just thinks you look down on him.

She shrugged again, chewing on her lower lip.

You have nothing to worry about with your appearance, Connell said.

Hm.

I don't just like you for your brains, trust me.

She laughed, feeling silly.

He rubbed her ear with his nose and added: I would miss you if you didn't want to see me anymore.

Would you miss sleeping with me? she said.

He touched his hand against her hipbone, rocking her back against his body, and said quietly: Yeah, a lot.

Can we go back to your house now?

He nodded. For a few seconds they just stood there in stillness, his arms around her, his breath on her ear. Most people go through their whole lives, Marianne thought, without ever really feeling that close with anyone.

Finally, after her third gin and tonic, the door bangs open and the boys arrive. The committee girls get up and start teasing them, scolding them for being late, things like that. Marianne hangs back, searching for Connell's eye contact, which he doesn't return. He's dressed in a white button-down shirt, the same Adidas sneakers he wears everywhere. The other boys are wearing shirts too, but more formal-looking, shinier, and worn with leather dress shoes. There's a heavy, stirring smell of aftershave in the air. Eric catches Marianne's eye and suddenly lets go of Karen, a move obvious enough that everyone else looks around too.

Look at you, Marianne, says Eric.

She can't tell immediately whether he's being sincere or mocking. All the boys are looking at her now except Connell.

I'm serious, Eric says. Great dress, very sexy.

Rachel starts laughing, leans in to say something in Connell's ear. He turns his face away slightly and doesn't laugh along. Marianne feels a certain pressure in her head that she wants to relieve by screaming or crying.

Let's go and have a dance, says Karen.

I've never seen Marianne dancing, Rachel says.

Well, you can see her now, says Karen.

Karen takes Marianne's hand and pulls her towards the dance floor. There's a Kanye West song playing, the one with the Curtis Mayfield sample. Marianne is still holding the raffle book in one hand, and she feels the other hand damp inside Karen's. The dance floor is crowded and sends shudders of bass up through her shoes into her legs. Karen props an arm on Marianne's shoulder, drunkenly, and says in her ear: Don't mind Rachel, she's in foul humour. Marianne nods her head, moving her body in time with the music. Feeling drunk now, she turns to search the room, wanting to know where Connell is. Right away she sees him, standing at the top of the steps. He's watching her. The music is so loud it throbs inside her body. Around him the others are talking and laughing. He's just looking at her and saying nothing. Under his gaze her movements feel magnified, scandalous, and the weight of Karen's arm on her shoulder is sensual and hot. She rocks her hips forward and runs a hand loosely through her hair.

In her ear Karen says: He's been watching you the whole time.

Marianne looks at him and then back at Karen, saying nothing, trying not to let her face say anything.

Now you see why Rachel's in a bad mood with you, says Karen.

She can smell the wine spritzer on Karen's breath when she speaks, she can see her fillings. She likes her so much at that moment. They dance a little more and then go back upstairs together, hand in hand, out of breath now, grinning about nothing. Eric and Rob are pretending to have an argument. Connell moves towards Marianne almost imperceptibly, and their arms touch. She wants to pick up his hand and suck on his fingertips one after another.

Rachel turns to her then and says: You might try actually selling some raffle tickets at some point?

Marianne smiles, and the smile that comes out is smug, almost derisive, and she says: Okay.

I think these lads might want to buy some, says Eric.

He nods over at the door, where some older guys have arrived. They're not supposed to be here, the nightclub said it would be ticket-holders only. Marianne doesn't know who they are, someone's brothers or cousins maybe, or just men in their twenties who like to hang around school fundraisers. They see Eric waving and come over. Marianne looks in her purse for the cash pouch in case they do want to buy raffle tickets.

How are things, Eric? says one of the men. Who's your friend here?

That's Marianne Sheridan, Eric says. You'd know her brother, I'd say. Alan, he would've been in Mick's year.

The man just nods, looking Marianne up and down. She feels indifferent to his attention. The music is too loud to hear what Rob is saying in Eric's ear, but Marianne feels it has to do with her.

Let me get you a drink, the man says. What are you having?

No, thanks, says Marianne.

The man slips an arm around her shoulders then. He's very tall, she notices. Taller than Connell. His fingers rub her bare arm. She tries to shrug him off but he doesn't let go. One of his friends starts laughing, and Eric laughs along.

Nice dress, the man says.

Can you let go of me? she says.

Very low-cut there, isn't it?

In one motion he moves his hand down from her shoulder and squeezes the flesh of her right breast, in front of everyone. Instantly she jerks away from him, pulling her dress up to her collarbone, feeling her face fill with blood. Her eyes are stinging and she feels a pain where he grabbed her. Behind her the others are laughing. She can hear them. Rachel is laughing, a high fluting noise in Marianne's ears.

Without turning around, Marianne walks out the door, lets it slam behind her. She's in the hallway now with the cloakroom and can't remember whether the exit is right or left. She's shaking all over her body. The cloakroom attendant asks if she's alright. Marianne doesn't know anymore how drunk she is. She walks a few steps towards a door on the left and then puts her back against the wall and starts sliding down towards a seated position on the floor. Her breast is aching where that man grabbed it. He wasn't joking, he wanted to hurt her. She's on the floor now hugging her knees against her chest.

Up the hall the door comes open again and Karen comes out, with Eric and Rachel and Connell following. They see Marianne on the floor and Karen runs over to her while the other three stay standing where they are, not knowing what to do maybe, or not wanting to do anything. Karen hunches down in front of Marianne and touches her hand. Marianne's eyes are sore and she doesn't know where to look.

Are you alright? Karen says.

I'm fine, says Marianne. I'm sorry. I think I just had too much to drink.

Leave her, says Rachel.

Here, look, it was just a bit of fun, says Eric. Pat's actually a sound enough guy if you get to know him.

I think it was funny, says Rachel.

At this Karen snaps around and looks at them. Why are you

even out here if you think it was so funny? she says. Why don't you go and pal around with your best friend Pat? If you think it's so funny to molest young girls?

How is Marianne *young*? says Eric.

We were all laughing at the time, says Rachel.

That's not true, says Connell.

Everyone looks around at him then. Marianne looks at him. Their eyes meet.

Are you okay, are you? he says.

Oh, do you want to kiss her better? says Rachel.

His face is flushed now, and he touches a hand to his brow. Everyone is still watching him. The wall feels cold against Marianne's back.

Rachel, he says, would you ever fuck off?

Karen and Eric exchange a look then, eyes wide, Marianne can see them. Connell never speaks or acts like this in school. In all these years she has never seen him behave at all aggressively, even when taunted. Rachel just tosses her head and walks back inside the club. The door falls shut heavily on its hinges. Connell continues rubbing his brow for a second. Karen mouths something at Eric, Marianne doesn't know what it is. Then Connell looks at Marianne and says: Do you want to go home? I'm driving, I can drop you. She nods her head. Karen helps her up from the floor. Connell puts his hands in his pockets as if to prevent himself touching her by accident. Sorry for making a fuss, Marianne says to Karen. I feel stupid. I'm not used to drinking.

It's not your fault, says Karen.

Thank you for being so nice, Marianne says.

They squeeze hands once more. Marianne follows Connell

towards the exit then and around the side of the hotel, to where his car is parked. It's dark and cool out here, with the sound of music from the nightclub pulsing faintly behind them. She gets in the passenger seat and puts her seatbelt on. He closes the driver's door and puts his keys in the ignition.

Sorry for making a fuss, she says again.

You didn't, says Connell. I'm sorry the others were being so stupid about it. They just think Pat is great because he has these parties in his house sometimes. Apparently if you have house parties it's okay to mess with people, I don't know.

It really hurt. What he did.

Connell says nothing then. He just kneads the steering wheel with his hands. He looks down into his lap, and exhales quickly, almost like a cough. Sorry, he says. Then he starts the car. They drive for a few minutes in silence, Marianne cooling her forehead against the window.

Do you want to come back to my house for a bit? he says.

Is Lorraine not there?

He shrugs. He taps his fingers on the wheel. She's probably in bed already, he says. I mean we could just hang out for a bit before I drop you home. It's okay if you don't want to.

What if she's still up?

Honestly she's pretty relaxed about this sort of stuff anyway. Like I really don't think she would care.

Marianne stares out the window at the passing town. She knows what he's saying: that he doesn't mind if his mother finds out about them. Maybe she already knows.

Lorraine seems like a really good parent, Marianne remarks.

Yeah. I think so.

She must be proud of you. You're the only boy in school

who's actually turned out well as an adult.

Connell glances over at her. How have I turned out well? he says.

What do you mean? Everyone likes you. And unlike most people you're actually a nice person.

He makes a facial expression she can't interpret, kind of raising his eyebrows, or frowning. When they get back to his house the windows are all dark and Lorraine is in bed. In Connell's room he and Marianne lie down together whispering. He tells her that she's beautiful. She has never heard that before, though she has sometimes privately suspected it of herself, but it feels different to hear it from another person. She touches his hand to her breast where it hurts, and he kisses her. Her face is wet, she's been crying. He kisses her neck. Are you okay? he says. When she nods, he smooths her hair back and says: It's alright to be upset, you know. She lies with her face against his chest. She feels like a soft piece of cloth that is wrung out and dripping.

You would never hit a girl, would you? she says.

God, no. Of course not. Why would you ask that?

I don't know.

Do you think I'm the kind of person who would go around hitting girls? he says.

She presses her face very hard against his chest. My dad used to hit my mum, she says. For a few seconds, which seems like an unbelievably long time, Connell says nothing. Then he says: Jesus. I'm sorry. I didn't know that.

It's okay, she says.

Did he ever hit you?

Sometimes.

Connell is silent again. He leans down and kisses her on the forehead. I would never hurt you, okay? he says. Never. She nods and says nothing. You make me really happy, he says. His hand moves over her hair and he adds: I love you. I'm not just saying that, I really do. Her eyes fill up with tears again and she closes them. Even in memory she will find this moment unbearably intense, and she's aware of this now, while it's happening. She has never believed herself fit to be loved by any person. But now she has a new life, of which this is the first moment, and even after many years have passed she will still think: Yes, that was it, the beginning of my life.

Two Days Later

(APRIL 2011)

He stands at the side of the bed while his mother goes to find one of the nurses. Is that all you have on you? his grandmother says.

Hm? says Connell.

Is that jumper all you have on you?

Oh, he says. Yeah.

You'll freeze. You'll be in here yourself.

His grandmother slipped in the Aldi car park this morning and fell on her hip. She's not old like some of the other patients, she's only fifty-eight. The same age as Marianne's mother, Connell thinks. Anyway, it looks like his grandmother's hip is kind of messed up now and possibly broken, and Connell had to drive Lorraine into Sligo town to visit the hospital. In the bed across the ward someone is coughing.

I'm alright, he says. It's warm out.

His grandmother sighs, like his commentary on the weather is painful to her. It probably is, because everything he does is painful to her, because she hates him for being alive. She looks him up and down with a critical expression.

Well, you certainly don't take after your mother, do you? she says.

Yeah, he says. No.

Physically Lorraine and Connell are different types. Lorraine is blonde and has a soft face without edges. The guys in school

45

think she's attractive, which they tell Connell often. She probably is attractive, so what, it doesn't offend him. Connell has darker hair and a hard-looking face, like an artist's impression of a criminal. He knows, however, that his grandmother's point is unrelated to his physical appearance and is meant as a remark on his paternity. So, okay, he has nothing to say on that.

No one except Lorraine knows who Connell's father is. She says he can ask any time he wants to know, but he really doesn't care to. On nights out his friends sometimes raise the subject of his father, like it's something deep and meaningful they can only talk about when they're drunk. Connell finds this depressing. He never thinks about the man who got Lorraine pregnant, why would he? His friends seem so obsessed with their own fathers, obsessed with emulating them or being different from them in specific ways. When they fight with their fathers, the fights always seem to mean one thing on the surface but conceal another secret meaning beneath. When Connell fights with Lorraine, it's usually about something like leaving a wet towel on the couch, and that's it, it's really about the towel, or at most it's about whether Connell is fundamentally careless in his tendencies, because he wants Lorraine to see him as a responsible person despite his habit of leaving towels everywhere, and Lorraine says if it was so important to him to be seen as responsible, he would show it in his actions, that kind of thing.

He drove Lorraine to the polling station to vote at the end of February, and on the way she asked who he was going to vote for. One of the independent candidates, he said vaguely. She laughed. Don't tell me, she said. The communist Declan Bree. Connell, unprovoked, continued watching the road. We could do with a bit more communism in this country if you ask me, he said. From the corner of his eye he could see Lorraine smiling. Come on now, comrade, she said. I was the one who raised you with your good socialist values, remember? It's true Lorraine has values. She's interested in Cuba, and the cause of Palestinian liberation. In the end Connell did vote for Declan Bree, who went on to be eliminated in the fifth count. Two of the seats went to Fine Gael and the other to Sinn Féin. Lorraine said it was a disgrace. Swapping one crowd of criminals for another, she said. He texted Marianne: fg in government, fucks sake. She texted back: The party of Franco. He had to look up what that meant.

The other night Marianne told him that she thought he'd turned out well as a person. She said he was nice, and that everyone liked him. He found himself thinking about that a lot. It was a pleasant thing to have in his thoughts. *You're a nice person and everyone likes you.* To test himself he would try not thinking about it for a bit, and then go back and think about it again to see if it still made him feel good, and it did. For some reason he wished he could tell Lorraine what she'd said. He felt it would reassure her somehow, but about what? That her only son was not a worthless person after all? That she hadn't wasted her life?

And I hear you're off to Trinity College, his grandmother says.

Yeah, if I get the points.

What put Trinity into your head?

He shrugs. She laughs, but it's like a scoffing laugh. Oh, good enough for you, she says. What are you going to study?

Connell resists the impulse to take his phone from his

pocket and check the time. English, he says. His aunts and uncles are all very impressed with his decision to put Trinity as his first choice, which embarrasses him. He'll qualify for the full maintenance grant if he does get in, but even at that he'll have to work full-time over the summer and at least part-time during term. Lorraine says she doesn't want him having to work too much through college, she wants him to focus on his degree. That makes him feel bad, because it's not like English is a real degree you can get a job out of, it's just a joke, and then he thinks he probably should have applied for Law after all.

Lorraine comes back into the ward now. Her shoes make a flat, clapping noise on the tiles. She starts to talk to his grandmother about the consultant who's on leave and about Dr O'Malley and the X-ray. She relays all this information very carefully, writing down the most important things on a piece of notepaper. Finally, after his grandmother kisses his face, they leave the ward. He disinfects his hands in the corridor while Lorraine waits. Then they go down the stairs and out of the hospital, into the bright, clammy sunshine.

After the fundraiser the other night, Marianne told him this thing about her family. He didn't know what to say. He started telling her that he loved her. It just happened, like drawing your hand back when you touch something hot. She was crying and everything, and he just said it without thinking. Was it true? He didn't know enough to know that. At first he thought it must have been true, since he said it, and why would he lie? But then he remembered he does lie sometimes, without planning to or knowing why. It wasn't the first time he'd had the urge to tell Marianne that he loved her, whether or not it was true, but it was the first time he'd given in and said it. He noticed how long it took her to say anything in response, and how her pause had bothered him, as if she might not say it back, and when she did say it he felt better, but maybe that meant nothing. Connell wished he knew how other people conducted their private lives, so that he could copy from example.

The next morning they woke up to the sound of Lorraine's keys in the door. It was bright outside, his mouth was dry, and Marianne was sitting up and pulling her clothes on. All she said was: Sorry, I'm sorry. They must have fallen asleep without meaning to. He had been planning to drop her home the night before. She put her shoes on and he got dressed too. Lorraine was standing in the hallway with two plastic bags of groceries when they reached the stairs. Marianne was wearing her dress from the night before, the black one with the straps.

Hello, sweetheart, said Lorraine.

Marianne's face looked bright like a light bulb. Sorry to intrude, she said.

Connell didn't touch her or speak to her. His chest hurt. She walked out the front door saying: Bye, sorry, thanks, sorry again. She shut the door behind her before he was even down the stairs.

Lorraine pressed her lips together like she was trying not to laugh. You can help me with the groceries, she said. She handed him one of the bags. He followed her into the kitchen and put the bag down on the table without looking at it. Rubbing his neck, he watched her unwrapping and putting away the items.

What's so funny? he said.

There's no need for her to run off like that just because I'm home, said Lorraine. I'm only delighted to see her, you know I'm very fond of Marianne.

He watched his mother fold away the reusable plastic bag.

Did you think I didn't know? she said.

He closed his eyes for a few seconds and then opened them again. He shrugged.

Well, I knew someone was coming over here in the afternoons, said Lorraine. And I do work in her house, you know.

He nodded, unable to speak.

You must really like her, said Lorraine.

Why do you say that?

Isn't that why you're going to Trinity?

He put his face in his hands. Lorraine was laughing then, he could hear her. You're making me not want to go there now, he said.

Oh, stop that.

He looked in the grocery bag he had left on the table and removed a packet of dried spaghetti. Self-consciously he brought it over to the press beside the fridge and put it with the other pasta.

So is Marianne your girlfriend, then? said Lorraine.

No.

What does that mean? You're having sex with her but she's not your girlfriend?

You're prying into my life now, he said. I don't like that, it's not your business.

He returned to the bag and removed a carton of eggs, which he placed on the countertop beside the sunflower oil.

Is it because of her mother? said Lorraine. You think she'd frown on you?

What?

Because she might, you know.

Frown on me? said Connell. That's insane, what have I ever done?

I think she might consider us a little bit beneath her station.

He stared at his mother across the kitchen while she put a box of own-brand cornflakes into the press. The idea that Marianne's family considered themselves superior to himself and Lorraine, too good to be associated with them, had never occurred to him before. He found, to his surprise, that the idea made him furious.

What, she thinks we're not good enough for them? he said.

I don't know. We might find out.

She doesn't mind you cleaning their house but she doesn't want your son hanging around with her daughter? What an absolute joke. That's like something from nineteenth-century times, I'm actually laughing at that.

You don't sound like you're laughing, said Lorraine.

Believe me, I am. It's hilarious to me.

Lorraine closed the press and turned to look at him curiously.

What's all the secrecy about, then? she said. If not for Denise Sheridan's sake. Does Marianne have a boyfriend or something, and you don't want him to find out?

You're getting so intrusive with these questions.

So she does have a boyfriend, then.

No, he said. But that's the last question I'm answering from you.

Lorraine's eyebrows moved around but she said nothing.

He crumpled up the empty plastic bag on the table and then paused there with the bag screwed up in his hand.

You're hardly going to tell anyone, are you? he said.

This is starting to sound very shady. Why shouldn't I tell anyone?

Feeling quite hard-hearted, he replied: Because there would be no benefit to you, and a lot of annoyance for me. He thought for a moment and added shrewdly: And Marianne.

Oh god, said Lorraine. I don't even think I want to know.

He continued waiting, feeling that she hadn't quite unambiguously promised not to tell anyone, and she threw her hands up in exasperation and said: I have more interesting things to gossip about than your sex life, okay? Don't worry.

He went upstairs then and sat on his bed. He didn't know how much time passed while he sat there like that. He was thinking about Marianne's family, about the idea that she was too good for him, and also about what she had told him the night before. He'd heard from guys in school that sometimes girls made up stories about themselves for attention, saying bad things had happened to them and stuff like that. And it was a pretty attention-grabbing story Marianne had told him, about her dad beating her up when she was a small child. Also, the dad was dead now, so he wasn't around to defend himself. Connell could see it was possible that Marianne had just lied to get his sympathy, but he also knew, as clearly as he knew anything, that she hadn't. If anything he felt like she'd been holding back on telling him how bad it really was. It gave him a queasy feeling, to have this information about her, to be tied to her in this way.

That was yesterday. This morning he was early to school, as

usual, and Rob and Eric started fake-cheering when he came to put his books in his locker. He dumped his bag on the floor, ignoring them. Eric slung an arm around his shoulder and said: Go on, tell us. Did you get the ride the other night? Connell felt in his pocket for his locker key and shrugged off Eric's arm. Funny, he said.

I heard you looked very cosy heading off together, said Rob.

Did anything happen? Eric said. Be honest.

No, obviously, said Connell.

Why is that obvious? Rachel said. Everyone knows she fancies you.

Rachel was sitting up on the windowsill with her legs swinging slowly back and forth, long and inky-black in opaque tights. Connell didn't meet her eye. Lisa was sitting on the floor against the lockers, finishing homework. Karen wasn't in yet. He wished Karen would come in.

I bet he did get a cheeky ride, said Rob. He'd never tell us anyway.

I wouldn't hold it against you, Eric said, she's not a bad-looking girl when she makes an effort.

Yeah, she's just mentally deranged, said Rachel.

Connell pretended to look for something in his locker. A thin white sweat had broken out on his hands and under his collar.

You're all being nasty, said Lisa. What has she ever done to any of you?

The question is what she's done to Waldron, said Eric. Look at him hiding in his locker there. Come on, spit it out. Did you shift her?

No, he said.

Well, I feel sorry for her, said Lisa.

Me too, said Eric. I think you should make it up to her, Connell. I think you should ask her to the Debs.

They all erupted in laughter. Connell closed his locker and walked out of the room carrying his schoolbag limply in his right hand. He heard the others calling after him, but he didn't turn around. When he got to the bathroom he locked himself in a cubicle. The yellow walls bore down on him and his face was slick with sweat. He kept thinking of himself saying to Marianne in bed: I love you. It was terrifying, like watching himself committing a terrible crime on CCTV. And soon she would be in school, putting her books in her bag, smiling to herself, never knowing anything. *You're a nice person and everyone likes you.* He took one deep uncomfortable breath and then threw up.

He indicates left coming out of the hospital to get back on the N16. A pain has settled behind his eyes. They drive along the Mall with banks of dark trees flanking them on either side.

Are you alright? says Lorraine.

Yeah.

You've got a look on you.

He breathes in, so his seatbelt digs into his ribs a little bit, and then exhales.

I asked Rachel to the Debs, he says.

What?

I asked Rachel Moran to go to the Debs with me.

They're about to pass a garage and Lorraine taps the window quickly and says: Pull in here. Connell looks over, confused. What? he says. She taps the window again, harder, and her nails click on the glass. Pull in, she says again. He hits the indicator quickly, checks the mirror, and then pulls in and stops the car. By the side of the garage someone is hosing down a van, water running off in dark rivers.

Do you want something from the shop? he says.

Who is Marianne going to the Debs with?

Connell squeezes the steering wheel absently. I don't know, he says. You hardly made me park here just to have a discussion, did you?

So maybe no one will ask her, says Lorraine. And she just won't go.

Yeah, maybe. I don't know.

On the walk back from lunch today he hung back behind the others. He knew Rachel would see him and wait with him, he knew that. And when she did, he screwed his eyes almost shut so the world was a whitish-grey colour and said: Here, do you have a date to the Debs yet? She said no. He asked if she wanted to go with him. Alright then, she said. I have to say, I was hoping for something a bit more romantic. He didn't reply to that, because he felt as if he had just jumped off a high precipice and fallen to his death, and he was glad he was dead, he never wanted to be alive again.

Does Marianne know you're taking someone else? says Lorraine.

Not as of yet. I will tell her.

Lorraine covers her mouth with her hand, so he can't make out her expression: she might be surprised, or concerned, or she might be about to get sick.

And you don't think maybe you should have asked her? she says. Seeing as how you fuck her every day after school.

That is vile language to use.

Lorraine's nostrils flare white when she inhales. How would you like me to put it? she says. I suppose I should say you've been using her for sex, is that more accurate?

Would you relax for a second? No one is using anyone.

How did you get her to keep quiet about it? Did you tell her something bad would happen if she told on you?

Jesus, he says. Obviously not. It was agreed, okay? You're getting it way out of proportion now.

Lorraine nods to herself, staring out the windshield. Nervously he waits for her to say something.

People in school don't like her, do they? says Lorraine. So I suppose you were afraid of what they would say about you, if they found out.

He doesn't respond.

Well, I'll tell what I have to say about you, Lorraine says. I think you're a disgrace. I'm ashamed of you.

He wipes his forehead with his sleeve. Lorraine, he says.

She opens the passenger door.

Where are you going? he says.

I'll get the bus home.

What are you talking about? Act normal, will you?

If I stay in the car, I'm only going to say things I'll regret.

What is this? he says. Why do you care if I go with someone or I don't, anyway? It's nothing to do with you.

She pushes the door wide and climbs out of the car. You're being so weird, he says. In response she slams the door shut, hard. He tightens his hands painfully on the steering wheel but stays quiet. It's my fucking car! he could say. Did I say you could slam the door, did I? Lorraine is walking away already, her handbag knocking against her hip with the pace of her stride. He watches her until she turns the corner. Two and a half years he worked in the garage after school to buy this car, and all he uses it for is driving his mother around because she doesn't have a licence. He could go after her now, roll the window down, shout at her to get back in. He almost feels like doing it, though she'd only ignore him. Instead he sits in the driver's seat, head tipped back against the headrest, listening to his own idiotic breathing. A crow on the forecourt picks at a discarded crisp packet. A family comes out of the shop holding ice creams. The smell of petrol infiltrates the car interior, heavy like a headache. He starts the engine.

Four Months Later

(AUGUST 2011)

She's in the garden, wearing sunglasses. The weather has been fine for a few days now, and her arms are getting freckled. She hears the back door open but doesn't move. Alan's voice calls from the patio: Annie Kearney's after getting five-seventy! Marianne doesn't respond. She feels in the grass beside her chair for the sun lotion, and when she sits up to apply it, she notices that Alan is on the phone.

Someone in your year got six hundred, hey! he yells.

She pours a little lotion into the palm of her left hand.

Marianne! Alan says. Someone got six A1s, I said!

She nods. She smooths the lotion slowly over her right arm, so it glistens. Alan is trying to find out who got six hundred points. Marianne knows right away who it must be, but she says nothing. She applies some lotion to her left arm and then, quietly, lies back down in the deckchair, face to the sun, and closes her eyes. Behind her eyelids waves of light move in green and red.

She hasn't eaten breakfast or lunch today, except two cups of sweetened coffee with milk. Her appetite is small this summer. When she wakes up in the morning she opens her laptop on the opposite pillow and waits for her eyes to adjust to the rectangle glow of the screen so she can read the news. She reads long articles about Syria and then researches the ideological backgrounds of the journalists who have written them. She reads long articles about the sovereign debt crisis in Europe and zooms in to see the small print on the graphs. After that she usually either goes back to sleep or gets in the shower, or maybe lies down and makes herself come. The rest of the day follows a similar pattern, with minor variations: maybe she opens her curtains, maybe not; maybe breakfast, or maybe just coffee, which she takes upstairs to her room so she doesn't have to see her family. This morning was different, of course.

Here, Marianne, says Alan. It's Waldron! Connell Waldron got six hundred points!

She doesn't move. Into the phone Alan says: No, she only got five-ninety. I'd say she's raging now someone did better than her. Are you raging, Marianne? She hears him but says nothing. Under the lenses of her sunglasses her eyelids feel greasy. An insect whirrs past her ear and away.

Is Waldron there with you, is he? says Alan. Put him on to me.

Why are you calling him 'Waldron' like he's your friend? Marianne says. You hardly know him.

Alan looks up from the phone, smirking. I know him well, he says. I saw him at Eric's gaff there the last day.

She regrets speaking. Alan is pacing up and down the patio, she can hear the gritty sound of his footsteps as he comes down towards the grass. Someone on the other end of the line starts talking, and Alan breaks into a bright, strained-looking smile. How are you now? he says. Fair play, congratulations. Connell's voice is quiet, so Marianne can't hear it. Alan is still smiling the effortful smile. He always gets like this around other people, cringing and sycophantic.

Yeah, Alan says. She did well, yeah. Not as well as yourself! Five-ninety she got. Do you want me to put her on to you?

Marianne looks up. Alan is joking. He thinks Connell will say no. He can't think of any reason why Connell would want to speak to Marianne, a friendless loser, on the phone; particularly not on this special day. Instead he says yes. Alan's smile falters. Yeah, he says, no bother. He holds the phone out for Marianne to take it. Marianne shakes her head. Alan's eyes widen. He jerks his hand towards her. Here, he says. He wants to talk to you. She shakes her head again. Alan prods the phone into her chest now, roughly. He's on the phone for you, Marianne, says Alan.

I don't want to speak to him, says Marianne.

Alan's face takes on a wild expression of fury, with the whites of his eyes showing all around. He jabs the phone harder into her sternum, hurting her. Say hello, he says. She can hear Connell's voice buzzing in the receiver. The sun glares down onto her face. She takes the phone from Alan's hand and, with a swipe of her finger, hangs up the call. Alan stands over the deckchair staring. There is no sound in the garden for a few seconds. Then, in a low voice, he says: What the fuck did you do that for?

I didn't want to speak to him, she says. I told you.

He wanted to speak to you.

Yes, I know he did.

It's unusually bright today, and Alan's shadow on the grass has a vivid, stark quality. She's still holding out the phone, loose in the palm of her hand, waiting for her brother to accept it.

In April, Connell told her he was taking Rachel Moran to the Debs. Marianne was sitting on the side of his bed at the time, acting very cold and humorous, which made him awkward. He told her it wasn't 'romantic', and that he and Rachel were just friends.

You mean like we're just friends, said Marianne.

Well, no, he said. Different.

But are you sleeping with her?

No. When would I even have time?

Do you want to? said Marianne.

I'm not hugely gone on the idea. I don't feel like I'm that insatiable really, I do already have you.

Marianne stared down at her fingernails.

That was a joke, Connell said.

I don't get what the joke part was.

I know you're pissed off with me.

I don't really care, she said. I just think if you want to sleep with her you should tell me.

Yeah, and I will tell you, if I ever want to do that. You're saying that's what the issue is, but I honestly don't think that's what it is.

Marianne snapped: What is it, then? He just stared at her. She went back to looking at her fingernails, flushed. He didn't say anything. Eventually she laughed, because she wasn't totally without spirit, and it obviously was kind of funny, just how savagely he had humiliated her, and his inability to apologise or even admit he had done it. She went home then and straight to bed, where she slept for thirteen hours without waking.

The next morning she quit school. It wasn't possible to go

back, however she looked at it. No one else would invite her to the Debs, that was clear. She had organised the fundraisers, she had booked the venue, but she wouldn't be able to attend the event. Everyone would know that, and some of them would be glad, and even the most sympathetic ones could only feel a terrible second-hand embarrassment. Instead she stayed home in her room all day with the curtains closed, studying and sleeping at strange hours. Her mother was furious. Doors were slammed. On two separate occasions Marianne's dinner was scraped into the bin. Still, she was an adult woman, and no one could make her dress up in a uniform anymore and submit to being stared at or whispered about.

A week after she left school she walked into the kitchen and saw Lorraine kneeling on the floor to clean the oven. Lorraine straightened up slightly, and wiped her forehead with the part of her wrist exposed above her rubber glove. Marianne swallowed.

Hello, sweetheart, Lorraine said. I hear you've been out of school for a few days. Is everything okay?

Yeah, I'm fine, said Marianne. Actually I'm not going back to school. I find I get more done if I just stay at home and study.

Lorraine nodded and said: Suit yourself. Then she went back to scrubbing the inside of the oven. Marianne opened the fridge to look for the orange juice.

My son tells me you're ignoring his phone calls, Lorraine added.

Marianne paused, and the silence in the kitchen was loud in her ears, like the white noise of rushing water. Yes, she said. I am, I suppose.

Good for you, said Lorraine. He doesn't deserve you.

Marianne felt a relief so high and sudden that it was almost like panic. She put the orange juice on the counter and closed the fridge.

Lorraine, she said, can you ask him not to come over here anymore? Like if he has to collect you or anything, is it okay if he doesn't come in the house?

Oh, he's permanently barred as far as I'm concerned. You don't need to worry about that. I have half a mind to kick him out of my own house.

Marianne smiled, feeling awkward. He didn't do anything that bad, she said. I mean, compared to the other people in school he was actually pretty nice, to be honest.

At this Lorraine stood up and stripped off her gloves. Without speaking, she put her arms around Marianne and embraced her very tightly. In a strange, cramped voice Marianne said: It's okay. I'm fine. Don't worry about me.

It was true what she had said about Connell. He didn't do anything that bad. He had never tried to delude her into thinking she was socially acceptable; she'd deluded herself. He had just been using her as a kind of private experiment, and her willingness to be used had probably shocked him. He pitied her in the end, but she also repulsed him. In a way she feels sorry for him now, because he has to live with the fact that he had sex with her, of his own free choice, and he liked it. That says more about him, the supposedly ordinary and healthy person, than it does about her. She never went back to school again except to sit the exams. By then people were saying she had been in the mental hospital. None of that mattered now anyway.

Are you angry he did better than you? says her brother.

Marianne laughs. And why shouldn't she laugh? Her life here in Carricklea is over, and either a new life will begin, or it won't. Soon she will be packing things into suitcases: woollen jumpers, skirts, her two silk dresses. A set of teacups and saucers patterned with flowers. A hairdryer, a frying pan, four white cotton towels. A coffee pot. The objects of a new existence.

No, she says.

Why wouldn't you say hello to him, then?

Ask him. If you're such good friends with him, you should ask him. He knows.

Alan makes a fist with his left hand. It doesn't matter, it's over. Lately Marianne walks around Carricklea and thinks how beautiful it is in sunny weather, white clouds like chalk dust over the library, long avenues lined with trees. The arc of a tennis ball through blue air. Cars slowing at traffic lights with their windows rolled down, music bleating from the speakers. Marianne wonders what it would be like to belong here, to walk down the street greeting people and smiling. To feel that life was happening here, in this place, and not somewhere else far away.

What does that mean? says Alan.

Ask Connell Waldron why we're not speaking anymore. Call him back now if you want to, I'd be interested to hear what he has to say.

Alan bites down on the knuckle of his index finger. His arm is shaking. In just a few weeks' time Marianne will live with different people, and life will be different. But she herself will not be different. She'll be the same person, trapped inside her own body. There's nowhere she can go that would free her from this. A different place, different people, what does that matter? Alan releases his knuckle from his mouth.

Like he fucking cares, says Alan. I'm surprised he even knows your name.

Oh, we used to be quite close actually. You can ask him about that too, if you want. Might make you a bit uncomfortable, though.

Before Alan can respond, they hear someone calling out from inside the house, and a door closing. Their mother is home. Alan looks up, his expression changes, and Marianne feels her own face moving around involuntarily. He glances down at her. You shouldn't tell lies about people, he says. Marianne nods, says nothing. Don't tell Mam about this, he says. Marianne shakes her head. No, she agrees. But it wouldn't matter if she did tell her, not really. Denise decided a long time ago that it is acceptable for men to use aggression towards Marianne as a way of expressing themselves. As a child Marianne resisted, but now she simply detaches, as if it isn't of any interest to her, which in a way it isn't. Denise considers this a symptom of her daughter's frigid and unlovable personality. She believes Marianne lacks 'warmth', by which she means the ability to beg for love from people who hate her. Alan goes back inside now. Marianne hears the patio door slide shut.

Three Months Later

(NOVEMBER 2011)

Connell doesn't know anyone at the party. The person who invited him isn't the same person who answered the door and, with an indifferent shrug, let him inside. He still hasn't seen the person who invited him, a person called Gareth, who's in his Critical Theory seminar. Connell knew going to a party on his own would be a bad idea, but on the phone Lorraine said it would be a good idea. I won't know anyone, he told her. And she said patiently: You won't get to know anyone if you don't go out and meet people. Now he's here, standing on his own in a crowded room not knowing whether to take his jacket off. It feels practically scandalous to be lingering here in solitude. He feels as if everyone around him is disturbed by his presence, and trying not to stare.

Finally, just as he decides to leave, Gareth comes in. Connell's intense relief at seeing Gareth triggers another wave of self-loathing, since he doesn't even know Gareth very well or particularly like him. Gareth puts his hand out and desperately, bizarrely, Connell finds himself shaking it. It's a low moment in his adult life. People are watching them shake hands, Connell is certain of this. Good to see you, man, says Gareth. Good to see you. I like the backpack, very nineties. Connell is wearing a completely plain navy backpack with no features to distinguish it from any of the other numerous backpacks at the party.

Uh, he says. Yeah, thanks.

Gareth is one of these popular people who's involved in college societies. He went to one of the big private schools in Dublin and people are always greeting him on campus, like: Hey, Gareth! Gareth, hey! They'll greet him from all the way across Front Square, just to get him to wave hello. Connell has seen it. People used to like me, he feels like saying as a joke. I used to be on my school football team. No one would laugh at that joke here.

Can I get you a drink? says Gareth.

Connell has a six-pack of cider with him, but he's reluctant to do anything that would draw attention to his backpack, in case Gareth might feel prompted to comment on it further. Cheers, he says. Gareth navigates over to the table at the side of the room and returns with a bottle of Corona. This okay? says Gareth. Connell looks at him for a second, wondering if the question is ironic or genuinely servile. Unable to decide, Connell says: Yeah, it'll do, thanks. People in college are like this, unpleasantly smug one minute and then abasing themselves to show off their good manners the next. He sips the beer while Gareth watches him. Without any apparent sarcasm Gareth grins and says: Enjoy.

This is what it's like in Dublin. All Connell's classmates have identical accents and carry the same size MacBook under their arms. In seminars they express their opinions passionately and conduct impromptu debates. Unable to form such straightforward views or express them with any force, Connell initially felt a sense of crushing inferiority to his fellow students, as if he had upgraded himself accidentally to an intellectual level far above his own, where he had to strain to make sense of the most basic premises. He did gradually start to wonder why all their classroom discussions were so abstract and lacking in textual detail, and eventually he realised that most people were not actually doing the reading. They were coming into college every day to have heated debates about books they had not read. He understands now that his classmates are not like him. It's easy for them to have opinions, and to express them with confidence. They don't worry about appearing ignorant or conceited. They are not stupid people, but they're not so much smarter than him either. They just move through the world in a different way, and he'll probably never really understand them, and he knows they will never understand him, or even try.

He only has a few classes every week anyway, so he fills the rest of the time by reading. In the evenings he stays late in the library, reading assigned texts, novels, works of literary criticism. Not having friends to eat with, he reads over lunch. At the weekends when there's football on, he checks the team news and then goes back to reading instead of watching the build-up. One night the library started closing just as he reached the passage in *Emma* when it seems like Mr Knightley is going to marry Harriet, and he had to close the book and walk home in a state of strange emotional agitation. He's amused at himself, getting wrapped up in the drama of novels like that. It feels intellectually unserious to concern himself with fictional people marrying one another. But there it is: literature moves him. One of his professors calls it 'the pleasure of being touched by great art'. In those words it almost sounds sexual. And in a way, the feeling provoked in Connell when Mr Knightley kisses Emma's hand is not completely asexual, though its relation to sexuality is indirect. It suggests to Connell that the same imagination he uses as a reader is necessary to understand real people also, and to be intimate with them.

You're not from Dublin, are you? says Gareth.

No. Sligo.

Oh yeah? My girlfriend's from Sligo.

Connell isn't sure what Gareth expects him to say to this.

Oh, he replies weakly. Well, there you go.

People in Dublin often mention the west of Ireland in this strange tone of voice, as if it's a foreign country, but one they consider themselves very knowledgeable about. In the Workmans the other night, Connell told a girl he was from Sligo and she made a funny face and said: Yeah, you look like it. Increasingly it seems as if Connell is actually drawn towards this supercilious type of person. Sometimes on a night out, among a crowd of smiling women in tight dresses and perfectly applied lipstick, his flatmate Niall will point out one person and say: I bet you think she's attractive. And it will always be some flat-chested girl wearing ugly shoes and disdainfully smoking a cigarette. And Connell has to admit, yes, he does find her attractive, and he may even try to talk to her, and he will go home feeling even worse than before.

Awkwardly he looks around the room and says: You live here, do you?

Yeah, says Gareth. Not bad for campus accommodation, is it?

No, yeah. It's really nice actually.

Whereabouts are you living yourself?

Connell tells him. It's a flat near college, just off Brunswick Place. He and Niall have one box room between them, with two single beds pushed up against opposite walls. They share a kitchen with two Portuguese students who are never home. The flat has some problems with damp and often gets so cold at night that Connell can see his own breath in the dark, but Niall is a decent person at least. He's from Belfast, and he also thinks people in Trinity are weird, which is reassuring. Connell half-knows some of Niall's friends by now, and he's acquainted with most of his own classmates, but no one he would have a proper conversation with.

Back home, Connell's shyness never seemed like much of an obstacle to his social life, because everyone knew who he was already, and there was never any need to introduce himself or create impressions about his personality. If anything, his personality seemed like something external to himself, managed by the opinions of others, rather than anything he individually did or produced. Now he has a sense of invisibility, nothingness, with no reputation to recommend him to anyone. Though his physical appearance has not changed, he feels objectively worse-looking than he used to be. He has become self-conscious about his clothes. All the guys in his class wear the same waxed hunting jackets and plum-coloured chinos, not that Connell has a problem with people dressing how they want, but he would feel like a complete prick wearing that stuff. At the same time, it forces him to acknowledge that his own clothes are cheap and unfashionable. His only shoes are an ancient pair of Adidas trainers, which he wears everywhere, even to the gym.

He still goes home at the weekends, because he works in the garage Saturday afternoons and Sunday mornings. Most people from school have left town now, for college or for work.

Karen is living down in Castlebar with her sister, Connell hasn't seen her since the Leaving Cert. Rob and Eric are both studying Business in Galway and never seem to be in town. Some weekends Connell doesn't see anyone from school at all. He sits at home in the evening watching television with his mother. What's it like living on your own? he asked her last week. She smiled. Oh, it's fantastic, she said. No one leaving towels on the couch. No dirty dishes in the sink, it's great. He nodded, humourless. She gave him a playful little shove. What do you want me to say? she says. I'm crying myself to sleep at night? He rolled his eyes. Obviously not, he muttered. She told him she was glad he had moved away, she thought it would be good for him. What's good about moving away? he said. You've lived here all your life and you turned out fine. She gawked at him. Oh, and you're planning to bury me here, are you? she said. Jesus, I'm only thirty-five. He tried not to smile, but he did find it funny. I could move away tomorrow, thanks very much, she added. It would save me looking at your miserable face every weekend. He had to laugh then, he couldn't help it.

Gareth is saying something Connell can't hear now. *Watch the Throne* is playing very loudly over a tinny pair of speakers. Connell leans forward a little, towards Gareth, and says: What?

My girlfriend, you should meet her, says Gareth. I'll introduce you.

Glad of a break in the conversation, Connell follows Gareth out the main door and onto the front steps. The building faces the tennis courts, which are locked now for the night and look eerily cool in the emptiness, reddish under the street lights. Down the steps some people are smoking and talking.

Hey, Marianne, says Gareth.

She looks up from her cigarette, mid-sentence. She's wearing a corduroy jacket over a dress, and her hair is pinned back. Her hand, holding the cigarette, looks long and ethereal in the light.

Oh, right, says Connell. Hi.

Instantly, unbelievably, Marianne's face breaks into a gigantic smile, exposing her crooked front teeth. She's wearing lipstick. Everyone is watching her now. She had been speaking, but she's stopped to stare at him.

Jesus Christ, she says. Connell Waldron! From beyond the grave.

He coughs and, in a panic to appear normal, says: When did you take up smoking?

To Gareth, to her friends, she adds: We went to school together. Fixing her gaze on Connell again, looking radiantly pleased, she says: Well, how are you? He shrugs and mumbles: Yeah, alright, good. She looks at him as if her eyes have a message in them. Would you like a drink? she says. He holds up the bottle Gareth gave him. I'll get you a glass, she says. Come on inside. She goes up the steps to him. Over her shoulder she says: Back in a second. From this remark, and from the way she was standing on the steps, he can tell that all these people at the party are her friends, she has a lot of friends, and she's happy. Then the front door shuts behind them and they're in the hallway, alone.

He follows her to the kitchen, which is empty and hygienically quiet. Matching teal surfaces and labelled appliances. The closed window reflects the lighted interior, blue and white. He doesn't need a glass but she takes one from the cupboard and he doesn't protest. Taking her jacket off, she asks him how he knows Gareth. Connell says they have classes together. She hangs her jacket on the back of a chair. She's wearing a longish grey dress, in which her body looks narrow and delicate.

Everyone seems to know him, she says. He's extroverted.

He's one of these campus celebrities, says Connell.

That makes her laugh, and it's like everything is fine between them, like they live in a slightly different universe where nothing bad has happened but Marianne suddenly has a cool boyfriend and Connell is the lonely, unpopular one.

He'd love that, says Marianne.

He seems to be on a lot of like, committees for things.

She smiles, she squints up at him. Her lipstick is very dark, a wine colour, and she's wearing make-up on her eyes.

I've missed you, she says.

This directness, coming so soon and so unexpectedly, makes him blush. He starts pouring the beer into the glass to divert his attention.

Yeah, you too, he says. I was kind of worried when you left school and all that. You know, I was pretty down about it.

Well, we never hung out much during school hours.

No. Yeah. Obviously.

And what about you and Rachel? says Marianne. Are you still together?

No, we broke up there during the summer.

In a voice just false enough to sound nearly sincere, Marianne says: Oh. I'm sorry.

After Marianne left school in April, Connell entered a period of low spirits. Teachers spoke to him about it. The guidance counsellor told Lorraine she was 'concerned'. People in school were probably talking about it too, he didn't know. He couldn't summon up the energy to act normal. At lunch he sat in the same place as always, eating sad mouthfuls of food, not listening to his friends when they spoke. Sometimes he wouldn't notice even when they called his name, and they would have to throw something at him or clip him on the head to get his attention. Everyone must have known there was something wrong with him. He felt a debilitating shame about the kind of person he'd turned out to be, and he missed the way Marianne had made him feel, and he missed her company. He called her phone all the time, he sent her text messages every day, but she never replied. His mother said he was barred from visiting her house, though he didn't think he would have tried that anyway.

For a while he tried to get over it by drinking too much and having anxious, upsetting sex with other girls. At a house party in May he slept with Barry Kenny's sister Sinead, who was twenty-three and had a degree in Speech and Language Therapy. Afterwards he felt so bad he threw up, and he had to tell Sinead he was drunk even though he wasn't really. There was no one he could talk to about that. He was excruciatingly lonely. He had recurring dreams about being with Marianne again, holding her peacefully the way he used to when they were tired, and speaking with her in low voices. Then he'd remember what had happened, and wake up feeling so depressed he couldn't move a single muscle in his body.

One night in June he came home drunk and asked Lorraine if she saw Marianne much at work.

Sometimes, said Lorraine. Why?

And is she alright, or what?

I've already told you I think she's upset.

She won't reply to any of my texts or anything, he said. When I call her, like if she sees it's me, she won't pick up.

Because you hurt her feelings.

Yeah, but it's kind of overreacting, isn't it?

Lorraine shrugged and looked back at the TV.

Do you think it is? he said.

Do I think what?

Do you think it's overreacting, what she's doing?

Lorraine kept looking straight at the TV. Connell was drunk, he doesn't remember what she was watching. Slowly she said: You know, Marianne is a very vulnerable person. And you did something very exploitative there and you hurt her. So maybe it's good that you're feeling bad about it.

I didn't say I felt bad about it, he said.

He and Rachel started seeing each other in July. Everyone in school had known she liked him, and she seemed to view the attachment between them as a personal achievement on her part. As to the actual relationship, it mostly took place before nights out, when she would put make-up on and complain about her friends and Connell would sit around drinking cans. Sometimes he looked at his phone while she was talking and she would say: You're not even *listening*. He hated the way he acted around her, because she was right, he really didn't listen, but when he did, he didn't like anything she actually said. He only had sex with her twice, neither time enjoyable, and when they lay in bed together he felt a constricting pain in his chest and throat that made it difficult to breathe. He had thought that being with her would make him feel less lonely, but it only gave his loneliness a new stubborn quality, like it was planted down inside him and impossible to kill.

Eventually the night of the Debs came. Rachel wore an extravagantly expensive dress and Connell stood in her front garden while her mother took their photograph. Rachel kept mentioning that he was going to Trinity, and her father showed him some golf clubs. Then they went to the hotel and ate dinner. Everyone got very drunk and Lisa passed out before dessert. Under the table Rob showed Eric and Connell naked photographs of Lisa on his phone. Eric laughed and tapped parts of Lisa's body on-screen with his fingers. Connell sat there looking at the phone and then said quietly: Bit fucked-up showing these to people, isn't it? With a loud sigh Rob locked the phone and put it back in his pocket. You've gotten awfully fucking gay about things lately, he said.

At midnight, sloppy drunk but hypocritically disgusted by the drunkenness of everyone around him, Connell wandered out of the ballroom and down a corridor into the smoking garden. He had lit a cigarette and was in the process of shredding some low-hanging leaves from a nearby tree when the door slid open and Eric came out to join him. Eric gave a knowing laugh on seeing him, and then sat on an upturned flowerpot and lit a cigarette himself.

Shame Marianne didn't come in the end, Eric said.

Connell nodded, hating to hear her name mentioned and unwilling to indulge it with a response.

What was going on there? said Eric.

Connell looked at him silently. A beam of white light was shining down from the bulb above the door and illuminating Eric's face with a ghostly pallor.

What do you mean? said Connell.

With herself and yourself.

Connell hardly recognised his own voice when he said: I don't know what you're talking about.

Eric grinned and his teeth glittered wetly in the light.

Do you think we don't know you were riding her? he said. Sure everyone knows.

Connell paused and took another drag on his cigarette. This was probably the most horrifying thing Eric could have said to him, not because it ended his life, but because it didn't. He knew then that the secret for which he had sacrificed his own happiness and the happiness of another person had been trivial all along, and worthless. He and Marianne could have walked down the school corridors hand in hand, and with what consequence? Nothing really. No one cared.

Fair enough, said Connell.

How long was that going on for?

I don't know. A while.

And what's the story there? said Eric. You were just doing it for the laugh, or what?

You know me.

He stubbed out his cigarette and went back inside to collect his jacket. After that he left without saying goodbye to anyone, including Rachel, who broke up with him shortly afterwards. That was it, people moved away, he moved away. Their life in Carricklea, which they had imbued with such drama and significance, just ended like that with no conclusion, and it would never be picked back up again, never in the same way.

Yeah, well, he says to Marianne. I wasn't that compatible with Rachel, I don't think.

Marianne smiles now, a coy little smile. Hm, she says.

What?

I probably could have told you that.

Yeah, you should have, he says. You weren't really replying to my texts at the time.

Well, I felt somewhat abandoned.

I felt a bit abandoned myself, didn't I? says Connell. You disappeared. And I never had anything to do with Rachel until ages after that, by the way. Not that it matters now or anything, but I didn't.

Marianne sighs and moves her head from side to side, ambivalently.

That wasn't really why I left school, she says.

Right. I suppose you were better off out of it.

It was more of a last-straw thing.

Yeah, he says. I wondered if that was what it was.

She smiles again, a lopsided smile like she's flirting. Really? she says. Maybe you're telepathic.

I did used to think I could read your mind at times, Connell says.

In bed, you mean.

He takes a sip from his glass now. The beer is cold but the glass is room temperature. Before this evening he didn't know how Marianne would act if he ever met her in college, but now it seems inevitable, of course it would be like this. Of course she would talk drolly about their sex life, like it's a cute joke between them and not awkward. And in a way he likes it, he likes knowing how to act around her.

Yeah, Connell says. And afterwards. But maybe that's normal.

It's not.

They both smile, a half-repressed smile of amusement. Connell puts the empty bottle on the countertop and looks at Marianne. She smooths down her dress.

You look really well, he says.

I know. It's classic me, I came to college and got pretty.

He starts laughing. He doesn't even want to laugh but something about the weird dynamic between them is making him do it. 'Classic me' is a very Marianne thing to say, a little self-mocking, and at the same time gesturing to some mutual understanding between them, an understanding that she is special. Her dress is cut low at the front, showing her pale collarbones like two white hyphens.

You were always pretty, he says. I should know, I'm a shallow guy. You're very pretty, you're beautiful.

She's not laughing now. She makes a kind of funny expression with her face and pushes her hair back off her forehead.

Oh well, she says. I haven't heard that one in a while.

Does Gareth not tell you you're beautiful? Or he's too busy with like, amateur drama or something.

Debating. And you're being very cruel.

Debating? says Connell. Jesus, don't tell me he's involved in this Nazi thing, is he?

Marianne's lips become a thin line. Connell doesn't read the campus papers much, but he has still managed to hear about the debating society inviting a neo-Nazi to give a speech. It's all over social media. There was even an article in *The Irish Times*. Connell hasn't commented on any of the Facebook threads, but he has liked several comments calling for the invite to be rescinded, which is probably the most strident political action he has ever taken in his life.

Well, we don't see eye to eye on everything, she says.

Connell laughs, happy for some reason to find her being so uncharacteristically weak and unscrupulous.

I thought I was bad going out with Rachel Moran, he says. Your boyfriend's a Holocaust denier.

Oh, he's just into free speech.

Yeah, that's good. Thank god for white moderates. As I believe Dr King once wrote.

She laughs then, sincerely. Her little teeth flash again and she lifts a hand to cover her mouth. He swallows some more of the drink and takes in her sweet expression, which he has missed, and it feels like a nice scene between them, although later on he'll probably hate everything he said to her. Okay, she says, we've both failed on ideological purity. Connell considers saying: I hope he's really good in bed, Marianne. She would definitely find it funny. For some reason, probably shyness, he doesn't say it. She looks at him with narrowed eyes and says: Are you seeing anyone problematic at the moment?

No, he says. Not even anyone good.

Marianne gives a curious smile. Finding it hard to meet people? she says.

He shrugs and then, vaguely, nods his head. Bit different from home, isn't it? he says.

I have some girlfriends I could introduce you to.

Oh yeah?

Yeah, I have those now, she says.

Not sure I'd be their type.

They look at one another. She's a little flushed, and her

lipstick is smudged just slightly on her lower lip. Her gaze unsettles him like it used to, like looking into a mirror, seeing something that has no secrets from you.

What does that mean? she says.

I don't know.

What's not to like about you?

He smiles and looks into his glass. If Niall could see Marianne, he would say: Don't tell me. You like her. It's true she is Connell's type, maybe even the originary model of the type: elegant, bored-looking, with an impression of perfect self-assurance. And he's attracted to her, he can admit that. After these months away from home, life seems much larger, and his personal dramas less significant. He's not the same anxious, repressed person he was in school, when his attraction to her felt terrifying, like an oncoming train, and he threw her under it. He knows she's acting funny and coy because she wants to show him that she's not bitter. He could say: I'm really sorry for what I did to you, Marianne. He always thought, if he did see her again, that's what he would say. Somehow she doesn't seem to admit that possibility, or maybe he's being cowardly, or both.

I don't know, he says. Good question, I don't know.

Three Months Later

(FEBRUARY 2012)

Marianne gets in the front seat of Connell's car and closes the door. Her hair is unwashed and she pulls her feet up onto the seat to tie her shoelaces. She smells like fruit liqueur, not in a bad way but not in a fully good way either. Connell gets in and starts the engine. She glances at him.

Is your seatbelt on? he says.

He's looking in the rear-view mirror like it's a normal day. Actually it's the morning after a house party in Swords and Connell wasn't drinking and Marianne was, so nothing is normal. She puts her seatbelt on obediently, to show that they're still friends.

Sorry about last night, she says.

She tries to pronounce this in a way that communicates several things: apology, painful embarrassment, some additional feigned embarrassment that serves to ironise and dilute the painful kind, a sense that she knows she will be forgiven or is already, a desire not to 'make a big deal'.

Forget about it, he says.

Well, I'm sorry.

It's alright.

Connell is pulling out of the driveway now. He has seemingly dismissed the incident, but for some reason this doesn't satisfy her. She wants him to acknowledge what happened before he lets her move on, or maybe she just wants to make herself suffer unduly.

It wasn't appropriate, she says.

Look, you were pretty drunk.

That's not an excuse.

And high out of your mind, he says, which I only found out later.

Yeah. I felt like an attacker.

Now he laughs. She pulls her knees against her chest and holds her elbows in her hands.

You didn't attack me, he says. These things happen.

This is the thing that happened. Connell drove Marianne to a mutual friend's house for a birthday party. They had arranged to stay the night there and Connell would drive her back the next morning. On the way they listened to Vampire Weekend and Marianne drank from a silver flask of gin and talked about the Reagan administration. You're getting drunk, Connell told her in the car. You know, you have a very nice face, she said. Other people have actually said that to me, about your face.

By midnight Connell had wandered off somewhere at the party and Marianne had found her friends Peggy and Joanna in the shed. They were drinking a bottle of Cointreau together and smoking. Peggy was wearing a beaten-up leather jacket and striped linen trousers. Her hair was loose around her shoulders, and she was constantly throwing it to one side and raking a hand through it. Joanna was sitting on top of the freezer unit in her socks. She was wearing a long shapeless garment like a maternity dress, with a shirt underneath. Marianne leaned against the washing machine and retrieved her gin flask from her pocket. Peggy and Joanna had been talking about men's fashion, and in particular the fashion sense of their own male friends. Marianne was content just to stand there, allowing the washing machine to support most of her body weight, swishing gin around the inside of her mouth, and listening to her friends speaking.

Both Peggy and Joanna are studying History and Politics with Marianne. Joanna is already planning her final-year thesis on James Connolly and the Irish Trades Union Congress. She's always recommending books and articles, which Marianne reads or half-reads or reads summaries of. People see Joanna as a serious person, which she is, but she can also be very funny. Peggy doesn't really 'get' Joanna's humour, because Peggy's form of charisma is more terrifying and sexy than it is comic. At a party before Christmas, Peggy cut Marianne a line of cocaine in their friend Declan's bathroom, and Marianne actually took it, or most of it anyway. It had no appreciable effect on her mood, except that for days afterwards she felt alternately amused at the idea that she had done it and guilty. She hasn't told Joanna about that. She knows Joanna would disapprove, because Marianne herself also disapproves, but when Joanna disapproves of things she doesn't go ahead and do them anyway.

Joanna wants to work in journalism, while Peggy doesn't seem to want to work at all. So far this hasn't been an issue for her, because she meets a lot of men who like to fund her lifestyle by buying her handbags and expensive drugs. She favours slightly older men who work for investment banks or accounting agencies, twenty-seven-year-olds with lots of money and sensible lawyer girlfriends at home. Joanna once asked Peggy if she ever thought she herself might one day be a twenty-seven-year-old whose boyfriend would stay out all night taking cocaine with a teenager. Peggy wasn't remotely insulted, she thought it was really funny. She said she would be married to a Russian oligarch by then anyway and she didn't care how many girlfriends he had. It makes Marianne wonder what she herself is going to do after college. Almost no paths seem definitively closed to her, not even the path of marrying an oligarch. When she goes out at night, men shout the most outrageously vulgar things at her on the street, so obviously they're not ashamed to desire her, quite the contrary. And in college she often feels there's no limit to what her brain can do, it can synthesise everything she puts into it, it's like having a powerful machine inside her head. Really she has everything going for her. She has no idea what she's going to do with her life.

In the shed, Peggy asked where Connell was.

Upstairs, said Marianne. With Teresa, I guess.

Connell has been casually seeing a friend of theirs called Teresa. Marianne has no real problem with Teresa, but finds herself frequently prompting Connell to say bad things about her for no reason, which he always refuses to do.

He wears nice clothes, volunteered Joanna.

Not *really*, said Peggy. I mean, he has a look, but it's just tracksuits most of the time. I doubt he even owns a suit.

Joanna sought Marianne's eye contact again, and this time Marianne returned it. Peggy, watching, took a performatively large mouthful of Cointreau and wiped her lips with the hand she was using to hold the bottle. What? she said.

Well, isn't he from a fairly working-class background? said Joanna.

That's so oversensitive, Peggy said. I can't criticise some-one's dress sense because of their socio-economic status? Come on.

No, that's not what she meant, said Marianne.

Because you know, we're all actually very nice to him, said Peggy.

Marianne found she couldn't look at either of her friends then. Who's 'we'? she wanted to say. Instead she took the bottle of Cointreau from Peggy's hand and swallowed two mouthfuls, lukewarm and repulsively sweet.

Some time around two o'clock in the morning, after she had become extremely drunk and Peggy had convinced her to share a joint with her in the bathroom, she saw Connell on the third-storey landing. No one else was up there. Hey, he said. She leaned against the wall, drunk and wanting his attention. He was at the top of the stairs.

You've been off with Teresa, she said.

Have I? he said. That's interesting. You're completely out of it, are you?

You smell like perfume.

Teresa's not here, said Connell. As in, she's not at the party.

Then Marianne laughed. She felt stupid, but in a good way. Come here, she said. He came over to stand in front of her.

What? he said.

Do you like her better than me? said Marianne.

He tucked a strand of hair behind her ear.

No, he said. To be fair, I don't know her very well.

But is she better in bed than I am?

You're drunk, Marianne. If you were sober you wouldn't even want to know the answer to that question.

86

So it's not the answer I want, she said.

She was engaging in this dialogue in a basically linear fashion, while at the same time trying to unbutton one of Connell's shirt buttons, not even in a sexy way, but just because she was so drunk and high. Also she hadn't managed to fully undo the button yet.

No, of course it's the answer you want, he said.

Then she kissed him. He didn't recoil like he was horrified, but he did pull away pretty firmly and said: No, come on.

Let's go upstairs, she said.

Yeah. We actually are upstairs.

I want you to fuck me.

He made a kind of frowning expression, which if she had been sober would have induced her to pretend she had only been joking.

Not tonight, he said. You're wasted.

Is that the only reason?

He looked down at her. She repressed a comment she had been saving up about the shape of his mouth, how perfect it was, because she wanted him to answer the question.

Yeah, he said. That's it.

So you otherwise would do it.

You should go to bed.

I'll give you drugs, she said.

You don't even— Marianne, you don't even have drugs. That's just one level of what's wrong with what you're saying. Go to bed.

Just kiss me.

He kissed her. It was a nice kiss, but friendly. Then he said goodnight and went downstairs lightly, with his light sober body walking in straight lines. Marianne went to find a bathroom, where she drank straight from the tap until her head stopped hurting and afterwards fell asleep on the bathroom floor. That's where she woke up twenty minutes ago when Connell asked one of the girls to find her.

Now he's flipping through the radio stations while they wait at a set of traffic lights. He finds a Van Morrison song and leaves it playing.

Anyway, I'm sorry, says Marianne again. I wasn't trying to make things weird with Teresa.

She's not my girlfriend.

Okay. But it was disrespectful of our friendship.

I didn't realise you were even close with her, he says.

I meant my friendship with you.

He looks around at her. She tightens her arms around her knees and tucks her chin into her shoulder. Lately she and Connell have been seeing a lot of each other. In Dublin they can walk down long stately streets together for the first time, confident that nobody they pass knows or cares who they are. Marianne lives alone in a one-bedroom apartment belonging to her grandmother, and in the evenings she and Connell sit in her living room drinking wine together. He complains to her, seemingly without reservation, about how hard it is to make friends in Trinity. The other day he lay on her couch and rolled the dregs of wine around in his glass and said: People here are such snobs. Even if they liked me I honestly wouldn't want to be friends with them. He put his glass down and looked at Marianne. That's why it's easy for you, by the way, he said. Because you're from a rich family, that's why people like you. She frowned and nodded, and then Connell started laughing. I'm messing with you, he said. Their eyes met. She wanted to laugh, but she didn't know if the joke was on her.

He always comes to her parties, though he says he doesn't really understand her friendship group. Her female friends like him a lot, and for some reason feel very comfortable sitting on his lap during conversations and tousling his hair fondly. The men have not warmed to him in the same way. He is tolerated through his association with Marianne, but he's not considered in his own right particularly interesting. He's not even smart! one of her male friends exclaimed the other night when Connell wasn't there. He's smarter than I am, said Marianne. No one knew what to say then. It's true that Connell is quiet at parties, stubbornly quiet even, and not interested in showing off how many books he has read or how many wars he knows about. But Marianne is aware, deep down, that that's not why people think he's stupid.

How was it disrespectful to our friendship? he says.

I think it would be difficult to stay friends if we started sleeping together.

He makes a devilish grinning expression. Confused, she hides her face in her arm.

Would it? he says.

I don't know.

Well, alright.

One night in the basement of Bruxelles, two of Marianne's friends were playing a clumsy game of pool while the others sat around drinking and watching. After Jamie won he said:

Who wants to play the winner? And Connell put his pint down quietly and said: Alright, yeah. Jamie broke but didn't pot anything. Without engaging in any conversation at all, Connell then potted four of the yellow balls in a row. Marianne started laughing, but Connell was expressionless, just focused-looking. In the short time after his turn he drank silently and watched Jamie send a red ball spinning off the cushion. Then Connell chalked his cue briskly and resumed pocketing the final three yellows. There was something so satisfying about the way he studied the table and lined the shots up, and the quiet kiss of the chalk against the smooth surface of the cue ball. The girls all sat around watching him take shots, watching him lean over the table with his hard, silent face lit by the overhead lamp. It's like a Diet Coke ad, said Marianne. Everyone laughed then, even Connell did. When it was just the black ball left he pointed at the top right-hand pocket and, gratifyingly, said: Alright, Marianne, are you watching? Then he potted it. Everyone applauded.

Instead of walking home that night, Connell came back to stay at hers. They lay in her bed looking up at the ceiling and talking. Until then they had always avoided discussing what had happened between them the year before, but that night Connell said: Do your friends know about us?

Marianne paused. What about us? she said eventually.

What happened in school and all that.

No, I don't think so. Maybe they've picked up on something but I never told them.

For a few seconds Connell said nothing. She was attuned to his silence in the darkness.

Would you be embarrassed if they found out? he said.

In some ways, yeah.

He turned over then, so he wasn't looking up at the ceiling anymore but facing her. Why? he said.

Because it was humiliating.

You mean like, the way I treated you.

Well, yeah, she said. And just the fact that I put up with it.

Carefully he felt for her hand under the quilt and she let him hold it. A shiver ran along her jaw and she tried to make her voice sound light and humorous.

Did you ever think about asking me to the Debs? she said. It's such a stupid thing but I'm curious whether you thought about it.

To be honest, no. I wish I did.

She nodded. She continued looking up at the black ceiling, swallowing, worried that he could make out her expression.

Would you have said yes? he asked.

She nodded again. She tried to roll her eyes at herself but it felt ugly and self-pitying rather than funny.

I'm really sorry, he said. I did the wrong thing there. And you know, apparently people in school kind of knew about us anyway. I don't know if you heard that.

She sat up on her elbow and stared down at him in the darkness.

Knew what? she said.

That we were seeing each other and all that.

I didn't tell anyone, Connell, I swear to god.

She could see him wince even in the dark.

No, I know, he said. My point is more that it wouldn't have mattered even if you did tell people. But I know you didn't.

Were they horrible about it?

No, no. Eric just mentioned it at the Debs, that people knew. No one cared, really.

There was another short silence between them.

I feel guilty for all the stuff I said to you, Connell added. About how bad it would be if anyone found out. Obviously that was more in my head than anything. I mean, there was no reason why people would care. But I kind of suffer from anxiety with these things. Not that I'm making excuses, but I think I projected some anxiety onto you, if that makes sense. I don't know. I'm still thinking about it a lot, why I acted in such a fucked-up way.

She squeezed his hand and he squeezed back, so tightly it almost hurt her, and this small gesture of desperation on his part made her smile.

I forgive you, she said.

Thank you. I think I did learn from it. And hopefully I have changed, you know, as a person. But honestly, if I have, it's because of you.

They kept holding hands underneath the quilt, even after they went to sleep.

When they get to her apartment now she asks if he wants to come in. He says he needs to eat something and she says there are breakfast things in the fridge. They go upstairs together. Connell starts looking in the fridge while she goes to take a shower. She strips all her clothes off, turns the water pressure up as high as it goes and showers for nearly twenty minutes. Then she feels better. When she comes out, wrapped in a white bathrobe, her hair towelled dry, Connell has eaten already. His plate is clean and he's checking his email. The room smells like coffee and frying. She goes towards him and he wipes his mouth with the back of his hand, as if he's nervous suddenly. She stands at his chair and, looking up at her, he undoes the sash of her bathrobe. It's been nearly a year. He touches his lips to her skin and she feels holy, like a shrine. Come to bed, then, she says. He goes with her.

Afterwards she switches on the hairdryer and he gets in the shower. Then she lies down again, listening to the sound of the pipes. She's smiling. When Connell comes out he lies beside her, they face one another, and he touches her. Hm, she says. They have sex again, not speaking very much. After that she feels peaceful and wants to sleep. He kisses her closed eyelids. It's not like this with other people, she says. Yeah, he says. I know. She senses there are things he isn't saying to her. She can't tell whether he's holding back a desire to pull away from her, or a desire to make himself more vulnerable somehow. He kisses her neck. Her eyes are getting heavy. I think we'll be fine, he says. She doesn't know or can't remember what he's talking about. She falls asleep.

Two Months Later

(APRIL 2012)

He's just come back from the library. Marianne has had friends over but they're heading off when he arrives, taking their jackets from the hooks in the hallway. Peggy is the only one still sitting at the table, draining a bottle of rosé into a huge glass. Marianne is wiping down the countertop with a wet cloth. The window over the kitchen sink shows an oblong of sky, denim-blue. Connell sits at the table and Marianne takes a beer out of the fridge and opens it for him. She asks if he's hungry and he says no. It's warm out and the cool of the bottle feels good. Their exams are starting soon, and he usually stays in the library now until the man comes around ringing the bell to say it's closing.

Can I just ask something? says Peggy.

He can tell she's drunk and that Marianne would like her to leave. He would like her to leave too.

Sure, says Marianne.

You guys are fucking each other, right? Peggy says. Like, you sleep together.

Connell says nothing. He runs his thumb over the label on the beer bottle, feeling for a corner to peel off. He has no idea what Marianne will come up with: something funny, he thinks, something that will make Peggy laugh and forget the question. Instead, unexpectedly, Marianne says: Oh, yeah. He starts smiling to himself. The corner of the beer label comes away from the glass under his thumb.

Peggy laughs. Okay, she says. Good to know. Everyone is speculating, by the way.

Well, yeah, says Marianne. But it's not a new thing, we used to hook up in school.

Oh really? Peggy says.

Marianne is pouring herself a glass of water. When she turns around, holding the glass, she looks at Connell.

I hope you don't mind me saying that now, she says.

He shrugs, but he's smiling at her, and she smiles back. They don't advertise the relationship, but his friends know about it. He doesn't like public displays, that's all. Marianne asked him once if he was 'ashamed' of her but she was just joking. That's funny, he said. Niall thinks I brag about you too much. She loved that. He doesn't really brag about her as such, though as it happens she is very popular and a lot of other men want to sleep with her. He might brag about her occasionally, but only in a tasteful way.

You actually make a very cute couple, says Peggy.

Thanks, Connell says.

I didn't say couple, says Marianne.

Oh, says Peggy. You mean like, you're not exclusive? That's cool. I wanted to try an open-relationship thing with Lorcan but he was really against it.

Marianne drags a chair back from the table and sits down. Men can be possessive, she says.

I know! says Peggy. It's crazy. You'd think they would jump at the idea of multiple partners.

Generally I find men are a lot more concerned with limiting the freedoms of women than exercising personal freedom for themselves, says Marianne.

Is that true? Peggy says to Connell.

He looks at Marianne with a little nod, preferring her to continue. He has come to know Peggy as the loud friend who interrupts all the time. Marianne has other, preferable friends, but they never stay as late or talk as much.

I mean, when you look at the lives men are really living, it's sad, Marianne says. They control the whole social system and this is the best they can come up with for themselves? They're not even having fun.

Peggy laughs. Are you having fun, Connell? she says.

Hm, he says. A reasonable amount, I would say. But I agree with the point.

Would you rather live under a matriarchy? says Peggy.

Difficult to know. I'd give it a go anyway, see what it was like.

Peggy keeps laughing, as if Connell is being unbelievably witty. Don't you enjoy your male privilege? she says.

It's like Marianne was saying, he replies. It's not that enjoyable to have. I mean, it is what it is, I don't get much fun out of it.

Peggy gives a toothy grin. If I were a man, she says, I would have as many as three girlfriends. If not more.

The last corner of the label peels off Connell's beer bottle now. It comes off more easily when the bottle is very cold, because the condensation dissolves the glue. He puts the beer on the table and starts to fold the label up into a small square. Peggy goes on talking but it doesn't seem important to listen to her.

Things are pretty good between him and Marianne at the moment. After the library closes in the evening he walks back to her apartment, maybe picking up some food or a four-euro bottle of wine on the way. When the weather is good, the sky feels miles away, and birds wheel through limitless air and light overhead. When it rains, the city closes in, gathers around with mists; cars move slower, their headlights glowing darkly, and the faces that pass are pink with cold. Marianne cooks dinner, spaghetti or risotto, and then he washes up and tidies the kitchen. He wipes crumbs out from under the toaster and she reads him jokes from Twitter. After that they go to bed. He likes to get very deep inside her, slowly, until her breathing is loud and hard and she clutches at the pillowcase with one hand. Her body feels so small then and so open. Like this? he says. And she's nodding her head and maybe punching her hand on the pillow, making little gasps whenever he moves.

The conversations that follow are gratifying for Connell, often taking unexpected turns and prompting him to express ideas he had never consciously formulated before. They talk about the novels he's reading, the research she studies, the precise historical moment that they are currently living in, the difficulty of observing such a moment in process. At times he has the sensation that he and Marianne are like figure-skaters, improvising their discussions so adeptly and in such perfect synchronisation that it surprises them both. She tosses herself gracefully into the air, and each time, without knowing how he's going to do it, he catches her. Knowing that they'll probably have sex again before they sleep probably makes the talking more pleasurable, and he suspects that the intimacy of their discussions, often moving back and forth from the conceptual to the personal, also makes the sex feel better. Last Friday, when they were lying there afterwards, she said: That was intense, wasn't it? He told her he always found it pretty intense. But I mean practically romantic, said Marianne. I think I was starting to have feelings for you there at one point. He smiled at the ceiling. You just have to repress all that stuff, Marianne, he said. That's what I do.

Marianne knows how he feels about her really. Just because he gets shy in front of her friends doesn't mean it's not serious between them – it is. Occasionally he worries he hasn't been sufficiently clear on this point, and after letting this worry build up for a day or so, wondering how he can approach the issue, he'll finally say something sheepish like: You know I really like you, don't you? And his tone will sound almost annoyed for some reason, and she'll just laugh. Marianne has a lot of other romantic options, as everyone knows. Politics students who turn up to her parties with bottles of Moët and anecdotes about their summers in India. Committee members of college clubs, who are dressed up in black tie very frequently, and who inexplicably believe that the internal workings of student societies are interesting to normal people. Guys who make a habit of touching Marianne casually during conversation, fixing her hair or placing a hand on her back. Once, when foolishly drunk, Connell asked Marianne why these people had to be so tactile with her, and she said: You won't touch me, but no one else is allowed to either? That put him in a terrible mood.

He doesn't go home at the weekends anymore because their friend Sophie got him a new job in her dad's restaurant. Connell just sits in an upstairs office at the weekends answering emails and writing bookings down in a big leather appointment book. Sometimes minor celebrities call in, like people from RTÉ and that kind of thing, but most weeknights the place is dead. It's obvious to Connell that the business is haemorrhaging money and will have to close down, but the job was so easy to come by that he can't work up any real anxiety about this prospect. If and when he's out of work, one of Marianne's other rich friends will just come up with another job for him to do. Rich people look out for each other, and being Marianne's best friend and suspected sexual partner has elevated Connell to the status of rich-adjacent: someone for whom surprise birthday parties are thrown and cushy jobs are procured out of nowhere.

Before term ended he had to give a class presentation on the *Morte Darthur*, and while he spoke his hands were shaking and he couldn't look up from the printouts to see if anyone was actually listening to him. His voice wavered several times and he had the sense that if he hadn't been seated, he would have fallen to the ground. Only later did he find out that this presentation was considered very impressive. One of his classmates actually called him 'a genius' to his face afterwards, in a dismissive tone of voice, like geniuses were slightly despicable people. It is generally known in their year group that Connell has received the highest grade in all but one module, and he finds he likes to be thought of as intelligent, if only because it makes his interactions with other people more legible. He likes when someone is struggling to remember the name of a book or an author, and he can provide it for them readily, not showing off, just remembering it. He likes when Marianne tells her friends – people whose fathers are judges and government ministers, people who went to inordinately expensive schools – that Connell is the smartest person they will 'ever meet'.

What about you, Connell? says Peggy.

He has not been listening, and all he can say in response is: What?

Tempted by the idea of multiple partners? she says.

He looks at her. She has an arch expression on her face.

Uh, he says. I don't know. What do you mean?

Do you not fantasise about having your own harem? says Peggy. I thought that was a universal thing for men.

Oh, right. No, not really.

Maybe just two, then, Peggy says.

Two what, two women?

Peggy looks at Marianne and makes a mischievous kind of giggling noise. Marianne sips her water calmly.

We can if you want to, says Peggy.

Wait, sorry, Connell says. We can what?

Well, whatever you call it, she says. A threesome or whatever.

Oh, he says. And he laughs at his own stupidity. Right, he says. Right, sorry. He folds the label over again, not knowing what else to say. I missed that, he adds. He can't do it. He's not indecisive on the question of whether he'd like to do it or not, he actually can't do it. For some reason, and he can't explain it to himself, he thinks maybe he could fuck Peggy in front of Marianne, although it would be awkward, and not necessarily enjoyable. But he could not, he's immediately certain, ever do anything to Marianne with Peggy watching, or any of her friends watching, or anyone at all. He feels shameful and confused even to think about it. It's something he doesn't understand in himself. For the privacy between himself and

Marianne to be invaded by Peggy, or by another person, would destroy something inside him, a part of his selfhood, which doesn't seem to have a name and which he has never tried to identify before. He folds the damp beer label up one more time so it's very small and tightly folded now. Hm, he says.

Oh no, says Marianne. I'm much too self-conscious. I'd die.

Peggy says: Really? She says this in a pleasant, interested tone of voice, like she's just as happy discussing Marianne's self-consciousness as she would be engaging in group sex. Connell tries not to display any outward relief.

I have all kinds of hang-ups, says Marianne. Very neurotic.

Peggy compliments Marianne's appearance in a routine, effeminate way and asks what her hang-ups are about.

Marianne pinches her lower lip and then says: Well, I don't feel lovable. I think I have an unlovable sort of . . . I have a coldness about me, I'm difficult to like. She gestures one of her long, thin hands in the air, like she's only approximating what she means rather than really nailing it.

I don't believe that, says Peggy. Is she cold with you?

Connell coughs and says: No.

She and Marianne continue talking and he rolls the folded label between his fingers, feeling anxious.

Marianne went home for a couple of days this week, and when she came back to Dublin last night she seemed quiet. They watched *The Umbrellas of Cherbourg* together in her apartment. At the end Marianne cried, but she turned her face away so it looked like she wasn't crying. This unsettled Connell. The film had a pretty sad ending but he didn't really see what there was to cry about. Are you okay? he said. She nodded, with her face turned, so he could see a white tendon in her neck pressing outwards.

Hey, he said. Is something upsetting you?

She shook her head but didn't turn around. He went to make her a cup of tea and by the time he brought it to her she had stopped crying. He touched her hair and she smiled, weakly. The character in the film had become pregnant unexpectedly, and Connell was trying to remember when Marianne had last had her period. The longer he thought about it, the longer ago it seemed to have been. Eventually, in a panic, he said: Hey, you're not pregnant or anything, are you? Marianne laughed. That settled his nerves.

No, she said. I got my period this morning.

Okay. Well, that's good.

What would you do if I was?

He smiled, he inhaled through his mouth. Kind of depends on what you would want to do, he said.

I admit I would have a slight temptation to keep it. But I wouldn't do that to you, don't worry.

Really? What would the temptation be? Sorry if that's insensitive to say.

I don't know, she said. In a way I like the idea of something so dramatic happening to me. I would like to upset people's expectations. Do you think I'd be a bad mother?

No, you'd be great, obviously. You're great at everything you do.

She smiled. You wouldn't have to be involved, she said.

Well, I would support you, whatever you decided.

He didn't know why he was saying he would support her, since he had virtually no spare income and no prospect of having any. It felt like the thing to say, that was all. Really he had never considered it. Marianne seemed like the kind of straightforward person who would arrange the whole procedure herself, and at most maybe he would go with her on the plane.

Imagine what they'd say in Carricklea, she said.

Oh, yeah. Lorraine would never forgive me.

Marianne looked up quickly and said: Why, she doesn't like me?

No, she loves you. I mean she wouldn't forgive me for doing that to you. She loves you, don't worry. You know that. She thinks you're much too good for me.

Marianne smiled again then, and touched his face with her hand. He liked that, so he moved towards her a little and stroked the pale underside of her wrist.

What about your family? he said. I guess they'd never forgive me either.

She shrugged, she dropped her hand back into her lap.

Do they know we're seeing each other now? he said.

She shook her head. She looked away, she held her hand against her cheek.

Not that you have to tell them, he said. Maybe they'd disapprove of me anyway. They probably want you going out with a doctor or a lawyer or something, do they?

I don't think they care very much what I do.

She covered her face using her flattened hands for a moment, and then she rubbed her nose briskly and sniffed. Connell knew she had a strained relationship with her family. He first came to realise this when they were still in school, and it didn't strike him as unusual, because Marianne had strained relationships with everyone then. Her brother Alan was a few years older, and had what Lorraine called a 'weak personality'. Honestly it was hard to imagine him standing his ground in a conflict with Marianne. But now they're both grown up and still she almost never goes home, or she goes and then comes back like this, distracted and sullen, saying she had a fight with her family again, and not wanting to talk about it.

You had another falling-out with them, did you? Connell said.

She nodded. They don't like me very much, she said.

I know it probably feels like they don't, he said. But at the end of the day they're your family, they love you.

Marianne said nothing. She didn't nod or shake her head, she just sat there. Soon after that they went to bed. She was having cramps and she said it might hurt to have sex, so he just touched her until she came. Then she was in a good mood and making luxurious moaning noises and saying: God, that was so nice. He got out of bed and went to wash his hands in the en suite, a small pink-tiled room with a potted plant in the corner and little jars of face cream and perfume everywhere. Rinsing his hands under the tap, he asked Marianne if she was feeling better. And from bed she said: I feel wonderful, thank you. In the mirror he noticed he had a little blood on his lower lip. He must have brushed it with his hand by accident. He rubbed at it with the wet part of his knuckle, and from the other room Marianne said: Imagine how bitter I'm going to be when you meet someone else and fall in love. She often makes little jokes like this. He dried his hands and switched off the bathroom light.

I don't know, he said. This is a pretty good arrangement, from my point of view.

Well, I do my best.

He got back into bed beside her and kissed her face. She had been sad before, after the film, but now she was happy. It was in Connell's power to make her happy. It was something he could just give to her, like money or sex. With other people she seemed so independent and remote, but with Connell she was different, a different person. He was the only one who knew her like that.

Eventually Peggy finishes her wine and leaves. Connell sits at the table while Marianne sees her out. The outside door closes and Marianne re-enters the kitchen. She rinses her water glass and leaves it upside down on the draining board. He's waiting for her to look at him.

You saved my life, he says.

She turns around, smiling, rolling her sleeves back down.

I wouldn't have enjoyed it either, she says. I would have done it if you wanted, but I could see you didn't.

He looks at her. He keeps looking at her until she says: What?

You shouldn't do things you don't want to do, he says.

Oh, I didn't mean that.

She throws her hands up, like the issue is irrelevant. In a direct sense he understands that it is. He tries to soften his manner since anyway it's not like he's annoyed at her.

Well, it was a good intervention on your part, he says. Very attentive to my preferences.

I try to be.

Yeah, you are. Come here.

She comes to sit down with him and he touches her cheek. He has a terrible sense all of a sudden that he could hit her face, very hard even, and she would just sit there and let him. The idea frightens him so badly that he pulls his chair back and stands up. His hands are shaking. He doesn't know why he thought about it. Maybe he wants to do it. But it makes him feel sick.

What's wrong? she says.

He feels a kind of tingling in his fingers now and he can't breathe right.

Oh, I don't know, he says. I don't know, sorry.

Did I do something?

No, no. Sorry. I had a weird . . . I feel weird. I don't know.

She doesn't get up. But she would, wouldn't she, if he told her to get up. His heart is pounding now and he feels dizzy.

Do you feel sick? she says. You've gone kind of white.

Here, Marianne. You're not cold, you know. You're not like that, not at all.

She gives him a strange look, screwing her face up. Well, maybe cold was the wrong word, she says. It doesn't really matter.

But you're not hard to like. You know? Everyone likes you. I didn't explain it well. Forget about it.

He nods. He still can't breathe normally. Well, what did you mean? he says. She's looking at him now, and finally she does stand up. You look morbidly pale, she says. Are you feeling faint? He says no. She takes his hand and tells him it feels damp. He nods, he's breathing hard. Quietly Marianne says: If I've done something to upset you, I'm really sorry. He forces a laugh and takes his hand away. No, a weird feeling came over me, he says. I don't know what it was. I'm okay now.

Three Months Later

(JULY 2012)

Marianne is reading the back of a yoghurt pot in the supermarket. With her other hand she's holding her phone, through which Joanna is telling an anecdote about her job. When Joanna gets into an anecdote she can really monologue at length, so Marianne isn't worried about taking her attention off the conversation for a few seconds to read the yoghurt pot. It's a warm day outside, she's wearing a light blouse and skirt, and the chill of the freezer aisle raises goosebumps on her arms. She has no reason to be in the supermarket, except that she doesn't want to be in her family home, and there aren't many spaces in which a solitary person can be inconspicuous in Carricklea. She can't go for a drink alone, or get a cup of coffee on Main Street. Even the supermarket will exhaust its usefulness when people notice she's not really buying groceries, or when she sees someone she knows and has to go through the motions of conversation.

The office is half-empty so nothing really gets done, Joanna is saying. But I'm still getting paid so I don't mind.

Because Joanna has a job now, most of their conversations take place over the phone, even though they're both living in Dublin. Marianne's only home for the weekend, but that's Joanna's only time off work. On the phone Joanna frequently describes her office, the various characters who work there, the dramas that erupt between them, and it's as if she's a citizen of a country Marianne has never visited, the country of paid employment. Marianne replaces the yoghurt pot in the freezer now and asks Joanna if she finds it strange, to be paid for her hours at work – to exchange, in other words, blocks of her extremely limited time on this earth for the human invention known as money.

It's time you'll never get back, Marianne adds. I mean, the time is real.

The money is also real.

Well, but the time is more real. Time consists of physics, money is just a social construct.

Yes, but I'm still alive at work, says Joanna. It's still me, I'm still having experiences. You're not working, okay, but the time is passing for you too. You'll never get it back either.

But I can decide what I do with it.

To that I would venture that your decision-making is also a social construct.

Marianne laughs. She wanders out of the freezer aisle and towards the snacks.

I don't buy into the morality of work, she says. Some work maybe, but you're just moving paper around an office, you're not contributing to the human effort.

I didn't say anything about morality.

Marianne lifts a packet of dried fruit and examines it, but it contains raisins so she puts it back down and picks up another.

Do you think I judge you for being so idle? says Joanna.

Deep down I think you do. You judge Peggy.

Peggy has an idle mind, which is different.

Marianne clicks her tongue as if to scold Joanna for her

cruelty, but not with any great investment. She's reading the back of a dried apple packet.

I wouldn't want you to turn into Peggy, says Joanna. I like you the way you are.

Oh, Peggy's not that bad. I'm going to the supermarket checkout now so I'm going to hang up.

Okay. You can call tomorrow after the thing if you feel like talking.

Thanks, says Marianne. You're a good friend. Bye.

Marianne makes her way to the self-service checkout, picking up a bottle of iced tea on the way and carrying the dried apples. When she reaches the row of self-service machines, she sees Lorraine unloading a basket of various groceries. Lorraine stops when she sees Marianne and says: Hello there! Marianne clutches the dried fruit against her ribcage and says hi.

How are you getting on? says Lorraine.

Good, thanks. And you?

Connell tells me you're top of your class. Winning prizes and all kinds of things. Doesn't surprise me, of course.

Marianne smiles. Her smile feels gummy and childish. She squeezes the package of dried fruit, feels it crackle under her damp grip, and scans it on the machine. The supermarket lights are chlorine-white and she's not wearing any make-up.

Oh, she says. Nothing major.

Connell comes around the corner, of course he does. He's carrying a six-pack of crisps, salt and vinegar flavour. He's wearing a white T-shirt and those sweatpants with the stripes down the side. His shoulders seem bigger now. And he looks at her. He's been in the supermarket the whole time; maybe he even saw her in the freezer aisle and walked past quickly to avoid making eye contact. Maybe he heard her talking on the phone.

Hello, says Marianne.

Oh, hey. I didn't know you were in town.

He glances at his mother, and then scans the crisps and puts them in the bagging area. His surprise at seeing Marianne seems genuine, or at least his reluctance to look at or speak to her does.

I hear you're very popular up there in Dublin, Lorraine says. See, I get all the gossip from Trinity now.

Connell doesn't look up. He's scanning the other items from the trolley: a box of teabags, a loaf of sliced pan.

Your son's just being kind, I'm sure, says Marianne.

She takes her purse out and pays for her items, which cost three euro eighty-nine. Lorraine and Connell are packing their groceries into reusable plastic bags.

Can we offer you a lift home? Lorraine says.

Oh, no, says Marianne. I'll walk. But thank you.

Walk! says Lorraine. Out to Blackfort Road? Do not. We'll give you a lift.

Connell takes both the plastic bags in his arms and cocks his head towards the door.

Come on, he says.

Marianne hasn't seen him since May. He moved home after the exams and she stayed in Dublin. He said he wanted to see other people and she said: Okay. Now, because she was never really his girlfriend, she's not even his ex-girlfriend. She's nothing. They all get in the car together, Marianne sitting in the back seat, while Connell and Lorraine have a conversation about someone they know who has died, but an elderly person so it's not that sad. Marianne stares out the window.

Well, I'm delighted we bumped into you, says Lorraine. It's great to see you looking so well.

Oh, thank you.

How long are you in town for?

Just the weekend, says Marianne.

Eventually Connell indicates at the entrance to the Foxfield estate and pulls in outside his house. Lorraine gets out. Connell glances at Marianne in the rear-view mirror and says: Here, get in the front, will you? I'm not a taxi driver. Wordlessly Marianne complies. Lorraine opens the boot and Connell twists around in his seat. Leave the bags, he says. I'll bring them in when I'm back. She puts up her hands in surrender, shuts the boot and then waves them off.

It's a short drive from Connell's house to Marianne's. He takes a left out of the estate, towards the roundabout. Only a few months ago he and Marianne used to stay up all night together talking and having sex. He used to pull the blankets off her in the morning and get on top of her with this little smiling expression like: Oh hey, hello. They were best friends. He told her that, when she asked him who his best friend was. You, he said. Then at the end of May he told her he was moving home for the summer.

How are things, anyway? he says.

Fine, thanks. How are you?

I'm alright, yeah.

He changes gears with a domineering gesture of his hand.

Are you still working in the garage? she asks.

No, no. You mean where I used to work? That place is closed now.

Is it?

Yeah, he says. No, I've been working in the Bistro. Actually your mam was in the other night with her, uh. Her boyfriend or whatever it is.

Marianne nods. They are driving past the football grounds now. A thin veil of rain begins to fall on the windshield, and Connell turns the wipers on, so they scrape out a mechanical rhythm on their voyage from side to side.

When Connell went home for Reading Week in the spring, he asked Marianne if she would send him naked pictures of herself. I'll delete them whenever you want obviously, he said. You can supervise. This suggested to Marianne a whole erotic ritual she had never heard of. Why would I want you to delete them? she said. They were talking on the phone, Connell at home in Foxfield and Marianne lying on her bed in Merrion Square. He explained briefly the politics of naked pictures, not showing them to people, deleting them on request, and so on.

Do you get these photos from a lot of girls? she asked him.

Well, I don't have any now. And I've never actually asked for any before, but sometimes you do get sent them.

She asked if he would send her back photographs of himself in return, and he made a 'hm' noise.

I don't know, he said. Would you really want a picture of my dick?

Comically, she felt the inside of her mouth get wet.

Yes, she said. But if you sent one I would honestly never delete it, so you probably shouldn't.

He laughed then. No, I don't care whether you delete it, he said.

She uncrossed her ankles. I mean I'll take it to my grave, she said. Like I will look at it probably every day until I die.

He was really laughing then. Marianne, he said, I'm not a religious person but I do sometimes think God made you for me.

The sports centre flashes past the driver's-side window through the blur of rainfall. Connell looks at Marianne again, then back at the road.

And you're with this guy Jamie now, aren't you? he says. So I hear.

Yeah.

He's not a bad-looking guy.

Oh, she says. Well, okay. Thanks.

She and Jamie have been together for a few weeks now. He has certain proclivities. They have certain shared proclivities. Sometimes in the middle of the day she remembers something Jamie has said or done to her, and all her energy leaves her completely, so her body feels like a carcass, something immensely heavy and awful that she has to carry around.

Yeah, says Connell. I actually beat him in a game of pool once. You probably don't remember.

I do.

Connell nods and adds: He always liked you. Marianne stares out the windshield at the car ahead. It's true, Jamie always liked her. He sent her a text once implying that Connell wasn't serious about her. She showed Connell the text and they laughed about it. They were in bed together at the time, Connell's face illuminated by the lit display on her phone screen. You should be with someone who takes you seriously, the message read.

What about you, are you seeing anyone? she says.

Not really. Nothing serious.

Embracing the single lifestyle.

You know me, he says.

I did once.

He frowns. That's a bit philosophical, he says. I haven't changed much in the last few months.

Neither have I. Actually, yeah. I haven't changed at all.

One night in May, Marianne's friend Sophie threw a house party to celebrate the end of the exams. Her parents were in Sicily or somewhere like that. Connell still had an exam left at the time, but he wasn't worried about it, so he came along too. All their friends were there, partly because Sophie had a heated swimming pool in her basement. They spent most of the night in their swimsuits, dipping in and out of the water, drinking and talking. Marianne sat at the side with a plastic cup of wine, while some of the others played a game in the pool. It seemed to involve people sitting on other people's shoulders and trying to knock each other into the water. Sophie got up onto Connell's shoulders for the second match, and said appreciatively: That's a nice solid torso you have. Marianne looked on, slightly drunk, admiring the way Sophie and Connell looked together, his hands on her smooth brown shins, and feeling a strange sense of nostalgia for a moment that was already in the process of happening. Sophie looked over at her then.

No need to worry, Marianne, she called. I'm not going to steal him away.

Marianne thought Connell would gaze off into the water, pretending not to hear, but instead he looked around at her and smiled.

She's not worried, he said.

She didn't know what that meant, really, but she smiled, and then the game began. She felt happy to be surrounded by people she liked, who liked her. She knew that if she wanted to speak, everyone would probably turn around and listen out of sincere interest, and that made her happy too, although she had nothing at all to say.

After the game was finished Connell came over to her, standing in the water where her legs were dangling. She looked down at him benignly. I was admiring you, she said. He pushed his wet hair back from his forehead. You're always admiring me, he said. She kicked her leg at him gently and he put his hand around her ankle and stroked it with his fingers. You and Sophie make an athletic team, she said. He kept stroking her leg under the water. It felt very nice. The others were calling him back to the deeper end then, they wanted to have another game. You're alright, he said. I'm having a break for this round. Then he hopped up onto the side of the pool, beside her. His body was glistening wet. He put his hand flat on the tiles behind her to steady himself.

Come here, he said.

He put his arm around her waist. He had never, ever touched her in front of anyone else before. Their friends had never seen them together like this, no one had. In the pool the others were still splashing and yelling.

That's nice, she said.

He turned his head and kissed her bare shoulder. She laughed again, shocked and gratified. He glanced back out at the water and then looked at her.

You're happy now, he said. You're smiling.

You're right, I am happy.

He nodded towards the pool, where Peggy had just fallen into the water, and people were laughing.

Is this what life is like? Connell said.

She looked at his face, but she couldn't tell from his expression if he was pleased or miserable. What do you mean? she said. But he only shrugged. A few days later he told her he was leaving Dublin for the summer.

You didn't tell me you were in town, he says now.

She nods slowly, like she's thinking about it, like it just now occurs to her that in fact she did not tell Connell she was in town, and it's an interesting thought.

So what, are we not friends anymore? he says.

Of course we are.

You don't reply to my messages very much.

Admittedly she has been ignoring him. She had to tell people what had happened between them, that he had broken up with her and moved away, and it mortified her. She was the one who had introduced Connell to everyone, who had told them all what great company he was, how sensitive and intelligent, and he had repaid her by staying in her apartment almost every night for three months, drinking the beer she bought for him, and then abruptly dumping her. It made her look like such a fool. Peggy laughed it off, of course, saying men were all the same. Joanna didn't seem to think the situation was funny at all, but puzzling, and sad. She kept asking what each of them had specifically said during the break-up, and then she would go quiet, as if she was re-enacting the scene in her mind to try and make sense of it.

Joanna wanted to know if Connell knew about Marianne's family. Everyone in Carricklea knows each other, Marianne said. Joanna shook her head and said: But I mean, does he know what they're like? Marianne couldn't answer that. She feels that even she doesn't know what her family are like, that she's never adequate in her attempts to describe them, that she oscillates between exaggerating their behaviour, which makes her feel guilty, or downplaying it, which also makes her feel guilty, but a different guilt, more inwardly directed. Joanna believes that she knows what Marianne's family are like, but how can she, how can anyone, when Marianne herself doesn't? Of course Connell can't. He's a well-adjusted person raised in a loving home. He just assumes the best of everyone and knows nothing.

I thought you would at least text me if you were coming home, he says. It's kind of weird running into you when I didn't know you were around.

At this moment she remembers leaving a flask in Connell's car the day they drove to Howth in April, and she never got the flask back. It might still be in his glovebox. She eyes the glovebox but doesn't feel she can open it, because he would ask what she was doing and she would have to bring up the trip to Howth. They went swimming in the sea that day and then parked his car somewhere out of sight and had sex in the back seat. It would be shameless to remind him of that day now that they're once again in the car together, even though she would really like her flask back, or maybe it's not about the flask, maybe she just wants to remind him he once fucked her in the back seat of the car they're now sitting in, she knows it would make him blush, and maybe she wants to force him to blush as a sadistic display of power, but that wouldn't be like her, so she says nothing.

What are you doing in town anyway? he says. Just visiting your family?

It's my father's anniversary Mass.

Oh, he says. He glances over at her, then back out the windshield. Sorry, he adds. I didn't realise. When is that, tomorrow morning?

She nods. Half ten, she says.

Sorry about that, Marianne. That was stupid of me.

It's alright. I didn't really want to come home for it but my mother kind of insists. I'm not a big Mass person.

No, he says. Yeah.

He coughs. She stares out the windshield. They're at the top of her street now. She and Connell have never spoken much about her father, or about his.

Do you want me to come? Connell says. Obviously if you don't want me there I won't go. But I wouldn't mind going, if you want.

She looks at him, and feels a certain weakening in her body.

Thank you for offering, she says. That's kind of you.

I don't mind.

You really don't have to.

It's no bother, he says. I'd like to go, to be honest.

He indicates and pulls into her gravel driveway. Her mother's car isn't there, she's not at home. The huge white facade of the house glares down at them. Something about the arrangement of windows gives Marianne's house a disapproving expression. Connell switches the engine off.

Sorry I was ignoring your messages, says Marianne. It was childish.

It's alright. Look, if you don't want to be friends anymore, we don't have to be.

Of course I want to be friends.

He nods, tapping his fingers on the steering wheel. His body is so big and gentle, like a Labrador. She wants to tell him things. But it's too late now, and anyway it has never done her any good to tell anyone.

Alright, says Connell. I'll see you tomorrow morning at the church, then, will I?

She swallows. Do you want to come inside for a bit? she says. We could have a cup of tea or something.

Oh, I would, but there's ice cream in the boot.

Marianne looks around, remembering the shopping bags, and feels disorientated suddenly.

Lorraine would kill me, he says.

Sure. Of course.

She gets out of the car then. He waves out the window. And he will come, tomorrow morning, and he will be wearing a navy sweatshirt with a white Oxford shirt underneath, looking innocent as a lamb, and he will stand with her in the vestibule afterwards, not saying very much but catching her eye supportively. Smiles will be exchanged, relieved smiles. And they will be friends again.

Six Weeks Later

(SEPTEMBER 2012)

He's late to meet her. The bus was caught in traffic because of some rally in town and now he's eight minutes late and he doesn't know where the cafe is. He has never met Marianne 'for coffee' before. The weather is too warm today, a scratchy and unseasonal heat. He finds the cafe on Capel Street and walks past the cashier towards the door at the back, checking his phone. It's nine minutes past three. Outside the back door Marianne is sitting in the smoking garden drinking her coffee already. No one else is out there, the place is quiet. She doesn't get up when she sees him.

Sorry I'm late, he says. There was some protest on so the bus was delayed.

He sits down opposite her. He hasn't ordered anything yet.

Don't worry about it, she says. What was the protest? It wasn't abortion or anything, was it?

He feels ashamed now that he didn't notice. No, I don't think so, he says. The household tax or something.

Well, best of luck to them. May the revolution be swift and brutal.

He hasn't seen her in person since July, when she came home for her father's Mass. Her lips look pale now and slightly chapped, and she has dark circles under her eyes. Although he takes pleasure in seeing her look good, he feels a special sympathy with her when she looks ill or her skin is bad, like when someone who's usually very good at sports has a poor game. It makes her seem nicer somehow. She's wearing a very elegant black blouse, her wrists look slender and white, and her hair is twisted back loosely at her neck.

Yeah, he says. I would have a bit more energy for protesting if it was more on the brutal side, to be honest.

You want to get beaten up by the Gardaí.

There are worse things than getting beaten up.

Marianne is taking a sip of coffee when he says this, and she seems to pause for a moment with the cup at her lips. He can't tell how he identifies this pause as distinct from the natural motion of her drinking, but he sees it. Then she replaces the cup on the saucer.

I agree, she says.

What does that mean?

I'm agreeing with you.

Have you recently been attacked by the guards or have I missed something? he says.

She taps a little extra sugar from a sachet into her cup and then stirs it. Finally she glances up at him as if remembering he's sitting there.

Aren't you going to have coffee? she says.

He nods. He's still feeling a little breathless after the walk from the bus, a little too warm under his clothes. He gets up from the table and goes back into the main room. It's cool in there and much dimmer. A woman in red lipstick takes his order and says she'll bring it right out.

Until April, Connell had been planning to work in Dublin for the summer and cover the rent with his wages, but a week before the exams his boss told him they were cutting back his hours. He could just about make rent that way but he'd have nothing left to live on. He'd always known that the place was going to go out of business, and he was furious with himself for not applying anywhere else. He thought about it constantly for weeks. In the end he decided he would have to move out for the summer. Niall was very nice about it, said the room would still be there for him in September and all of that. What about yourself and Marianne? Niall asked. And Connell said: Yeah, yeah. I don't know. I haven't told her yet.

The reality was that he stayed in Marianne's apartment most nights anyway. He could just tell her about the situation and ask if he could stay in her place until September. He knew she would say yes. He thought she would say yes, it was hard to imagine her not saying yes. But he found himself putting off the conversation, putting off Niall's enquiries about it, planning to bring it up with her and then at the last minute failing to. It just felt too much like asking her for money. He and Marianne never talked about money. They had never talked, for example, about the fact that her mother paid his mother money to scrub their floors and hang their laundry, or about the fact that this money circulated indirectly to Connell, who spent it, as often as not, on Marianne. He hated having to think about things like that. He knew Marianne never thought that way. She bought him things all the time, dinner, theatre tickets, things she would pay for and then instantly, permanently, forget about.

They went to a party in Sophie Whelan's house one night as the exams were ending. He knew he would finally have to tell Marianne that he was moving out of Niall's place, and he would have to ask her, outright, if he could stay with her instead. Most of the evening they spent by the swimming pool, immersed in the bewitching gravity of warm water. He watched Marianne splashing around in her strapless red swimsuit. A lock of wet hair had come loose from the knot at her neck and was sealed flat and shining against her skin. Everyone was laughing and drinking. It felt nothing like his real life. He didn't know these people at all, he hardly even believed in them, or in himself. At the side of the pool he kissed Marianne's shoulder impulsively and she smiled at him, delighted. No one looked at them. He thought he would tell her about the rent situation that night in bed. He felt very afraid of losing her. When they got to bed she wanted to have sex and afterwards she fell asleep. He thought of waking her up but he couldn't. He decided he would wait until after his last exam to talk to her about moving home.

Two days later, directly after his paper on Medieval and Renaissance Romance, he went over to Marianne's apartment and they sat at the table drinking coffee. He half-listened to her talking about some complicated relationship between Teresa and Lorcan, waiting for her to finish, and eventually he said: Hey, listen. By the way. It looks like I won't be able to pay rent up here this summer. Marianne looked up from her coffee and said flatly: What?

Yeah, he said. I'm going to have to move out of Niall's place.

When? said Marianne.

Pretty soon. Next week maybe.

Her face hardened, without displaying any particular emotion. Oh, she said. You'll be going home, then.

He rubbed at his breastbone then, feeling short of breath. Looks like it, yeah, he said.

She nodded, raised her eyebrows briefly and then lowered them again, and stared down into her cup of coffee. Well, she said. You'll be back in September, I assume.

His eyes were hurting and he closed them. He couldn't understand how this had happened, how he had let the discussion slip away like this. It was too late to say he wanted to stay with her, that was clear, but when had it become too late? It seemed to have happened immediately. He contemplated putting his face down on the table and just crying like a child. Instead he opened his eyes again.

Yeah, he said. I'm not dropping out, don't worry.

So you'll only be gone three months.

Yeah.

There was a long pause.

I don't know, he said. I guess you'll want to see other people, then, will you?

Finally, in a voice that struck him as truly cold, Marianne said: Sure.

He got up then and poured his coffee down the sink, although it wasn't finished. When he left her building he did cry, as much for his pathetic fantasy of living in her apartment as for their failed relationship, whatever that was.

Within a couple of weeks she was going out with someone else, a friend of hers called Jamie. Jamie's dad was one of the people who had caused the financial crisis – not figuratively, one of the actual people involved. It was Niall who told Connell they were together. He read it in a text message during work and had to go into the back room and press his forehead against a cool shelving unit for almost a full minute. Marianne had just wanted to see someone else all along, he thought. She was probably glad he'd had to leave Dublin because he was broke. She wanted a boyfriend whose family could take her on skiing holidays. And now that she had one, she wouldn't even answer Connell's emails anymore.

By July even Lorraine had heard that Marianne was seeing someone new. Connell knew people in town were talking about it, because Jamie had this nationally infamous father, and because there was nothing much else going on.

When did you two split up, then? Lorraine asked him.

We were never together.

You were seeing each other, I thought.

Casually, he replied.

Young people these days. I can't get my head around your relationships.

You're hardly ancient.

When I was in school, she said, you were either going out with someone or you weren't.

Connell moved his jaw around, staring at the television blandly.

Where did I come from, then? he said.

Lorraine gave him a nudge of reproach and he continued to look at the TV. It was a travel programme, long silver beaches and blue water.

Marianne Sheridan wouldn't go out with someone like me, he said.

What does that mean, someone like you?

I think her new boyfriend is a bit more in line with her social class.

Lorraine was silent for several seconds. Connell could feel his back teeth grinding together quietly.

I don't believe Marianne would act like that, Lorraine said. I don't think she's that kind of person.

He got up from the sofa. I can only tell you what happened, he said.

Well, maybe you're misinterpreting what happened.

But Connell had already left the room.

Back outside the cafe now, the sunlight is so strong it crunches all the colours up and makes them sting. Marianne's lighting a cigarette, with the box left open on the table. When he sits down she smiles at him through the small grey cloud of smoke. He feels she's being coy, but he doesn't know about what.

I don't think we've ever met for coffee before, he says. Have we?

Have we not? We must have.

He knows he's being unpleasant now but he can't stop. No, he says.

We have, she says. We got coffee before we went to see *Rear Window*. Although I guess that was more like a date.

This remark surprises him, and in response he just makes some non-committal noise like: Hm.

The door behind them opens and the woman comes out with his coffee. Connell thanks her and she smiles and goes back inside. The door swings shut. Marianne is saying that she hopes Connell and Jamie get to know each other better. I hope you get along with him, Marianne says. And she looks up at Connell nervously then, a sincere expression which touches him.

Yeah, I'm sure I will, he says. Why wouldn't I?

I know you'll be civil. But I mean I hope you get along.

I'll try.

And don't intimidate him, she says.

Connell pours a splash of milk in his coffee, letting the colour come up to the surface, and then replaces the jug on the table.

Oh, he says. Well, I hope you're telling him not to intimidate me either.

As if you could find him intimidating, Connell. He's shorter than I am.

It's not strictly a height thing, is it?

Seen from his point of view, she says, you're a lot taller, and you're the person who used to fuck his girlfriend.

That's a nice way of putting it. Is that what you told him about us, Connell's this tall guy who used to fuck me?

She laughs now. No, she says. But everyone knows.

Does he have some insecurities about his height? I won't exploit them, I'd just like to know.

Marianne lifts her coffee cup. Connell can't figure out what kind of relationship they are supposed to have now. Are they agreeing not to find each other attractive anymore? When were they supposed to have stopped? Nothing in Marianne's behaviour gives him any clue. In fact he suspects she is still attracted to him, and that she now finds it funny, like a private joke, to indulge an attraction to someone who could never belong in her world.

Back in July he went to the anniversary Mass for Marianne's father. The church in town was small, smelling of rain and incense, with stained-glass panels in the windows. He and Lorraine never went to Mass, he'd only been in there for funerals before. He saw Marianne in the vestibule when he arrived. She looked like a piece of religious art. It was so much more painful to look at her than anyone had warned him it would be, and he wanted to do something terrible, like set himself on fire or drive his car into a tree. He always reflexively imagined ways to cause himself extreme injury when he was distressed. It seemed to soothe him briefly, the act of imagining a much worse and more totalising pain than the one he really felt, maybe just the cognitive energy it required, the momentary break in his train of thought, but afterwards he would only feel worse.

That night, after Marianne went back to Dublin, he went out drinking with some people from school, to Kelleher's first, and then McGowan's, and then that awful nightclub Phantom around the back of the hotel. No one was around that he had ever been really close with, and after a few drinks he became aware that he wasn't there to socialise anyway, he was just there to drink himself into a kind of sedated nonconsciousness. He withdrew from the conversation gradually and focused on consuming as much alcohol as he could without passing out, not even laughing along with the jokes, not even listening.

It was in Phantom that they met Paula Neary, their old Economics teacher. By then Connell was so drunk that his vision was misaligned, and beside every solid object he could see another version of the object, like a ghost. Paula bought them all shots of tequila. She was wearing a black dress and a silver pendant. He licked a line of salt off the back of his own hand and saw the ghostly other of her necklace, a faint white trace on her shoulder. When she looked at him she did not have two eyes, but several, and they moved around exotically in the air, like jewels. He started laughing about it, and she leaned in close with her breath on his face to ask him what was so funny.

He doesn't remember how he got back to her house, whether they walked or took a taxi, he still doesn't know. The place had that strange unfurnished cleanliness that lonely houses sometimes have. She seemed like a person with no hobbies: no bookcases, no musical instruments. What do you do with yourself at the weekends, he remembers slurring. I go out and have fun, she said. This struck him even at the time as deeply depressing. She poured them both glasses of wine. Connell sat on the leather sofa and drank the wine for something to do with his hands.

How is the football team looking this year? he said.

It's not the same without you, said Paula.

She sat beside him on the couch. Her dress had slipped down slightly, exposing a mole over her right breast. He could have fucked her back when he was in school. People joked about it, but they would have been shocked if it had really happened, they would have been scared. They would have thought his shyness masked something steely and frightening.

Best years of your life, she said.

What?

Best years of your life, secondary school.

He tried to laugh, and it came out very goofy and nervous. I don't know, he said. That's a sad thought if that's true.

She started to kiss him then. This seemed like a strange thing to happen to him, unpleasant on the surface level, but also interesting in a way, as if his life was taking a new direction.

Her mouth tasted sour like tequila. Briefly he wondered if it was legal for her to kiss him, and he concluded it must be, he couldn't think of a reason why it wouldn't be, and yet it felt substantially wrong. Every time he pulled away from her she seemed to follow him forward, so that he found himself puzzled about the physics of what was going on, and he was no longer sure whether he was sitting upright on the sofa or reclining backwards against the arm. As an experiment he tried to sit up, which confirmed he was in fact sitting up already, and the small red light which he thought might have been on the ceiling above him was just a standby light on the stereo system across the room.

Back in school Miss Neary had made him feel so uncomfortable. But was he mastering that discomfort now by letting her kiss him on the sofa in her living room, or just succumbing to it? He'd hardly had time to formulate this question when she started unbuttoning his jeans. In a panic he tried to push her hand away, but with such an ineffectual gesture that she appeared to think he was helping her. She got the top button undone and he told her that he was really drunk, and maybe they should stop. She put her hand inside the waistband of his underwear and said it was okay, she didn't mind. He thought he would probably black out then, but he found he couldn't. He wished he could have. He heard Paula saying: You're so hard. That was an especially insane thing for her to say, because he actually wasn't.

I'm going to get sick, he said.

She jerked back then, pulling her dress after her, and he took the opportunity to stand up from the sofa and button his jeans back up. Cautiously she asked if he was okay. When he looked at her he could make out two separate Paulas sitting on the couch, so clearly delineated that it was no longer obvious which was the real Paula and which the ghost. Sorry, he said. He woke up the next day fully clothed on the floor of his living room. He still has no idea how he made it home.

He must be insecure about something, says Marianne now. I don't know what. Maybe he'd like to be more cerebral.

Maybe he just has good self-esteem.

No, definitely not that. He's . . .

Her eyes flick back and forth quickly. When she does this, she looks like an expert mathematician performing calculations in her head. She sets the coffee cup back in the saucer.

He's what? says Connell.

He's a sadist.

Connell stares at her across the table, simply allowing his face to express the alarm he feels at this remark, and she gives a cute little smile. She twists her cup around on the saucer.

Are you serious? says Connell.

Well, he likes to beat me up. Just during sex, that is. Not during arguments.

She laughs, a stupid laugh that doesn't suit her. Connell's visual field shudders violently for a second, like the beginning of a gigantic migraine, and he lifts a hand to his forehead. He realises he is scared. Around Marianne he often feels somehow innocent, though really he's a lot more sexually experienced than she is.

And you're into that, are you? he says.

She shrugs. Her cigarette is burning out in the ashtray. She picks it up quickly and drags on it before stubbing it out.

I don't know, she says. I don't know if I really like it.

Why do you let him do it, then?

It was my idea.

Connell picks up his cup and takes a large mouthful of very hot coffee, wanting to do something efficient with his hands. When he replaces the cup it splashes up and spills over into the saucer.

What do you mean? he says.

It was my idea, that I wanted to submit to him. It's difficult to explain.

Well, go on and try if you want. I'm interested.

She laughs again now. It's going to make you feel very awkward, she says.

Okay.

She looks at him, maybe to see if he's joking, and then she lifts her chin at an angle, and he knows she won't back down from telling him about it, because that would be giving in to something she doesn't believe about herself.

It's not that I get off on being degraded as such, she says. I just like to know that I would degrade myself for someone if they wanted me to. Does that make sense? I don't know if it does, I've been thinking about it. It's about the dynamic, more than what actually happens. Anyway I suggested it to him, that I could try being more submissive. And it turns out he likes to beat me up.

Connell starts coughing. Marianne picks a small wooden coffee-stirrer out of a jar on the table and starts twisting it in her fingers. He waits for the coughing to subside and then says: What does he do to you?

Oh, I don't know, she says. He hits me with a belt sometimes. He likes choking me, things like that.

Right.

I mean, I don't enjoy it. But then, you're not really submitting to someone if you only submit to things you enjoy.

Have you always had these ideas? Connell says.

She gives him a look. He feels like the fear has consumed him and turned him into something else now, like he has passed through the fear, and looking at her is like swimming towards her across a strip of water. He picks up the cigarette packet and looks into it. His teeth start chattering and he puts a cigarette on his lower lip and lights it. Marianne is the only one who ever triggers these feelings in him, the strange dissociative feeling, like he's drowning and time doesn't exist properly anymore.

I don't want you to think Jamie's a horrible guy, she says.

He sounds like one.

He's not really.

Connell drags on the cigarette and then lets his eyes half-close for a second. The sun is very warm, and he can sense Marianne's body close to him, and the mouthful of smoke, and the bitter aftertaste of coffee.

Maybe I want to be treated badly, she says. I don't know. Sometimes I think I deserve bad things because I'm a bad person.

He exhales. In the spring he would sometimes wake up at night beside Marianne, and if she was awake too they would move into each other's arms until he could feel himself inside her. He didn't have to say anything, except to ask her if it was alright, and she always said it was. Nothing else in his life compared to what he felt then. Often he wished he could fall asleep inside her body. It was something he could never have with anyone else, and he would never want to. Afterwards they'd just go back to sleep in each other's arms, without speaking.

You never said any of this to me, he says. When we were . . .

It was different with you. We were, you know. Things were different.

She twists the little strip of wood with both hands and then releases it on one side so it recoils from her fingers.

Should I be feeling insulted? he says.

No. If you want to hear the simplest explanation, I'll tell you.

Well, is it a lie?

No, she says.

She pauses. Carefully she sets down the wooden coffee-stirrer. She has no props now, and reaches to touch her hair instead.

I didn't need to play any games with you, she says. It was real. With Jamie it's like I'm acting a part, I just pretend to feel that way, like I'm in his power. But with you that really was the dynamic, I actually had those feelings, I would have done anything you wanted me to. Now, you see, you think I'm a bad girlfriend. I'm being disloyal. Who wouldn't want to beat me up?

She covers her eyes with her hand. She's smiling, a tired and self-hating smile. He wipes the palms of his hands on his lap.

I wouldn't, he says. Maybe I'm kind of unfashionable in that way.

She moves her hand away and looks at him, the same smile, and her lips still look dry.

I hope we can always take each other's sides, she says. It's very comforting for me.

Well, that's good.

She looks at him then, like she's seeing him for the first time since they sat down together.

Anyway, she says. How are you?

He knows the question is meant honestly. He's not someone who feels comfortable confiding in others, or demanding things from them. He needs Marianne for this reason. This fact strikes him newly. Marianne is someone he can ask things of. Even though there are certain difficulties and resentments in their relationship, the relationship carries on. This seems remarkable to him now, and almost moving.

Something kind of weird happened to me in the summer, he said. Can I tell you about it?

Four Months Later

(JANUARY 2013)

She's in her apartment with friends. The scholarship exams finished this week and term is about to start again on Monday. She feels drained, like a vessel turned out onto its rim. She's smoking her fourth cigarette of the evening, which gives her a curious acidic sensation in her chest, and she also hasn't eaten dinner. For lunch she had a tangerine and a piece of unbuttered toast. Peggy is on the sofa telling a story about interrailing in Europe, and for some reason she insists on explaining the difference between West and East Berlin. Marianne exhales and says absently: Yes, I've been there.

Peggy turns to her, eyes widened. You've been to Berlin? she says. I didn't think they let people from Connacht travel that far.

Some of their friends laugh politely. Marianne taps the ash off her cigarette into the ceramic tray on the arm of the sofa. Extremely hilarious, she says.

They must have given you time off from the farm, says Peggy.

Quite, says Marianne.

Peggy continues telling her story then. She has lately taken to sleeping over in Marianne's apartment when Jamie's not there, eating breakfast in her bed, and even following her to the bathroom when she showers, clipping her toenails blithely and complaining about men. Marianne likes to be singled out as her special friend, even when this expresses itself as a tendency to take up vast amounts of her leisure time. But at certain parties lately, Peggy has also started to make fun of her in front of others. For the sake of their friends, Marianne tries to laugh along, but the effort contorts her face, which only gives Peggy another chance to tease her. When everyone else has gone home she snuggles into Marianne's shoulder and says: Don't be mad with me. And Marianne says in a thin, defensive voice: I'm not mad at you. They are right now shaping up to have this exact exchange, yet again, in just a few short hours.

After the Berlin story concludes, Marianne gets another bottle of wine from the kitchen and refills people's glasses.

How did the exams go, by the way? Sophie asks her.

Marianne gives a humorous shrug and is rewarded with a little laughter. Her friends sometimes seem uncertain about her dynamic with Peggy, volunteering extra laughter when Marianne tries to be funny, but in a way that can seem sympathetic or even pitying rather than amused.

Tell the truth, says Peggy. You fucked them up, didn't you?

Marianne smiles, makes a face, puts the cap back on the wine bottle. The scholarship exams finished two days ago; Peggy and Marianne sat them together.

Well, they could have gone better, Marianne says diplomatically.

This is one hundred per cent typical you, says Peggy. You're the smartest person in the world but when it comes down to it, you're a bottler.

You can sit them again next year, says Sophie.

I doubt they went that badly, Joanna says.

Marianne avoids Joanna's eyes and puts the wine back in

the fridge. The scholarships offer five years of paid tuition, free accommodation on campus, and meals in the Dining Hall every evening with the other scholars. For Marianne, who doesn't pay her own rent or tuition and has no real concept of how much these things cost, it's just a matter of reputation. She would like her superior intellect to be affirmed in public by the transfer of large amounts of money. That way she could affect modesty without having anyone actually believe her. The fact is, the exams didn't go badly. They went fine.

My Stats professor was on at me to sit them, says Jamie. But I just couldn't be fucked studying over Christmas.

Marianne produces another vacant smile. Jamie didn't sit the exams because he knew he wouldn't pass them if he did. Everyone in the room knows this also. He's trying to brag, but he lacks the self-awareness to understand that what he's saying is legible as bragging, and that no one believes the brag anyway. There's something reassuring in how transparent he is to her.

Early in their relationship, without any apparent forethought, she told him she was 'a submissive'. She was surprised even hearing herself say it: maybe she did it to shock him. What do you mean? he asked. Feeling worldly, she replied: You know, I like guys to hurt me. After that he started to tie her up and beat her with various objects. When she thinks about how little she respects him, she feels disgusting and begins to hate herself, and these feelings trigger in her an overwhelming desire to be subjugated and in a way broken. When it happens her brain simply goes empty, like a room with the light turned off, and she shudders into orgasm without any perceptible joy. Then it begins again. When she thinks about breaking up with him, which she frequently does, it's not his reaction but Peggy's she finds herself thinking about most.

Peggy likes Jamie, which is to say that she thinks he's kind of a fascist, but a fascist with no essential power over Marianne. Marianne complains about him sometimes and Peggy just says things like: Well, he's a chauvinist pig, what do you expect? Peggy thinks men are disgusting animals with no impulse control, and that women should avoid relying on them for emotional support. It took a long time for it to dawn on Marianne that Peggy was using the guise of her general critique of men to defend Jamie whenever Marianne complained about him. What did you expect? Peggy would say. Or: You think that's bad? By male standards he's a prince. Marianne has no idea why she does this. Any time Marianne makes the suggestion, however tentative, that things might be coming to an end with Jamie, Peggy's temper flares up. They've even fought about it, fights that end with Peggy curiously declaring that she doesn't care whether they break up or not anyway, and Marianne, by then exhausted and confused, saying they probably won't.

When Marianne sits back down now, her phone starts ringing, a number she doesn't recognise. She stands up to get it, gesturing for the others to continue talking, and wanders back into the kitchen.

Hello? she says.

Hi, it's Connell. This is a bit awkward, but I've just had some of my things stolen. Like my wallet and my phone and stuff.

Jesus, how awful. What happened?

I'm just wondering— See, I'm all the way out in Dun Laoghaire now and I don't have money to get in a taxi or anything. I wonder if there's any way I could meet up with you and maybe borrow some cash or something.

All her friends are looking at her now and she waves them back to their conversation. From the armchair Jamie continues to watch her on the phone.

Of course, don't worry about that, she says. I'm at home, so do you want to get a taxi over here? I'll come outside and pay the driver, does that suit you? You can ring the bell when you're here.

Yeah. Alright, thanks. Thanks, Marianne. I'm borrowing this phone so I'd better give it back now. See you in a bit.

He hangs up. Her friends look at her expectantly as she holds the phone in one hand and turns to face them. She explains what's happened, and they all express sympathy for Connell. He still comes to her parties occasionally, just for a quick drink before heading on somewhere else. He told Marianne in September what had happened with Paula Neary, and it made Marianne feel unearthly, possessed of a violence she had never known before. I know I'm being dramatic, Connell said. It's not like she did anything that bad. But I feel fucked up about it. Marianne heard herself in a voice like hard ice saying: I would like to slit her throat. Connell looked up and laughed, just from shock. Jesus, Marianne, he said. But he was laughing. I would, she insisted. He shook his head. You have to tone down these violent impulses, he said. You can't be going around slashing people's throats, they'll put you in prison. Marianne let him laugh it off, but quietly she said: If she ever lays a hand on you again I will do it, I don't care.

She has only spare change in her purse, but in a drawer in her bedside cabinet she has three hundred euro in cash. She goes in there now, without switching the light on, and she can hear the voices of her friends murmur through the wall. The cash is there, six fifties. She takes three and folds them into her purse quietly. Then she sits on the side of the bed, not wanting to go back out right away.

Things at home were tense over Christmas. Alan gets anxious and highly strung whenever they have guests in the house. One night, after their aunt and uncle left, Alan followed Marianne down to the kitchen, where she had taken their empty cups of tea.

State of you, he said. Bragging about your exam results.

Marianne turned on the hot tap and measured the temperature with her fingers. Alan stood inside the doorway, arms folded.

I didn't bring it up, she said. They did.

If that's all you have to brag about in your life I feel sorry for you, said Alan.

The water from the tap got warmer and Marianne put the plug in the sink and squeezed a little dish soap onto a sponge.

Are you listening to me? said Alan.

Yes, you feel sorry for me, I'm listening.

You're fucking pathetic, so you are.

Message received, she said.

She placed one of the cups on the draining board to dry and dipped another into the hot water.

Do you think you're smarter than me? he said.

She ran the wet sponge around the inside of the teacup. That's a strange question, she said. I don't know, I've never thought about it.

Well, you're not, he said.

Okay, fair enough.

Okay, fair enough, he repeated in a cringing, girlish voice. No wonder you have no friends, you can't even have a normal conversation.

Right.

You should hear what people in town say about you.

Involuntarily, because this idea was so ridiculous to her, she laughed. Enraged now, Alan wrenched her back from the sink by her upper arm and, seemingly spontaneously, spat at her. Then he released her arm. A visible drop of spit had landed on the cloth of her skirt. Wow, she said, that's disgusting. Alan turned and left the room, and Marianne went back to rinsing the dishes. Lifting the fourth teacup onto the draining board she noticed a mild but perceptible tremor in her right hand.

On Christmas Day her mother gave her an envelope with five hundred euro in it. There was no card; it was one of the small brown-paper envelopes she used for Lorraine's wages. Marianne thanked her, and Denise said airily: I'm a bit concerned about you. Marianne fingered the envelope and tried to arrange her face into a suitable expression. What about me? she said.

Well, said Denise, what are you going to do with your life?

I don't know. I think I still have a lot of options open. I'm just focusing on college at the moment.

And then what?

Marianne pressed her thumb on the envelope and smudged

it until a faint dark smear appeared on the paper. As I said, she repeated, I don't know.

I'm worried the real world will come as a bit of a shock to you, said Denise.

In what way?

I don't know if you realise that university is a very protective environment. It's not like a workplace.

Well, I doubt anyone in the workplace will spit at me over a disagreement, said Marianne. It would be pretty frowned upon, as I understand.

Denise gave a tight-lipped smile. If you can't handle a little sibling rivalry, I don't know how you're going to manage adult life, darling, she said.

Let's see how it goes.

At this, Denise struck the kitchen table with her open palm. Marianne flinched, but didn't look up, didn't let go of the envelope.

You think you're special, do you? said Denise.

Marianne let her eyes close. No, she said. I don't.

It's almost one in the morning by the time Connell rings the buzzer. Marianne goes downstairs with her purse and finds the taxi is idling outside the building. In the square opposite, a mist wreathes itself around the trees. Winter nights are so exquisite, she thinks of saying to Connell. He's standing talking to the driver through the window, with his back turned. When he hears the door he turns around, and she sees his mouth cut and bloody, dark blood like dried ink. She steps back, clutching her collarbone, and Connell goes: I know, I saw myself in the mirror. But I'm okay actually, I just need to get cleaned up. In a state of confusion she pays the driver, almost dropping her change in the gutter. On the staircase inside she sees Connell's upper lip is swollen into a hard shiny mass on the right side. His teeth are the colour of blood. Oh god, she says. What happened? He takes her hand kindly, stroking her knuckles with his thumb.

Some guy came up and asked me for my wallet, he says. And I told him no, for some reason, and then he hit me in the face. I mean, it was a bad idea, I should have just given him the money. Sorry for calling you, it's the only number I knew off the top of my head.

Oh, Connell, how awful. I have friends round, but what suits you? Do you want to have a shower or something and you can stay here? Or do you want to just get some cash and go home?

They're outside the door of her apartment now, and they pause there.

Whatever's good for you, he says. I'm really drunk, by the way. Sorry.

Oh, how drunk?

Well, I haven't been home since the exams. I don't know, do I still have pupils?

She looks in his eyes, where his pupils are swollen to round black bullets.

Yes, she says. They're huge.

He strokes her hand again and says more quietly: Oh well. They get like that when I see you anyway.

She laughs, shaking her head.

You're definitely drunk if you're flirting with me, she says. Jamie's here, you know.

Connell breathes in through his nose and then glances over his own shoulder.

Maybe I'll just go back out and get punched in the face again, he says. It wasn't that bad.

She smiles, but he lets go of her hand. She opens the door.

In the living room her friends all gasp and make him retell the story, which he does, though without the desired drama. Marianne gets him a glass of water, which he swills in his mouth and then spits into the kitchen sink, pink like coral.

Fucking lowlife scum, says Jamie.

Who, me? Connell says. That's not very nice. We can't all go to private school, you know.

Joanna laughs. Connell isn't usually hostile and Marianne wonders if getting punched in the face has put him in a hostile mood, or else he's more drunk than she thought.

I was talking about the guy that robbed you, says Jamie. And he was probably stealing to buy drugs, by the way, that's what most of them do.

Connell touches his teeth with his fingers as if to ascertain that they're still in his mouth. Then he wipes his hands on a dishtowel.

Oh well, he says. It's not an easy life out there for a drug addict.

No, indeed, says Joanna.

They could always try, I don't know, giving up drugs? says Jamie.

Connell laughs and says: Yeah, I'm sure they've just never thought of that.

Everyone's quiet and Connell gives a bashful smile. His teeth are less insane-looking now that he's rinsed them with water. Sorry, everyone, he says. I'll get out of your way. They all insist he's not in their way, except Jamie, who says nothing. Marianne experiences a flash of maternalistic desire to run Connell a bath. Joanna asks him if he's in pain, and he responds by rubbing his front teeth with a fingertip again and then saying: It's not that bad. He's wearing a black jacket over a stained white T-shirt, under which Marianne recognises the glimmer of an unadorned silver neckchain he's had since school. Peggy once described the neckchain as 'Argos chic', which made Marianne cringe, though she couldn't tell which friend she was cringing for.

How much cash do you think you'll need? she says to Connell. The question is sensitive enough that her friends start to talk amongst themselves, so she feels she has him almost alone. He shrugs. You might not be able to make withdrawals without your bank card, she says. He squeezes his eyes shut and touches his forehead.

Fuck me, I'm so drunk, he says. I'm sorry, I feel like I'm hallucinating. What are you asking me?

Money. How much can I give you?

Oh, I don't know, ten quid?

Let me give you a hundred, she says.

What? No.

They argue like this for a while, until Jamie comes up and touches Marianne's arm. She is suddenly conscious of his ugliness, and wants to pull away from him. His hairline is receding and he has a weak, jawless face. Beside him, and even covered in blood, Connell radiates good health and charisma.

I'll probably have to head off shortly, says Jamie.

Well, I'll see you tomorrow, says Marianne.

Jamie looks at her in shock and she swallows the impulse to say: What? Instead she smiles. It's not like she's the world's best-looking person, far from it. In certain photographs she appears not only plain but garishly ugly, baring her crooked teeth for the camera like a piece of vermin. Guiltily she squeezes Jamie's wrist, as if she can perform the following impossible act of communication: to Jamie, that Connell is injured and regrettably requires her attention, while to Connell, that she would rather not be touching Jamie at all.

Alright, says Jamie. Well, goodnight, then.

He kisses the side of her face and goes to get his jacket. Everyone thanks Marianne for having them. Glasses are left on the draining board or in the sink. Then the front door closes and she and Connell are alone. She feels her shoulder muscles relaxing, like their solitude is a narcotic. She fills the kettle and takes cups down from the press, then places some more of the dirty glasses in the sink and empties the ashtray.

Is he still your boyfriend, then? says Connell.

She smiles, and so does he. She takes two teabags from the box and tamps them down into the cups while the kettle is boiling. She loves to be alone with him like this. It makes her life seem very manageable suddenly.

He is, yes, she says.

And why would that be the case?

Why is he my boyfriend?

Yeah, says Connell. What's going on there? In terms of like, why you're still going out with him.

Marianne snorts. I presume you'll have tea, she says. He nods. He puts his right hand in his pocket. She takes a carton of milk from the fridge, it's damp in her fingers. Connell is standing against the kitchen counter now, his mouth swollen but most of the blood rinsed off, and his face looks brutally handsome.

You could have a different boyfriend, you know, he says. I mean, guys are constantly falling in love with you, from what I hear.

Stop that.

You're the kind of person, people either love you or hate you.

The kettle clicks its switch and she lifts it out of the cradle. She fills one of the cups and then the other.

Well, you don't hate me, she says.

He doesn't say anything at first. Then he says: No, I'm immune to you, in a way. Because I knew you in school.

When I was an ugly loser, says Marianne.

No, you were never ugly.

She puts the kettle back down. She feels a certain power over him, a dangerous power.

Do you still think I'm pretty? she says.

He looks at her, probably knowing what she's doing, and then looks at his own hands, as if reminding himself of his physical stature in the room.

You're in a good mood, he says. Must have been a good party.

She ignores this. Fuck you, she thinks, but she doesn't mean it. She dumps the teabags in the sink with a spoon, then uses the milk and replaces it in the fridge, all with the rapid movements of someone dealing impatiently with a drunk friend.

I'd rather literally anyone else, says Connell. I'd rather the guy who mugged me was your boyfriend.

What do you care?

He says nothing. She thinks of the way she treated Jamie before he left, and rubs her face with her hands. Some milk-drinking culchie, Jamie called Connell once. It's true, she has seen Connell drink milk directly from the carton. He plays video games with aliens in them, he has opinions about football managers. He's wholesome like a big baby tooth. Probably never in his life has he thought about inflicting pain on someone for sexual purposes. He's a good person, he's a nice friend. So why does she go after him like this all the time, pressing him for something? Does she have to be her old desperate self around him always?

Do you love him? says Connell.

Her hand pauses on the door of the fridge.

Unlike you to take an interest in my feelings, Connell, she says. I kind of thought that stuff was off-limits for us, I have to say.

Alright. Okay.

He rubs at his mouth again, looking distracted now. Then he drops his hand and looks out the kitchen window.

Look, he says, I probably should have told you before, but I've been seeing someone. I've been with her for a while, I should have mentioned it to you.

Marianne is so shocked by this news that it feels physical. She looks at him, plainly, unable to disguise her astonishment. In the time they've been friends he has never had a girlfriend. She's never even given much thought to the idea that he might want one.

What? she says. How long have you been together?

About six weeks. Helen Brophy, I don't know would you know her. She studies Medicine.

Marianne turns her back on him and takes her cup from the counter. She tries to hold her shoulders very still, frightened that she'll cry and he'll see her.

Why are you trying to get me to break up with Jamie, then? she says.

I'm not, I'm not. I just want you to be happy, that's all.

Because you're such a good friend, is it?

Well, yeah, he says. I mean, I don't know.

The cup in Marianne's hands is too hot to hold, but instead of placing it down again she just lets the pain seep into her fingers, down into her flesh.

Are you in love with her? she says.

Yeah. I do love her, yeah.

Now Marianne starts crying, the most embarrassing thing that has happened to her in her entire adult life. Her back is turned but she feels her shoulders jerk upwards in a horrible involuntary spasm.

Jesus, says Connell. Marianne.

Fuck off.

Connell touches her back and she jolts away from him, like he's trying to hurt her. She puts the cup down on the counter to wipe her face roughly with her sleeve.

Just go away, she says. Leave me alone.

Marianne, don't. I feel awful, okay? I should have told you before, I'm sorry.

I don't want to talk to you. Just leave.

For a while nothing happens. She chews on the inside of her cheek until the pain begins to settle her nerves and she's not crying anymore. She dries her face again, with her hands this time, and turns around.

Please, she says. Please just go.

He sighs, he's looking at the floor. He rubs his eyes.

Yeah, he says. Look, I'm really sorry to ask, but I do kind of need that money to get home. Sorry.

She remembers then and feels bad. In fact she smiles at him, that's how bad she feels. Oh god, she says. In the excitement there I forgot you actually got assaulted. Can I give you two fifties, is that okay? He nods, but he's not looking at her. She knows that he feels bad; she wants to be a grown-up about things. She finds her purse and hands him the money, which he puts in his pocket. He looks down, blinking and clearing his throat, like he's going to cry too. I'm sorry, he says.

It's nothing, she says. Don't worry about it.

He rubs at his nose and looks around the room like he's never going to see it again.

You know, I didn't really know what was going on with us last summer, he says. Like, when I had to move home and that. I kind of thought maybe you would let me stay here or something. I don't really know what happened with us in the end.

She feels a sharp pain in her chest and her hand flies to her throat, clutching at nothing.

You told me you wanted us to see other people, she says. I had no idea you wanted to stay here. I thought you were breaking up with me.

He rubs his palm flat against his mouth for a second, and then breathes out.

You didn't say anything about wanting to stay here, she adds. You would have been welcome, obviously. You always were.

Right, okay, he says. Look, I'll head off, then. Have a good night, yeah?

He leaves. The door clicks shut behind him, not very loudly.

In the Arts Block the next morning Jamie kisses her in front of everyone and says she looks beautiful. How was Connell last night? he says. She grips Jamie's hand, she gives a conspiratorial roll of her eyes. Oh, he was so out of it, she says. I got rid of him eventually.

Six Months Later

(JULY 2013)

He wakes up just after eight. It's bright outside the window and the carriage is warming up, a heavy warmth of breath and sweat. Minor train stations with unreadable names flash past and vanish. Elaine is already awake but Niall is still sleeping. Connell rubs his left eye with his knuckles and sits up. Elaine is reading the one novel she has brought with her on the journey, a novel with a glossy cover and the words *Now a Major Motion Picture* along the top. The actress on the front has been their constant companion for weeks. Connell feels an almost friendly affinity with her pale period-drama face.

Whereabouts are we, do you know? says Connell.

Elaine looks up from the book. We passed Ljubljana about two hours ago, she says.

Oh, right, he says. We're not far, then.

Connell looks over at Niall, whose sleeping head is bobbing slightly on his neck. Elaine follows his gaze. Out for the count as usual, she says.

There were others at the beginning. Some friends of Elaine's went with them from Berlin to Prague, and they met a few of Niall's Engineering classmates in Bratislava before they crossed over to Vienna on the train. Hostels were cheap, and the cities they visited had a pleasantly temporary feeling about them. Nothing Connell did there seemed to stay with him. The whole trip felt like a series of short films, screened only once, and afterwards he had a sense of what they were about but no exact memories of the plot. He remembers seeing things out the windows of taxis.

In each city he finds an internet cafe and completes the same three rituals of communication: he calls Helen on Skype, he sends his mother a free text message from his phone network's website, and he writes Marianne an email.

Helen is on a J1 in Chicago for the summer. In the background of their calls he can hear her girlfriends chatting, doing things with each other's hair, and sometimes Helen will turn and say something to them like: Guys, please! I'm on the phone! He loves seeing her face on-screen, especially when the connection is good and her movements are smooth and lifelike. She has a great smile, great teeth. After the end of their call yesterday he paid at the counter, walked back out into the sunshine and bought himself an overpriced glass of Coke with ice. Sometimes when Helen has a lot of friends around or if the internet cafe is especially crowded, their conversations can get a little awkward, but even still he feels better after talking to her. He finds himself rushing to the end of the conversation so they can hang up, and then he can retrospectively savour how much he likes seeing her, without the moment-to-moment pressure of having to produce the right expressions and say the right things. Just to see Helen, her beautiful face, her smile, and to know that she continues loving him, this puts the gift of joy into his day, and for hours he feels nothing but a light-headed happiness.

Helen has given Connell a new way to live. It's as if an impossibly heavy lid has been lifted off his emotional life and suddenly he can breathe fresh air. It is physically possible to type and send a message reading: I love you! It had never seemed possible before, not remotely, but in fact it's easy. Of course if someone saw the messages he would be embarrassed, but he knows now that this is a normal kind of embarrassment, an almost protective impulse towards a particularly good part of life. He can sit down to dinner with Helen's parents, he can accompany her to her friends' parties, he can tolerate the smiling and the exchange of repetitive conversation. He can squeeze her hand while people ask him questions about his future. When she touches him spontaneously, applying a little pressure to his arm, or even reaching to brush a piece of lint off his collar, he feels a rush of pride, and hopes that people are watching them. To be known as her boyfriend plants him firmly in the social world, establishes him as an acceptable person, someone with a particular status, someone whose conversational silences are thoughtful rather than socially awkward.

The texts he sends Lorraine are fairly businesslike. He updates her when they see historic landmarks or cultural treasures. Yesterday:

hey from vienna. stephen's cathedral fairly overrated to be honest but the art history museum was good. hope things are ok at home.

She likes to ask how Helen's doing. The first time they met, Helen and his mother hit it off right away. Whenever Helen visits, Lorraine is always shaking her head at Connell's little behaviours and saying: How do you put up with him, sweetheart? But whatever, it's nice they get along. Helen is the first girlfriend he has introduced to his mother and he finds he's curiously eager to impress on Lorraine how normal their relationship is and how nice a person Helen considers him to be. He's not sure where this stems from exactly.

In the weeks they've been apart, his emails to Marianne have become lengthy. He's started drafting them on his phone in idle moments, while waiting for his clothes in a launderette, or lying in the hostel at night when he can't sleep for the heat. He reads over these drafts repeatedly, reviewing all the elements of prose, moving clauses around to make the sentences fit together correctly. Time softens out while he types, feeling slow and dilated while actually passing very rapidly, and more than once he's looked up to find that hours have gone by. He couldn't explain aloud what he finds so absorbing about his emails to Marianne, but he doesn't feel that it's trivial. The experience of writing them feels like an expression of a broader and more fundamental principle, something in his identity, or something even more abstract, to do with life itself. In his little grey journal he wrote recently: idea for a story told through emails? Then he crossed it out, deciding it was gimmicky. He finds himself crossing things out in his journal as if he imagines some future person poring over it in detail, as if he wants the future person to know which ideas he has thought better of.

His correspondence with Marianne includes a lot of links to news reports. At the moment they're both engrossed in the Edward Snowden story, Marianne because of her interest in the architecture of global surveillance, and Connell because of the fascinating personal drama. He reads all the speculation online, he watches the blurry footage from Sheremetyevo

Airport. He and Marianne can only talk about it over email, using the same communication technologies they now know are under surveillance, and it feels at times like their relationship has been captured in a complex network of state power, that the network is a form of intelligence in itself, containing them both, and containing their feelings for one another. I feel like the NSA agent reading these emails has the wrong impression of us, Marianne wrote once. They probably don't know about the time you didn't invite me to the Debs.

She writes to him a lot about the house where she's staying with Jamie and Peggy, outside Trieste. She recounts the goings-on, how she feels, how she surmises the others are feeling, and what she's reading and thinking about. He writes to her about the cities they visit, sometimes including a paragraph describing a particular sight or scene. He wrote about coming up from the U-Bahn station in Schönleinstraße to find it was suddenly dark out, and the fronds of trees waving over them like spooky fingers, and the noise from bars, and the smell of pizza and exhaust fumes. It feels powerful to him to put an experience down in words, like he's trapping it in a jar and it can never fully leave him. He told Marianne once that he'd been writing stories, and now she keeps asking to read them. If they're as good as your emails they must be superb, she wrote. That was a nice thing to read, though he responded honestly: They're not as good as my emails.

He and Niall and Elaine have arranged to get the train from Vienna to Trieste to spend their last few nights in Marianne's holiday home, before they all fly back to Dublin together. A day trip to Venice has been mentioned. Last night they got on the train with their backpacks and Connell texted Marianne:

should be there by tomorrow afternoon, won't have time to reply to your email properly before then. He has almost no clean clothes left by now. He's wearing a grey T-shirt, black jeans and dirty white trainers. In his backpack: various lightly soiled clothes, one clean white T-shirt, an empty plastic bottle for water, clean underwear, a rolled-up phone charger, his passport, two packets of generic paracetamol, a very beaten-up copy of a James Salter novel, and for Marianne, an edition of Frank O'Hara's selected poems he found in an English-language bookshop in Berlin. One soft-covered grey notebook.

Elaine nudges Niall until his head jerks forward and his eyes open. He asks what time it is and where they are, and Elaine tells him. Then Niall links his fingers together and stretches his arms out in front of him. His joints crack quietly. Connell looks out the window at the passing landscape: dry yellows and greens, the orange slant of a tiled roof, a window cut flat by the sun and flashing.

The university scholarships were announced back in April. The Provost stood on the steps of the Exam Hall and read out a list of the scholars. The sky was extremely blue that day, delirious, like flavoured ice. Connell was wearing his jacket and Helen had her arm wrapped around his. When it came to English they read out four names, alphabetically, and the last one was: Connell Waldron. Helen threw her arms around him. That was it, they said his name and moved on. He waited in the square until they announced History and Politics, and when he heard Marianne's name he looked around to see her. He could hear a circle of her friends cheering, and some applause. He put his hands in his pockets. Hearing Marianne's name he realised how real it was, he really had won the scholarship, they both had. He doesn't remember much of what happened then. He remembers calling Lorraine after the announcements and she was just quiet on the phone, shocked, and then she murmured: Oh my god, Jesus Christ.

Niall and Elaine arrived beside him, cheering and slapping his back and calling him 'an absolute fucking nerd'. Connell was laughing at nothing, just because so much excitement demanded some kind of outward expression and he didn't want to cry. That night all the new scholars had to go to a formal black-tie meal together in the Dining Hall. Connell borrowed a tux from someone in his class, it didn't fit very well, and at dinner he felt awkward trying to make conversation with the English professor seated next to him. He wanted to be with Helen, and with his friends, not with these people he had never met before and who knew nothing about him.

Everything is possible now because of the scholarship. His rent is paid, his tuition is covered, he has a free meal every day in college. This is why he's been able to spend half the summer travelling around Europe, disseminating currency with the carefree attitude of a rich person. He's explained it, or tried to explain it, in his emails to Marianne. For her the scholarship was a self-esteem boost, a happy confirmation of what she has always believed about herself anyway: that she's special. Connell has never really known whether to believe that about himself, and he still doesn't know. For him the scholarship is a gigantic material fact, like a vast cruise ship that has sailed into view out of nowhere, and suddenly he can do a postgraduate programme for free if he wants to, and live in Dublin for free, and never think about rent again until he finishes college.

Suddenly he can spend an afternoon in Vienna looking at Vermeer's *The Art of Painting*, and it's hot outside, and if he wants he can buy himself a cheap cold glass of beer afterwards. It's like something he assumed was just a painted backdrop all his life has revealed itself to be real: foreign cities are real, and famous artworks, and underground railway systems, and remnants of the Berlin Wall. That's money, the substance that makes the world real. There's something so corrupt and sexy about it.

They get to Marianne's house at three, in baking afternoon heat. The undergrowth outside the gate hums with insects and a ginger cat is lying on the bonnet of a car across the street. Through the gate Connell can see the house, the same way it looks in the photographs she's sent him, a stonework facade and white-shuttered windows. He sees the garden table with two cups left on its surface. Elaine rings the bell and after a few seconds someone appears from around the side of the house. It's Peggy. Lately Connell has become convinced that Peggy doesn't like him, and he finds himself watching her behaviour for evidence. He doesn't like her either, and never has, but that doesn't strike him as relevant. She races towards the gate, her sandals clapping on the gravel. The heat beats down on the back of Connell's neck like the feeling of human eyes staring. She unlocks the gate and lets them in, grinning and saying *ciao, ciao*. She's wearing a short denim dress and huge black sunglasses. They all walk up the gravel towards the house, Niall carrying Elaine's backpack as well as his own. Peggy fishes a set of keys from her dress pocket and unlocks the front door.

Inside the hall a stone archway leads down a short flight of steps. The kitchen is a long room with terracotta tiles, white cupboards and a table by the garden doors, flooded with sunlight. Marianne is standing outside, in the back garden among the cherry trees, with a laundry basket in her arms. She's wearing a white dress with a halter-neck and her skin looks tanned. She's been hanging washing on the line. The air outside is very still and the laundry hangs there in damp colours, not moving. Marianne puts her hand to the door handle and then sees them inside. This all seems to happen very slowly, though it only takes a few seconds. She opens the door and puts the basket on the table, and he feels a sort of enjoyably painful sensation in his throat. Her dress looks immaculate and he's conscious of how unwashed he must appear, not having showered since they left the hostel yesterday morning, and that his clothes aren't really clean.

Hello, says Elaine.

Marianne smiles and says *ciao*, as if she's making fun of herself, and she kisses Elaine's cheeks and then Niall's and asks about their journey and Connell stands there, overwhelmed by this feeling, which might only be total exhaustion, an exhaustion that has been accumulating for weeks. He can smell the scent of laundry. Up close he sees Marianne's arms are lightly freckled, her shoulders a bright rose colour. Presently she turns to him and they exchange kisses on each cheek. Looking in his eyes she says: Well, hello. He senses a certain receptivity in her expression, like she's gathering information about his feelings, something they have learned to do to each other over a long time, like speaking a private language. He can feel his face get warm as she looks at him but he doesn't want to look away. He can gather information from her face too. He gathers that she has things she wants to tell him.

Hi, he says.

Marianne has accepted an offer to spend her third year of college in Sweden. She'll be leaving in September and, depending on their plans for Christmas, Connell may not see her again until next June. People are always telling him he's going to miss her, but until now he's been looking forward to how long and intense their email correspondence will be while she's away. Now he looks into her cold interpretive eyes and thinks: Okay, I will miss her. He feels ambivalent about this, as if it's disloyal of him, because maybe he's enjoying how she looks or some physical aspect of her closeness. He's not sure what friends are allowed to enjoy about each other.

In a series of emails they exchanged recently about their own friendship, Marianne expressed her feelings about Connell mainly in terms of her sustained interest in his opinions and beliefs, the curiosity she feels about his life, and her instinct to survey his thoughts whenever she feels conflicted about anything. He expressed himself more in terms of identification, his sense of rooting for her and suffering with her when she suffers, his ability to perceive and sympathise with her motivations. Marianne thought this had something to do with gender roles. I think I just like you a lot as a person, he replied defensively. That's actually very sweet, she wrote back.

Jamie comes down the steps behind them now and they all turn around to greet him. Connell makes a half-nodding gesture, just barely inclining his chin upwards. Jamie gives him a mocking smile and says: You're looking rough, mate. Jamie has been a continual object of loathing and derision for Connell since he became Marianne's boyfriend. For several months after he first saw them together Connell had compulsive fantasies about kicking Jamie in the head until his skull was the texture of wet newspaper. Once, after speaking to Jamie briefly at a party, Connell left the building and punched a brick wall so hard his hand started bleeding. Jamie is somehow both boring and hostile at the same time, always yawning and rolling his eyes when other people are speaking. And yet he is the most effortlessly confident person Connell has ever met. Nothing fazes him. He doesn't seem capable of internal conflict. Connell can imagine him choking Marianne with his bare hands and feeling completely relaxed about it, which according to her he in fact does.

Marianne puts on a pot of coffee while Peggy cuts bread into slices and arranges olives and Parma ham onto plates. Elaine is telling them about Niall's antics and Marianne is laughing in a generous way, not because the stories are so funny but to make Elaine feel welcome. Peggy passes plates around the table and Marianne touches Connell's shoulder and hands him a cup of coffee. Because of the white dress and because of the small white china cup, he wants to say: You look like an angel. It's not even something Helen would mind him saying, but he can't talk like that in front of people anyway, saying whimsical affectionate things. He drinks the coffee, he eats some bread. The coffee is very hot and bitter and the bread is soft and fresh. He starts to feel tired.

After lunch he goes upstairs to shower. There are four bedrooms, so he has one to himself, with a huge sash window over the garden. After his shower he dresses in the only presentable clothes he has left: a plain white T-shirt and the blue jeans he has had since he was in school. His hair is wet. He feels clear-headed, an effect of the coffee, and the high water pressure in the shower, and the cool cotton on his skin. He hangs the damp towel over his shoulders and opens the window. Cherries hang on the dark-green trees like earrings. He thinks about this phrase once or twice. He would put it in an email to Marianne, but he can't email her when she's downstairs. Helen wears earrings, usually a pair of tiny gold hoops. He lets himself fantasise about her briefly because he can hear the others are downstairs anyway. He thinks about her lying on her back. He should have thought about it in the shower, but he was tired. He needs the WiFi code for this house.

Like Connell, Helen was popular in school. She still goes to lengths to keep in touch with old friends and extended family, remembering birthdays, posting nostalgic photographs on Facebook. She always RSVPs to parties and arrives on time, she's always taking group photographs again and again until there's one everybody is happy with. In other words she's a nice person, and Connell is beginning to understand that he actually likes nice people, that he even wants to be one. She's had one serious boyfriend in the past, a guy called Rory, who she broke up with in first year of college. He's in UCD so Connell has never bumped into him, but he has looked at his photographs on Facebook. He's not unlike Connell in build and complexion, but somehow gawky-looking and unfashionable. Connell admitted to Helen once that he'd looked him up online, and she asked what he'd made of him.

I don't know, said Connell. He seems kind of uncool, doesn't he?

She thought that was hilarious. They were lying in bed, Connell had his arm around her.

Is that your type, you like uncool guys? he said.

You tell me.

Why, am I uncool?

I think so, she said. I mean that in a nice way, I don't like cool people.

He sat up slightly to look down at her.

Am I really? he said. I'm not offended but honestly, I thought I was kind of cool.

You're such a culchie, though.

Am I? In what way am I?

You have the thickest Sligo accent, she said.

I do not. I can't believe that. No one's ever said that to me before. Do I really?

She was still laughing. He stroked his hand over her belly, grinning to himself because he was making her laugh.

I can hardly understand you half the time, she said. Thankfully you're the strong and silent type.

He had to laugh then too. Helen, that is brutal, he said.

She tucked a hand behind her head. Do you honestly think you're cool? she said.

Well, not anymore.

She smiled to herself. Good, she said. It's good that you're not.

Helen and Marianne first met back in February, on Dawson Street. He and Helen were walking along holding hands when he saw Marianne coming out of Hodges Figgis wearing a black beret. Oh, hi, he said in an agonised voice. He thought of dropping Helen's hand but he couldn't bring himself to do it. Hi, Marianne said. You must be Helen. The two women then made perfectly competent and genial conversation while he stood there panicking and staring at various objects in the surrounding environment.

Afterwards Helen asked him: So you and Marianne, were you always just friends, or . . . ? They were in his room then, off Pearse Street. Buses went by outside and threw a column of yellow light on the bedroom door.

Yeah, more or less, he said. Like, we were never together as such.

But you've slept together.

Yeah, kind of. No, yeah, to be fair, we have. Is that a big deal?

No, I'm just curious, said Helen. It was like a friends-with-benefits thing?

Basically. In final year of school, and for a while last year. It wasn't serious or anything.

Helen smiled at him. He was raking his bottom lip with his teeth, something he remembered to stop doing only after she'd already seen him.

She looks like she goes to art college, said Helen. I guess you think she's really chic.

He gave a little laugh, looked at the floor. It's not like that, he said. We've known each other since we were kids.

It doesn't have to be weird that she's your ex, Helen said.

She's not my ex. We're just friends.

But before you were friends, you were . . .

Well, she wasn't my girlfriend, he said.

But you had sex with her, though.

166

He covered his entire face in his hands. Helen laughed.

After that, Helen was determined to make friends with Marianne, as if to prove a point. When they saw her at parties Helen went out of her way to compliment her hair and clothing, and Marianne would nod vaguely and then continue expressing some in-depth opinion about the Magdalene Laundry report or the Denis O'Brien case. Objectively Connell did find Marianne's opinions interesting, but he could see how her fondness for expressing them at length, to the exclusion of lighter conversation, was not universally charming. One evening, after an overly long discussion about Israel, Helen became irritable, and on the walk home she told Connell that she found Marianne 'self-absorbed'.

Because she talks about politics too much? said Connell. I wouldn't call that self-absorbed, though.

Helen shrugged, but drew a breath inwards through her nose that indicated she didn't like his interpretation of her point.

She was the same way in school, he added. But she's not putting it on, she's genuinely interested in that stuff.

She really cares about Israeli peace talks?

Surprised, Connell replied simply: Yeah. After a few seconds of walking along in silence he added: As do I, to be honest. It is fairly important. Helen sighed aloud. He was surprised that she would sigh in that petulant way, and wondered how much she had had to drink. Her arms were folded up at her chest. Not being preachy, he went on. Obviously we're not going to save the Middle East by talking about it at a house party. I think Marianne just thinks about that stuff a lot.

You don't think maybe she does it for the attention? said Helen.

He frowned in a conscious effort to look thoughtful. Marianne was so totally uninterested in what people thought of her, so extremely secure in her own self-perception, that it was hard to imagine her caring for attention one way or another. She did not altogether, as far as Connell knew, actually like herself, but praise from other people seemed as irrelevant to her as disapproval had been in school.

Honestly? he said. Not really.

She seems to like your attention well enough.

Connell swallowed. He only then understood why Helen was so annoyed, and not trying to veil her annoyance. He didn't think Marianne had been paying him any special notice, though she did always listen when he spoke, a courtesy she occasionally failed to pay others. He turned his head to look at a passing car.

I didn't notice that, he said eventually.

To his relief, Helen dropped this specific theme and settled back into a more general critique of Marianne's behaviour.

Every time we see her at a party she's always flirting with like ten different guys, said Helen. Talk about craving male approval.

Pleased that he was no longer implicated in the censure, Connell smiled and said: Yeah. She wasn't like that in school at all.

You mean she didn't act so slutty? said Helen.

Feeling suddenly cornered, and regretting that he had let his guard down, Connell again fell silent. He knew that Helen was a nice person, but he forgot sometimes how old-fashioned her values were. After a time he said uncomfortably: Here, she's my friend, alright? Don't be talking about her like that. Helen didn't respond, but hiked her folded arms further up her chest. It was the wrong thing to say anyway. Later he would wonder if he was really defending Marianne or just defending himself from an implied accusation about his own sexuality, that he was tainted somehow, that he had unacceptable desires.

By now the unspoken consensus is that Helen and Marianne don't like each other very much. They're different people. Connell thinks the aspects of himself that are most compatible with Helen are his best aspects: his loyalty, his basically practical outlook, his desire to be thought of as a good guy. With Helen he doesn't feel shameful things, he doesn't find himself saying weird stuff during sex, he doesn't have that persistent sensation that he belongs nowhere, that he never will belong anywhere. Marianne had a wildness that got into him for a while and made him feel that he was like her, that they had the same unnameable spiritual injury, and that neither of them could ever fit into the world. But he was never damaged like she was. She just made him feel that way.

One night he was waiting for Helen in college, just outside the Graduates Memorial Building. She was coming from the gym at the other end of campus and they were going to get the bus to her house together. He was standing on the steps looking at his phone when the door behind him opened and a group of people came out in formal dresses and suits, all laughing and talking together. The light in the hallway behind them cast them into silhouette, so it took him a second to recognise Marianne. She was wearing a long dark-coloured dress and had her hair piled up high on her head, making her neck look slender and exposed. She caught his eye with a familiar expression. Hello, she said. He didn't know the people she was with; he guessed they were from the debating society or something. Hi, he said. How could his feeling for her ever be anything like his feeling for other people? But part of the feeling was knowing the terrible hold he'd had over her, and still had, and could not foresee ever losing.

Helen arrived then. He only noticed her when she called out to him. She was wearing her leggings and trainers, gym bag slung over one shoulder, a damp sheen on her forehead visible under the street light. He felt a vast rush of love for her, love and compassion, almost sympathy. He knew that he belonged with her. What they had together was normal, a good relationship. The life they were living was the right life. He took the bag off her shoulder and lifted a hand to wave Marianne goodbye. She didn't wave back, she just nodded. Have fun! Helen said. Then they went to get the bus. He was sad for Marianne after that, sad that nothing in her life had ever truly seemed healthy, and sad that he'd had to turn away from her. He knew that it had caused her pain. In a way he was even sad for himself. Sitting on the bus he continued to picture her standing in the doorway with the light behind her: how exquisite she looked, and what a glamorous, formidable person she was, and that subtle expression that came over her face when she looked at him. But he couldn't be what she wanted. After a time he realised Helen was speaking, and he stopped thinking about all that and started listening.

For dinner Peggy cooks pasta and they eat at the round garden table. The sky is a thrilling chlorine-blue, stretched taut and featureless like silk. Marianne brings a cold bottle of sparkling wine out from the house, with condensation running down the glass like sweat, and asks Niall to open it. Connell finds this decision judicious. Marianne is very smooth and sociable on these occasions, like a diplomat's wife. Connell is seated between her and Peggy. The cork sails over the garden wall and lands somewhere no one can see it. A crest of white spills over the lip of the bottle and Niall pours the wine into Elaine's glass. The glasses are broad and shallow like saucers. Jamie turns his empty one upside down and says: Do we not have proper champagne glasses?

These are champagne glasses, says Peggy.

No, I mean the tall ones, Jamie says.

You're thinking of flutes, says Peggy. These are coupes.

Helen would laugh at this conversation, and thinking of how much she would laugh, Connell smiles. Marianne says: It's not a matter of life and death, is it? Peggy fills her glass and passes the bottle to Connell.

I'm just saying, these aren't for champagne, says Jamie.

You're such a philistine, Peggy says.

I'm a philistine? he says. We're drinking champagne out of gravy boats.

Niall and Elaine start laughing, and Jamie smiles under the mistaken impression that they are laughing at his witticism. Marianne touches a fingertip to her eyelid lightly, as if removing a piece of dust or grit. Connell hands her the bottle and she accepts it.

It's an old style of champagne glass, says Marianne. They belonged to my dad. Go inside and get yourself a flute if you prefer, they're in the press over the sink.

Jamie makes wide ironic eyes and says: I didn't realise it was such an emotional issue for you. Marianne puts the bottle in the centre of the table and says nothing. Connell has never heard Marianne mention her father like that in casual conversation. Nobody else at the table seems aware of this; Elaine may not even know Marianne's father is dead. Connell tries to catch Marianne's eye, but he can't.

The pasta is delicious, says Elaine.

Oh, says Peggy. It's very al dente, isn't it? Maybe too al dente.

I think it's nice, Marianne says.

Connell takes a mouthful of wine, which foams cold in his mouth and then disappears like air. Jamie starts telling an anecdote about one of his friends, who is on a summer internship at Goldman Sachs. Connell finishes his wine and unobtrusively Marianne refills his glass. Thanks, he says quietly. Her hand hovers for a second as if she's going to touch him, and then she doesn't. She says nothing.

The morning after the scholarships were announced, he and Marianne went to the swearing-in ceremony together. She'd been out the night before and looked hungover, which pleased him, because the ceremony was so formal and they had to wear gowns and recite things in Latin. Afterwards they went for breakfast together in a cafe near college. They sat outside, at a table on the street, and people walked by carrying paper shopping bags and having loud conversations on the phone. Marianne drank a single cup of black coffee and ordered a croissant which she didn't finish. Connell had a large ham-and-cheese omelette with two slices of buttered toast, and tea with milk in it.

Marianne said she was worried about Peggy, who was the

only one of the three of them not to get the scholarship. She said it would be hard on her. Connell inhaled and said nothing. Peggy didn't need subsidised tuition or free on-campus accommodation, because she lived at home in Blackrock and her parents were both doctors, but Marianne was intent on seeing the scholarships as a matter of personal feeling rather than economic fact.

Anyway, I'm happy for you, Marianne said.

I'm happy for you too.

But you deserve it more.

He looked up at her. He wiped his mouth with the napkin. You mean in terms of the financial stuff? he said.

Oh, she replied. Well, I meant that you're a better student.

She looked down critically at her croissant. He watched her.

Though in terms of financial circumstances too, obviously, she said. I mean, it's kind of ridiculous they don't means-test these things.

I guess we're from very different backgrounds, class-wise.

I don't think about it much, she said. Quickly she added: Sorry, that's an ignorant thing to say. Maybe I should think about it more.

You don't consider me your working-class friend?

She gave a smile that was more like a grimace and said: I'm conscious of the fact that we got to know each other because your mother works for my family. I also don't think my mother is a good employer, I don't think she pays Lorraine very well.

No, she pays her fuck all.

He cut a thin slice of omelette with his knife. The egg was more rubbery than he would have liked.

I'm surprised this hasn't come up before, she said. I think it's totally fair if you resent me.

No, I don't resent you. Why would I?

He put his knife and fork down and looked at her. She had an anxious little expression on her face.

I just feel weird about all this, he said. I feel weird wearing black tie and saying things in Latin. You know at the dinner last night, those people serving us, they were students. They're working to put themselves through college while we sit there eating the free food they put in front of us. Is that not horrible?

Of course it is. The whole idea of 'meritocracy' or whatever, it's evil, you know I think that. But what are we supposed to do, give back the scholarship money? I don't see what that achieves.

Well, it's always easy to think of reasons not to do something.

You know you're not going to do it either, so don't guilt-trip me, she said.

They continued eating then, as if they were acting out an argument in which both sides were equally compelling, and they had chosen their positions more or less at random, only in order to have the discussion out. A large seagull landed at the base of a nearby street light, its plumage magnificently clean and soft-looking.

You need to get it straight in your mind what you think a good society would look like, said Marianne. And if you think people should be able to go to college and get English degrees, you shouldn't feel guilty for doing that yourself, because you have every right to.

That's okay for you, you don't feel guilty about anything.

She started rooting around in her handbag looking for something. Offhandedly she said: Is that how you see me?

No, he said. Then, uncertain of how guilty he thought Marianne felt about anything, he added: I don't know. I should have known coming to Trinity that it would be like this. I'm just looking at all this scholarship stuff thinking, Jesus, what would people in school say?

For a second Marianne said nothing. He felt in some obscure sense that he had expressed himself incorrectly, but he didn't know how. To be fair, she said, you were always very concerned with what people in school would say. He remembered then, about how people had treated her at that time, and how he himself had treated her, and he felt bad. It wasn't the conclusion he was hoping the conversation would have, but he smiled and said: Ouch. She smiled back at him and then lifted her coffee cup. At that moment he thought: just as their relationship in school had been on his terms, their relationship now was on hers. But she's more generous, he thought. She's a better person.

When Jamie's story is finished, Marianne goes inside and comes back out again with another bottle of sparkling wine, and one bottle of red. Niall starts unwrapping the wire on the first bottle and Marianne hands Connell a corkscrew. Peggy starts clearing away people's plates. Connell unpeels the foil from the top of the bottle as Jamie leans over and says something to Marianne. He sinks the screw into the cork and twists it downwards. Peggy takes his plate away and stacks it with the others. He folds down the arms of the corkscrew and lifts the cork from the neck of the bottle with the sound of lips smacking.

The sky has dimmed into a cooler blue now, with silver clouds on the rim of the horizon. Connell's face feels flushed and he wonders if he's sunburned. He likes imagining Marianne older sometimes, with children. He imagines they're all here in Italy together and she's making a salad or something and complaining to Connell about her husband, who is older, probably an intellectual, and Marianne finds him dull. Why didn't I marry you? she would say. He can see Marianne very clearly in this dream, he sees her face, and he feels that she has spent years as a journalist, maybe living in Lebanon. He doesn't see himself so well or know what he's been doing. But he knows what he would say to her. Money, he would say. And she would laugh without looking up from the salad.

At the table they're talking about their day trip to Venice: which trains they should take, which galleries are worth seeing. Marianne tells Connell he would like the Guggenheim, and Connell is pleased that she has spoken to him, pleased to be singled out as an appreciator of modern art.

I don't know why we're bothering with Venice, says Jamie. It's just full of Asians taking pictures of everything.

God forbid you might have to encounter an Asian person, Niall says.

There's a stillness at the table. Jamie says: What? It's clear from his voice and from the delayed pace of his response that he's now drunk.

It's kind of racist, what you just said about Asian people, Niall says. I'm not making a big thing of it.

Oh, because all the Asians at the table are going to get offended, are they? says Jamie.

Marianne stands up abruptly and says: I'll go get dessert.

Connell is disappointed by this display of spinelessness, but he says nothing either. Peggy follows Marianne into the house and everyone at the table is silent. A huge moth circles in the dark air and Jamie bats at it with his napkin. After a minute or two Peggy and Marianne bring dessert out from the kitchen: a gigantic glass bowl of halved strawberries with a stack of white china dishes and silver spoons. Two more bottles of wine. The dishes are passed around and people fill them with fruit.

She spent all afternoon halving these little bastards, Peggy says.

I feel so spoilt, says Elaine.

Where's the cream? Jamie says.

It's inside, says Marianne.

Why didn't you bring it out? he says.

Marianne pulls her chair back from the table coldly and stands up to go inside. It's almost dark out now. Jamie ranges his eyes around the table, trying to find someone who will look back at him and agree that he was right to ask for the cream, or that Marianne was overreacting to an innocent query. Instead people seem to avoid looking at him, and with a loud sigh he knocks his chair back and follows her. The chair tips over noiselessly onto the grass. He goes in the side door to the kitchen and slams it behind him. There's a back door too, which leads down into the other part of the garden, where the trees are. It's walled off from here, so only the tops of the trees are visible.

By the time Connell turns his attention back to the table Niall is staring at him. He doesn't know what Niall's stare means. He tries squinting his eyes to show Niall he's confused. Niall casts a significant look at the house and then back at him.

Connell looks over his right shoulder. The light is on in the kitchen, leaking a yellowish glow through the garden doors. He only has a sidelong view so he can't see what's going on inside. Elaine and Peggy are complimenting the strawberries. When they stop, Connell hears a raised voice coming from the house, almost a shriek. Everyone freezes. He stands up from the table to go to the house, and feels his blood pressure drop. He's had a bottle of wine to drink by now, or more.

When he reaches the garden doors he sees Jamie and Marianne are standing at the counter, having some kind of argument. They don't see Connell through the glass right away. He pauses with his hand on the door handle. Marianne is all flushed, maybe from too much sun, or maybe she's angry. Jamie is unsteadily refilling his champagne glass with red wine. Connell turns the handle and comes inside. Alright? he says. They both look at him, they both stop talking. He notices Marianne is shivering as if she's cold. Jamie lifts his glass sarcastically in Connell's direction, sloshing wine over the rim and onto the floor.

Put that down, says Marianne quietly.

I'm sorry, what? says Jamie.

Put that glass down, please, says Marianne.

Jamie smiles and nods to himself. You want me to put it down? he says. Okay. Okay, look, I'm putting it down.

He drops the glass on the floor and it shatters. Marianne screams, a real scream from her throat, and launches her body at Jamie, drawing her right arm behind her as if to strike him. Connell steps in between them, glass crunches under his shoe, and he grabs Marianne by her upper arms. Behind him Jamie is laughing. Marianne tries to push Connell aside, her whole body shudders, and her face is blotchy and discoloured like she's been crying. Come here, he says. Marianne. She looks at him. He remembers her in school, so bitter and stubborn with everyone. He knew things about her then. They look at each other and the rigidity leaves her and she goes slack like she's been shot.

You're a fucking mental case, you are, says Jamie. You need help.

Connell turns Marianne's body around and steers her towards the back door. She offers no resistance.

Where are you going? says Jamie.

Connell doesn't answer. He opens the door and Marianne goes through it without speaking. He closes it behind them. It's dark now in this part of the garden, with only the mottled window providing any light. The cherries glow dimly on the trees. Over the wall they can hear Peggy's voice. Together he and Marianne walk down the steps and say nothing. The kitchen light goes out behind them. They can hear Jamie on the other side of the wall then, rejoining the others. Marianne is wiping her nose on the back of her hand. The cherries hang around them gleaming like so many spectral planets. The air is light with scent, green like chlorophyll. They sell chlorophyll chewing gum in Europe, Connell has noticed. Overhead the sky is velvet-blue. Stars flicker and cast no light. They walk down a line of trees together, away from the house, and then stop.

Marianne leans against a slim silver tree trunk and Connell puts his arms around her. She feels thin, he thinks. Was she so thin before. She presses her face into his one remaining clean T-shirt. She's still wearing the white dress from earlier, with a gold embroidered shawl now. He holds her tightly, his body adjusting itself to hers like the kind of mattress that's supposedly good for you. She softens into his arms. She starts to seem calmer. Their breathing slows into one rhythm. The kitchen light goes on for a time and then off again, voices rise and recede. Connell feels certain about what he's doing, but it's a blank certainty, as if he's blankly performing a memorised task. He finds that his fingers are in Marianne's hair and he's stroking the back of her neck calmly. He doesn't know how long he has been doing this. She rubs at her eyes with her wrist.

Connell releases her. She feels in her pocket for a packet of cigarettes and a crushed box of matches. She offers him a cigarette and he accepts. She strikes a match and the flare of light illuminates her features in the darkness. Her skin looks dry and inflamed, her eyes are swollen. She breathes in and the cigarette paper hisses in the flame. He lights his own, then drops the match in the grass and compresses it under his foot. They smoke quietly. He walks away from the tree, surveying the bottom of the garden, but it's too dark to make much out. He returns to Marianne under the branches and absently pulls at a broad, waxy leaf. She hangs the cigarette on her lower lip and lifts her hair into her hands, twisting it into a knot that she secures with an elastic tie from her wrist. Eventually they finish their cigarettes and stub them out in the grass.

Can I stay in your room tonight? she says. I'll sleep on the floor.

The bed is massive, he says, don't worry about it.

The house is dark when they get back inside. In Connell's room they undress down to their underwear. Marianne is wearing a white cotton bra that makes her breasts look small and triangular. They lie side by side under the quilt. He's aware that he could have sex with her now if he wanted to. She wouldn't tell anyone. He finds it strangely comforting, and allows himself to think about what it would be like. Hey, he would say quietly. Lie on your back, okay? And she would just obediently lie on her back. So many things pass secretly between people anyway. What kind of person would he be if it happened now? Someone very different? Or exactly the same person, himself, with no difference at all.

After a time he hears her say something he can't make out. I didn't hear that, he says.

I don't know what's wrong with me, says Marianne. I don't know why I can't be like normal people.

Her voice sounds oddly cool and distant, like a recording of her voice played after she herself has gone away or departed for somewhere else.

In what way? he says.

I don't know why I can't make people love me. I think there was something wrong with me when I was born.

Lots of people love you, Marianne. Okay? Your family and friends love you.

For a few seconds she's silent and then she says: You don't know my family.

He had hardly even noticed himself using the word 'family'; he'd just been reaching for something reassuring and meaningless to say. Now he doesn't know what to do.

In the same strange unaccented voice she continues: They hate me.

He sits up in bed to see her better. I know you fight with

them, he says, but that doesn't mean they hate you.

Last time I was home my brother told me I should kill myself.

Mechanically Connell sits up straighter, pushing the quilt off his body as if he's about to get up. He runs his tongue around the inside of his mouth.

What did he say that for? he says.

I don't know. He said no one would miss me if I was dead because I have no friends.

Would you not tell your mother if he talked to you like that?

She was there, says Marianne.

Connell moves his jaw around. The pulse in his neck is throbbing. He's trying to visualise this scene, the Sheridans at home, Alan for some reason telling Marianne to commit suicide, but it's hard to picture any family behaving the way that she has described.

What did she say? he asks. As in, how did she react?

I think she said something like, oh, don't encourage her.

Slowly Connell breathes in through his nose and exhales the breath between his lips.

And what provoked this? he says. Like, how did the argument start?

He senses that something in Marianne's face changes now, or hardens, but he can't name what it is exactly.

You think I did something to deserve it, she says.

No, obviously I'm not saying that.

Sometimes I think I must deserve it. Otherwise I don't know why it would happen. But if he's in a bad mood he'll just follow me around the house. There's nothing I can do. He'll just come into my room, he doesn't care if I'm sleeping or anything.

Connell rubs his palms on the sheet.

Would he ever hit you? he says.

Sometimes. Less so since I moved away. To be honest I don't even mind it that much. The psychological stuff is more demoralising. I don't know how to explain it, really. I know it must sound . . .

He touches his hand to his forehead. His skin feels wet. She doesn't finish the sentence to explain how it must sound.

Why didn't you ever tell me about it before? he says. She says nothing. The light is dim but he can see her open eyes. Marianne, he says. The whole time we were together, why didn't you tell me any of this?

I don't know. I suppose I didn't want you to think I was damaged or something. I was probably afraid you wouldn't want me anymore.

Finally he puts his face in his hands. His fingers feel cold and clammy on his eyelids and there are tears in his eyes. The harder he presses with his fingers, the faster the tears seep out, wet, onto his skin. Jesus, he says. His voice sounds thick and he clears his throat. Come here, he says. And she comes to him. He feels terribly ashamed and confused. They lie face-to-face and he puts his arms around her body. In her ear he says: I'm sorry, okay? She holds onto him tightly, her arms winding around him, and he kisses her forehead. But he always thought she was damaged, he thought it anyway. He screws his eyes shut with guilt. Their faces feel hot and damp now. He thinks of her saying: I thought you wouldn't want me anymore. Her mouth is so close that her breath is wet on his lips. They start to kiss, and her mouth tastes dark like wine. Her body shifts against him, he touches her breast with his hand, and in a few seconds he could be inside her again, and then she says: No, we shouldn't. She draws away, just like that. He can hear himself breathing in the silence, the pathetic heaving of his breath. He waits until it slows down again, not wanting to have his voice break when he tries to speak. I'm really sorry, he says. She squeezes his hand. It's a very sad gesture. He can't believe the stupidity of what he's just done. Sorry, he says again. But Marianne has already turned away.

Five Months Later

(DECEMBER 2013)

In the lobby of the Languages and Literature building she sits down to check her email. She doesn't remove her overcoat because she'll be getting up in a minute. Beside her on the desk is her breakfast, which she just purchased from the supermarket across the street: one black coffee with brown sugar, one lemon pastry roll. She eats this exact breakfast regularly. Lately she has started to eat it slowly, in lavish sugary mouthfuls that congeal around her teeth. The more slowly she eats, and the more consideration she gives to the composition of her food, the less hungry she feels. She won't eat again until eight or nine in the evening.

She has two new emails, one from Connell and one from Joanna. She dabs her mouse back and forth between them, and then selects Joanna's.

no real news from here, as usual. I've recently taken to staying home at night and watching my way through a nine part documentary series about the american civil war. I have a lot of new information about various civil war generals to share with you next time we're on Skype. how are you? how is Lukas? did he take those photos yet or is that today? and the big question . . . can I see them when they're done?? or is that prurient. I await your word. xx

Marianne lifts the lemon pastry, takes a large, slow bite, and lets it dissolve in layers on her tongue. She chews, swallows, then lifts the coffee cup. One mouthful of coffee. She replaces the cup and opens Connell's message.

I don't know what you mean by your last sentence there exactly. Do you mean just because we're far away from each other or because we've actually changed as people? I do feel like a pretty different person now than I was then but maybe I don't seem that different, I don't know. By the way I looked your friend Lukas up on Facebook, he's what you would call 'Scandinavian looking'. Sadly Sweden did not qualify for the World Cup this time so if you end up with a Swedish boyfriend I'll have to think of another way to bond with him. Not that I'm saying this guy Lukas is going to be your boyfriend or would want to talk to me about football if he was, although it's something I am putting out as a possibility. I know you like the tall handsome guys as you say, so why not Lukas, who looks tall and is also handsome (Helen has seen his photo and agrees). But whatever, I'm not pushing the boyfriend thing, I just hope you have confirmed he's not a psychopath. You don't always have a good radar on that.

Unrelatedly we were getting a taxi through Phoenix Park last night and we saw a lot of deer. Deer are kind of strange looking creatures. In the night they have a ghostly appearance and their eyes can reflect headlights in an olive green or silver colour, like a special effect.

They paused to observe our taxi before moving on. To me it's weird when animals pause because they seem so intelligent, but maybe that's because I associate pausing with thought. Deer are elegant anyway I have to say. If you were an animal yourself, you could do worse than be a deer. They have those thoughtful faces and nice sleek bodies. But they also kind of startle off in unpredictable ways. They didn't remind me of you at the time but in retrospect I see a similarity there. I hope you're not offended by the comparison. I would tell you about the party prior to us getting the taxi through Phoenix Park but it was honestly boring and not as good as the deer. No one was there who you would know that well. Your last email was really good, thank you. I look forward to hearing more as always.

Marianne checks the time in the top-right corner of the screen: 09:49. She navigates back to Joanna's message and hits reply.

He's taking the photos today, I'm actually heading over there now. Of course I will send them to you when they are finished AND I expect long flattering commentary on each individual photograph. I'm excited to hear what you've learned about the US Civil War. All I've learned here is how to say 'no thank you' (nej tack) and 'really, no' (verkligen, nej). Talk soon xxx

Marianne closes her laptop, eats another two bites of the pastry and folds the rest up in its little greaseproof wrap. She slips her laptop into her satchel and removes her soft felt beret, which she pulls down over her ears. The pastry she disposes of in a nearby bin.

Outside it's still snowing. The exterior world looks like an old TV screen badly tuned. Visual noise breaks the landscape into soft fragments. Marianne buries her hands in her pockets. Flakes of snow fall on her face and dissolve there. A cold flake alights on her top lip and she feels for it with her tongue. Head down against the cold, she is on her way to Lukas's studio. Lukas's hair is so blonde that the individual strands look white. She finds them on her clothing sometimes, finer than thread. He dresses all in black: black shirts, black zip-up hoodies, black boots with thick black rubber soles. He's an artist. The first time they met, Marianne told him she was a writer. It was a lie. Now she avoids talking to him about it.

Lukas lives near the station. She takes her hand from her pocket, blows on her fingers and presses the buzzer. He answers, in English: Who is it?

It's Marianne, she says.

Ah, you're early, says Lukas. Come on in.

Why does he say 'you're early'? Marianne thinks as she climbs the stairs. The connection was fuzzy but he seemed to say it with a smile. Was he pointing it out to make her appear too eager? But she finds she doesn't care how eager she appears, because there is no secret eagerness to be discovered in her. She could be here, ascending the staircase to Lukas's studio, or she could be in the campus library, or in the dorm making herself coffee. For weeks now she has had this feeling, the feeling of moving around inside a protective film, floating like mercury. The outside world touches against her outside skin, but not the other part of herself, inside. So whatever Lukas's reason for saying 'you're early', she finds it doesn't matter to her.

Upstairs he's setting up. Marianne removes her hat and shakes it. Lukas looks up, then back at the tripod. Are you getting used to the weather? he says. She hangs her hat on the back of the door and shrugs. She begins to take off her coat. In Sweden we have a saying, he says. There's no such thing as bad weather, only bad clothes.

Marianne hangs her coat beside her hat. What's wrong with my clothes? she says mildly.

It's just an expression, says Lukas.

She honestly can't tell now if he meant to criticise her clothes or not. She's wearing a grey lambswool sweater and a thick black skirt with knee-high boots. Lukas has bad manners, which, to Marianne, makes him seem childish. He never offers her coffee or tea when she arrives, or even a glass of water. He starts talking right away about whatever he has been reading or doing since her last visit. He doesn't seem to crave her input, and sometimes her responses confuse or disorientate him, which he claims is an effect of his bad English. In fact his comprehension is very good. Anyway, today is different. She removes her boots and leaves them by the door.

There's a mattress in the corner of the studio, where Lukas sleeps. The windows are very tall and run almost to the floor, with blinds and thin trailing curtains. Various unrelated items are dotted around the room: several large potted plants, stacks of atlases, a bicycle wheel. This array impressed Marianne initially, but Lukas later explained he had gathered the items intentionally for a shoot, which made them seem artificial to her. Everything is an effect with you, Marianne told him once. He took this as a compliment about his art. He does have immaculate taste. He's sensitive to the most minuscule of aesthetic failures, in painting, in cinema, even in novels or television shows. Sometimes when Marianne mentions a film she has recently watched, he waves his hand and says: It fails for me. This quality of discernment, she has realised, does not make Lukas a good person. He has managed to nurture a fine artistic sensitivity without ever developing any real sense of right and wrong. The fact that this is even possible unsettles Marianne, and makes art seem pointless suddenly.

She and Lukas have had an arrangement for a few weeks now. Lukas calls it 'the game'. Like any game, there are some rules. Marianne is not allowed to talk or make eye contact while the game is going on. If she breaks the rules, she gets punished later. The game doesn't end when the sex is finished, the game ends when she gets in the shower. Sometimes after sex Lukas takes a long time before he lets her get in the shower, just talking to her. He tells her bad things about herself. It's hard to know whether Marianne likes to hear those things; she desires to hear them, but she's conscious by now of being able to desire in some sense what she does not want. The quality of gratification is thin and hard, arriving too quickly and then leaving her sick and shivery. You're worthless, Lukas likes to tell her. You're nothing. And she feels like nothing, an absence to be forcibly filled in. It isn't that she likes the feeling, but it relieves her somehow. Then she showers and the game is over. She experiences a depression so deep it is tranquillising, she eats whatever he tells her to eat, she experiences no more ownership over her own body than if it were a piece of litter.

Since she arrived here in Sweden, but particularly since the beginning of the game, people have seemed to her like coloured paper shapes, not real at all. At times a person will make eye contact with Marianne, a bus conductor or someone looking for change, and she'll be shocked briefly into the realisation that this is in fact her life, that she is actually visible to other people. This feeling opens her to certain longings: hunger and thirst, a desire to speak Swedish, a physical desire to swim or dance. But these fade away again quickly. In Lund she's never really hungry, and though she fills a plastic Evian bottle with water every morning, she empties most of it back into the sink at night.

She sits on the corner of the mattress now while Lukas switches a lamp on and off and does something with his camera. I still don't know with the light yet, he says. Maybe we can do, like, first one and then another one. Marianne shrugs. She doesn't understand the import of what he's saying. Because all his friends speak Swedish, it has been difficult for her to work out how popular or well regarded Lukas is. People spend time in his studio often and seem to move a lot of artistic equipment up and down his stairs, but are they fans of his work, grateful for his attention? Or are they exploiting him for the convenient location of his working space while making fun of him behind his back?

Okay, I think we're ready to go, says Lukas.

Do you want me to . . .

Maybe just the sweater now.

Marianne pulls her sweater off over her head. She places it in her lap, folds it, and then puts it to one side. She is wearing a black lace bra with little flowers embroidered on it. Lukas starts doing something with his camera.

She doesn't hear from the others much anymore: Peggy, Sophie, Teresa, that crowd. Jamie wasn't happy about the break-up, and he told people he wasn't happy, and people felt sorry for him. Things started to turn against Marianne, she could sense that before she left. At first it was unsettling, the way eyes turned away from her in a room, or conversation stopped short when she entered; the sense of having lost her footing in the social world, of being no longer admired and envied, how quickly it had all slipped away from her. But then she found it was easy to get used to. There's always been something inside her that men have wanted to dominate, and their desire for domination can look so much like attraction, even love. In school the boys had tried to break her with cruelty and disregard, and in college men had tried to do it with sex and popularity, all with the same aim of subjugating some force in her personality. It depressed her to think people were so predictable. Whether she was respected or despised, it didn't make much difference in the end. Would every stage of her life continue to reveal itself as the same thing, again and again, the same remorseless contest for dominance?

With Peggy it had been hard. *I'm your best friend*, Peggy kept saying at the time, in an increasingly weird voice. She couldn't accept Marianne's laissez-faire attitude to the situation. You realise people are talking about you, Peggy said one night while Marianne was packing. Marianne didn't know how to respond. After a pause, she replied thoughtfully: I don't think I always care about the same things you care about.

But I do care about you. Peggy threw her hands in the air wildly, walked around the coffee table twice.

I'm your best friend, she said. What am I supposed to do?

I don't really know what that question means.

I mean, what position does this put me in? Because honestly, I don't really want to take sides.

Marianne frowned, zipping a hairbrush into the pocket of her suitcase.

You mean, you don't want to take my side, she said.

Peggy looked at her, breathing hard now from her exertion around the coffee table. Marianne was kneeling down by her suitcase still.

I don't know if you really understand how people are feeling, Peggy said. People are upset about this.

About me breaking up with Jamie?

About the whole drama. People are actually upset.

Peggy looked at her, awaiting a response, and Marianne replied eventually: Okay. Peggy rubbed a hand over her face and said: I'll leave you to pack up. As she went out the door she added: You should consider seeing a therapist or something. Marianne didn't understand the suggestion. I should see a therapist because I'm *not* upset? she thought. But it was hard to dismiss something she had admittedly been hearing all her life from various sources: that she was mentally unwell and needed help.

Joanna is the only one who has kept in touch. In the evening they talk on Skype about their coursework, films they've seen, articles Joanna is working on for the student paper. On-screen her face always appears dimly lit against the same backdrop, her cream-coloured bedroom wall. She never wears make-up anymore, sometimes she doesn't even brush her hair. She has a girlfriend now called Evelyn, a graduate student in International Peace Studies. Marianne asked once if Joanna saw Peggy often, and she made a quick wincing expression, only for a fraction of a second, but long enough for Marianne to see. No, said Joanna. I don't see any of those people. They know I was on your side anyway.

I'm sorry, said Marianne. I didn't want you to fall out with anyone because of me.

Joanna made a face again, this time a less legible expression, either because of the poor lighting, the pixelation on-screen, or the ambivalent feeling she was trying to express.

Well, I was never really friends with them anyway, said Joanna. They were more your friends.

I thought we were all friends.

You were the only one I got on with. Frankly I don't think Jamie or Peggy are particularly good people. It's not my business if you want to be friends with them, that's just my opinion.

No, I agree with you, said Marianne. I guess I just got caught up in how much they seemed to like me.

Yeah. I think in your better judgement you did realise how obnoxious they were. But it was easier for me because they never really liked me that much.

Marianne was surprised by this matter-of-fact turn in the conversation, and felt a little castigated, though Joanna's tone remained friendly. It was true, Peggy and Jamie were not very good people; bad people even, who took joy in putting others down. Marianne feels aggrieved that she fell for it, aggrieved that she thought she had anything in common with them, that she'd participated in the commodity market they passed off as friendship. In school she had believed herself to be above such frank exchanges of social capital, but her college life indicated that if anyone in school had actually been willing to speak to her, she would have behaved just as badly as anyone else. There is nothing superior about her at all.

Can you turn and face to the window? says Lukas.

Sure.

Marianne turns on the mattress, legs pulled up to her chest.

Can you move, like . . . legs down in some way? says Lukas.

Marianne crosses her legs in front of her. Lukas scoots the tripod forward and readjusts the angle. Marianne thinks of Connell's email comparing her to a deer. She liked the line about thoughtful faces and sleek bodies. She has lost even more weight in Sweden, she's thinner now, very sleek.

She's decided not to go home for Christmas this year. She thinks a lot about how to extricate herself from 'the family situation'. In bed at night she imagines scenarios in which she is completely free of her mother and brother, on neither good nor bad terms with them, simply a neutral non-participant in their lives. She spent much of her childhood and adolescence planning elaborate schemes to remove herself from family conflict: staying completely silent, keeping her face and body expressionless and immobile, wordlessly leaving the room and making her way to her bedroom, closing the door quietly behind her. Locking herself in the toilet. Leaving the house for an indefinite number of hours and sitting in the school car park by herself. None of these strategies had ever proven successful. In fact her tactics only seemed to increase the possibility that she would be punished as the primary instigator.

Now she can see that her attempt to avoid a family Christmas, always a peak occasion for hostilities, will be entered into the domestic accounting book as yet another example of offensive behaviour on her part.

When she thinks of Christmastime now she thinks of Carricklea, lights strung up over Main Street, the glowing plastic Santa Claus in the window of Kelleher's with its animated arm waving a stiff, repetitive greeting. Tinfoil snowflakes hanging in the town pharmacy. The door of the butcher shop swinging open and shut, voices calling out on the corner. Breath rising as mist in the church car park at night. Foxfield in the evening, houses quiet as sleeping cats, windows bright. The Christmas tree in Connell's front room, tinsel bristling, furniture cramped to make space, and the high, delighted sound of laughter. He said he would be sorry not to see her. Won't be the same without you, he wrote. She felt stupid then and wanted to cry. Her life is so sterile now and has no beauty in it anymore.

I think maybe take this off, Lukas says now.

He's gesturing to her bra. She reaches behind her back and snaps open the clasp, then slips the straps off her shoulders. She discards it out of view of the camera. Lukas takes a few pictures, lowers the camera's position on the tripod, moves it forward an inch, and continues. Marianne stares at the window. The sound of the camera shutter stops eventually and she turns around. Lukas is opening a drawer underneath the table. He takes out a coil of thick black ribbon, made of some coarse cotton or linen fibre.

What's that? Marianne says.

You know what it is.

Don't start this now.

Lukas just stands there unwinding the cloth, indifferent. Marianne's bones begin to feel very heavy, a familiar feeling. They are so heavy she can hardly move. Silently she holds out her arms in front of her, elbows together. Good, he says. He kneels down and wraps the cloth tightly. Her wrists are thin but the ribbon is pulled so tight that a little flesh still swells on either side. This looks ugly to her and instinctively she turns away, towards the window again. Very good, he says. He goes back to the camera. The shutter clicks. She closes her eyes but he tells her to open them. She's tired now. The inside of her body seems to be gravitating further and further downwards, towards the floor, towards the centre of the earth. When she looks up, Lukas is unwrapping another length of ribbon.

No, she says.

Don't make it hard on yourself.

I don't want to do this.

I know, he says.

He kneels down again. She draws her head back, avoiding his touch, and quickly he puts his hand around her throat. This gesture doesn't frighten her, it only exhausts her so entirely that she can't speak or move anymore. Her chin drops forward, slack. She's tired of making evasive efforts when it's easier, effortless, to give in. He squeezes her throat slightly and she coughs. Then, not speaking, he lets go of her. He takes up the cloth again and wraps it as a blindfold around her eyes. Even her breathing feels laboured now. Her eyes itch. He touches her cheek gently with the back of his hand and she feels sick.

You see, I love you, he says. And I know you love me.

Horrified, she pulls away from him, striking the back of her head on the wall. She scrabbles with her bound wrists to pull the blindfold back from her eyes, managing to lift it far enough so that she can see.

What's wrong? he says.

Untie me.

Marianne.

Untie me now or I'll call the police, she says.

This doesn't seem a particularly realistic threat, since her hands are still bound, but maybe sensing that the mood has changed, Lukas starts to unwrap the cloth from her wrists. She's shivering violently now. As soon as the binding is loose enough that she can draw her arms apart, she does. She pulls the blindfold off and grabs her sweater, tugs it over her head, threads her arms through the sleeves. She's standing up straight now, feet on the mattress.

Why are you acting like this? he says.

Get away from me. Don't ever talk to me like that again.

Like what? What did I say?

She takes her bra from the mattress, crumples it in her hand and walks across the room to thrust it down into her handbag. She starts to pull her boots on, hopping stupidly on one foot.

Marianne, he says. What have I done?

Are you being serious or is this some kind of artistic technique?

All of life is an artistic technique.

She stares at him. Improbably, he follows this remark up with: I think you are a very gifted writer. She laughs, out of horror.

You don't feel the same way for me, he says.

I want to be very clear, she says. I feel nothing for you. Nothing. Okay?

He returns to his camera, back turned to her, as if to disguise some expression. Malicious laughter at her distress? she thinks. Rage? He could not, it's too appalling to consider, actually have hurt feelings? He starts to remove the device from the tripod. She opens the door of the apartment and makes her way down the staircase. Could he really do the gruesome things he does to her and believe at the same time that he's acting out of love? Is the world such an evil place, that love should be indistinguishable from the basest and most abusive forms of violence? Outside her breath rises in a fine mist and the snow keeps falling, like a ceaseless repetition of the same infinitesimally small mistake.

Three Months Later

(MARCH 2014)

In the waiting room he has to fill out a questionnaire. The seats are brightly coloured, arranged around a coffee table with a children's abacus toy on it. The coffee table is much too low for him to lean forward and fill out the pages on its surface, so he arranges them awkwardly in his lap instead. On the very first question he pierces the page with his ballpoint pen and leaves a tiny tear in the paper. He looks up at the receptionist who provided him with the form but she's not watching, so he looks back down again. The second question is headed 'Pessimism'. He has to circle the number beside one of the following statements:

- 0　I am not discouraged about my future
- 1　I feel more discouraged about my future than I used to be
- 2　I do not expect things to work out for me
- 3　I feel my future is hopeless and will only get worse

It seems to him that any of these statements could plausibly be true, or more than one of them could be true at the same time. He puts the end of his pen between his teeth. Reading the fourth sentence, which for some reason is labelled '3', gives Connell a prickling feeling inside the soft tissue of his nose, like the sentence is calling out to him. It's true, he feels his future is hopeless and will only get worse. The more he thinks about it, the more it resonates. He doesn't even have to think about it, because he feels it: its syntax seems to have originated inside him. He rubs his tongue hard on the roof of his mouth, trying to settle his face into a neutral frown of concentration. Not wanting to alarm the woman who will receive the questionnaire, he circles statement 2 instead.

It was Niall who told him about the service. What he said specifically was: It's free, so you might as well. Niall is a practical person, and he shows compassion in practical ways. Connell hasn't been seeing much of him lately, because Connell lives in his scholarship accommodation now and doesn't see much of anyone anymore. Last night he spent an hour and a half lying on the floor of his room, because he was too tired to complete the journey from his en suite back to his bed. There was the en suite, behind him, and there was the bed, in front of him, both well within view, but somehow it was impossible to move either forward or backwards, only downwards, onto the floor, until his body was arranged motionless on the carpet. Well, here I am on the floor, he thought. Is life so much worse here than it would be on the bed, or even in a totally different location? No, life is exactly the same. Life is the thing you bring with you inside your own head. I might as well be lying here, breathing the vile dust of the carpet into my lungs, gradually feeling my right arm go numb under the weight of my body, because it's essentially the same as every other possible experience.

0 I feel the same about myself as ever
1 I have lost confidence in myself

2 I am disappointed in myself
3 I dislike myself

He looks up at the woman behind the glass. It strikes him now for the first time that they've placed a glass screen between this woman and the people in the waiting room. Do they imagine that people like Connell pose a risk to the woman behind the glass? Do they imagine that the students who come in here and patiently fill out the questionnaires, who repeat their own names again and again for the woman to type into her computer – do they imagine that these people want to hurt the woman behind the desk? Do they think that because Connell sometimes lies on his own floor for hours, he might one day purchase a semi-automatic machine gun online and commit mass murder in a shopping centre? Nothing could be further from his mind than committing mass murder. He feels guilty after he stammers a word on the phone. Still, he can see the logic: mentally unhealthy people are contaminated in some way and possibly dangerous. If they don't attack the woman behind the desk due to uncontrollable violent impulses, they might breathe some kind of microbe in her direction, causing her to dwell unhealthily on all the failed relationships in her past. He circles 3 and moves on.

o I don't have any thoughts of killing myself
1 I have thoughts of killing myself, but I would not carry them out
2 I would like to kill myself
3 I would kill myself if I had the chance

He glances back over at the woman again. He doesn't want to confess to her, a total stranger, that he would like to kill himself. Last night on the floor he fantasised about lying completely still until he died of dehydration, however long that took. Days maybe, but relaxing days in which he wouldn't have to do anything or focus very hard. Who would find his body? He didn't care. The fantasy, purified by weeks of repetition, ends at the moment of death: the calm, silent eyelid that closes over everything for good. He circles statement 1.

After completing the rest of the questions, all of which are intensely personal and the last one is about his sex life, he folds the pages over and hands them back to the receptionist. He doesn't know what to expect, handing over this extremely sensitive information to a stranger. He swallows and his throat is so tight it hurts. The woman takes the sheets like he's handing over a delayed college assignment and gives him a bland, cheerful smile. Thanks, she says. You can wait for the counsellor to call you now. He stands there limply. In her hand she holds the most deeply private information he has ever shared with anyone. Seeing her nonchalance, he experiences an impulse to ask for it back, as if he must have misunderstood the nature of this exchange, and maybe he should fill it out differently after all. Instead he says: Okay. He sits down again.

For a while nothing happens. His stomach is making a low whining noise now because he hasn't eaten breakfast. Lately he's too tired to cook for himself in the evenings, so he finds himself signing in for dinner on the scholars' website and eating Commons in the Dining Hall. Before the meal everyone stands for grace, which is recited in Latin. Then the food is served by other students, who are dressed all in black to differentiate them from the otherwise identical students who are being served. The meals are always the same: salty orange soup to start, with a bread roll and a square of butter wrapped in foil. Then a piece of meat in gravy, with silver dishes of potatoes passed around. Then dessert, some kind of wet sugary cake, or the fruit salad which is mostly grapes. These are all served rapidly and whisked away rapidly, while portraits of men from different centuries glare down from the walls in expensive regalia. Eating alone like this, over-hearing the conversations of others but unable to join in, Connell feels profoundly and almost unendurably alienated from his own body. After the meal another grace is recited, with the ugly noise of chairs pulled back from tables. By seven he has emerged into the darkness of Front Square, and the lamps have been lit.

A middle-aged woman comes out to the waiting room now, wearing a long grey cardigan, and says: Connell? He tries to contort his face into a smile, and then, giving up, rubs his jaw with his hand instead, nodding. My name is Yvonne, she says. Would you like to come with me? He rises from the couch and follows her into a small office. She closes the door behind them. On one side of the office is a desk with an ancient Microsoft computer humming audibly; on the other side, two low mint-coloured armchairs facing one another. Now then, Connell, she says. You can sit down wherever you like. He sits on the chair facing the window, out of which he can see the back of a concrete building and a rusting drain-pipe. She sits down opposite him and picks up a pair of glasses from a chain around her neck. She fixes them on her face and looks down at her clipboard.

Okay, she says. Why don't we talk about how you're feeling?

Yeah. Not great.

I'm sorry to hear that. When did you start feeling this way?

Uh, he says. A couple of months ago. January, I suppose.

She clicks a pen and writes something down. January, she says. Okay. Did something happen then, or it just came on out of nowhere?

A few days into the new year, Connell got a text message from Rachel Moran. It was two o'clock in the morning then, and he and Helen were coming back from a night out. Angling his phone away, he opened the text: it was a group message that went out to all their school friends, asking if anyone had seen or been in contact with Rob Hegarty. It said he hadn't been seen for a few hours. Helen asked him what the text said and for some reason Connell replied: Oh, nothing, just a group message. Happy New Year. The next day Rob's body was recovered from the River Corrib.

Connell later heard from friends that Rob had been drinking a lot in the preceding weeks and seemed out of sorts. Connell hadn't known anything about it, he hadn't been home much last term, he hadn't really been seeing people. He checked his Facebook to find the last time Rob had sent him a message, and it was from early 2012: a photograph from a night out, Connell pictured with his arm around the waist of Marianne's friend Teresa. In the message Rob had written: are u riding her?? NICE haha. Connell had never replied. He hadn't seen Rob at Christmas, he couldn't remember for certain whether he'd even seen him last summer or not. Trying to summon an exact mental picture of Rob's face, Connell found that he couldn't: an image would appear at first, whole and recognisable, but on any closer inspection the features would float away from one another, blur, become confused.

In the following days, people from school posted status updates about suicide awareness. Since then Connell's mental state has steadily, week after week, continued to deteriorate. His anxiety, which was previously chronic and low-level, serving as a kind of all-purpose inhibiting impulse, has become severe. His hands start tingling when he has to perform minor interactions like ordering coffee or answering a question in class. Once or twice he's had major panic attacks: hyperventilation, chest pain, pins and needles all over his body. A feeling of dissociation from his senses, an inability to think straight or interpret what he sees and hears. Things begin to look and sound different, slower, artificial, unreal. The first time it happened he thought he was losing his mind, that the whole cognitive framework by which he made sense of the world had disintegrated for good, and everything from then on would just be undifferentiated sound and colour. Then within a couple of minutes it passed, and left him lying on his mattress coated in sweat.

Now he looks up at Yvonne, the person assigned by the university to listen to his problems for money.

One of my friends committed suicide in January, he says. A friend from school.

Oh, how sad. I'm very sorry to hear that, Connell.

We hadn't really kept up with each other in college. He was in Galway and I was here and everything. I guess I feel guilty now that I wasn't in touch with him more.

I can understand that, Yvonne says. But however sad you

might be feeling about your friend, what happened to him is not your fault. You're not responsible for the decisions he made.

I never even replied to the last message he sent me. I mean, that was years ago, but I didn't even reply.

I know that must feel very painful for you, of course that's very painful. You feel you missed an opportunity to help someone who was suffering.

Connell nods, dumbly, and rubs his eye.

When you lose someone to suicide, it's natural to wonder if there's anything you could have done to help this person, Yvonne says. I'm sure everyone in your friend's life is asking themselves the same questions now.

But at least other people tried to help.

This sounds more aggressive, or more wheedling, than Connell intended it to. He's surprised to see that instead of responding directly, Yvonne just looks at him, looks through the lenses of her glasses, and her eyes are narrowed. She's nodding. Then she lifts a sheaf of paper off the table and holds it upright, businesslike.

Well, I've had a look at this inventory you filled out for us, she says. And I'll be honest with you, Connell, what I'm seeing here would be pretty concerning.

Right. Would it?

She shuffles the sheets of paper. He can see on the first sheet where his pen made the small tear.

This is what we call the Beck Depression Inventory, she says. I'm sure you've figured out how it works, we just assign a score from zero to three for each item. Now, someone like me might score between, say, zero and five on a test like this, and someone who's going through a mild depressive episode could expect to see a score of maybe fifteen or sixteen.

Okay, he says. Right.

And what we're seeing here is a score of forty-three.

Yeah. Okay.

So that would put us in the territory of a very serious depression, she says. Do you think that matches up with your experience?

He rubs at his eye again. Quietly he manages to say: Yeah.

I'm seeing that you're feeling very negatively towards yourself, you're having some suicidal thoughts, things like that. So those are things we'd have to take very seriously.

Right.

At this point she starts talking about treatment options. She says she's going to recommend that he should see a GP in college to talk about the option of medication. You understand I'm not in a position to make any prescriptions here, she says. He nods, restless now. Yeah, I know that, he says. He keeps rubbing at his eyes, they're itchy. She offers him a glass of water but he declines. She starts to ask questions about his family, about his mother and where she lives and whether he has brothers and sisters.

Any girlfriend or boyfriend on the scene at the moment? Yvonne says.

No, says Connell. No one like that.

Helen came back to Carricklea with him for the funeral. The morning of the ceremony they dressed in his room together in silence, with the noise of Lorraine's hairdryer humming through the wall. Connell was wearing the only suit he owned, which he had bought for a cousin's communion when he was sixteen. The jacket was tight around his shoulders, he could feel it when he lifted his arms. The sensation that he looked bad preoccupied him. Helen was sitting at the mirror putting on her make-up, and Connell stood behind her to knot his tie. She reached up to touch his face. You look handsome, she said. For some reason that made him angry, like it was the most insensitive, vulgar thing she possibly could have said, and he didn't respond. She dropped her hand then and went to put her shoes on.

They stopped in the vestibule of the church to speak to someone Lorraine knew. Connell's hair was wet from the rain and he kept smoothing it, not looking at Helen, not speaking. Then, through the opened church doors, he saw Marianne. He'd known she was coming back from Sweden for the funeral. In the doorway she looked very slim and pale, wearing a black coat, carrying a wet umbrella. He hadn't seen her since Italy. She looked, he thought, almost frail. She started putting her umbrella in the stand inside the door.

Marianne, he said.

He said this aloud without thinking about it. She looked up and saw him then. Her face was like a small white flower. She put her arms around his neck, and he held her tightly. He could smell the inside of her house on her clothes. The last time he'd seen her, everything had been normal. Rob was still alive then, Connell could have sent him a message or even called him and talked to him on the phone, it was possible then, it had been possible. Marianne touched the back of Connell's head with her hand. Everyone stood there watching them, he felt that. When they knew it couldn't go on any longer, they let go of one another. Helen patted his arm quickly. People were moving in and out of the vestibule, coats and umbrellas dripping silently onto the tiles.

We'd better go and pay our respects, Lorraine said.

They lined up with everyone else to shake hands with the family. Rob's mother Eileen was just crying and crying, they could hear her the whole way down the church. By the time they got halfway up the queue Connell's legs were shaking. He wished Lorraine were standing with him and not Helen. He felt like he was going to be sick. When it was finally his turn, Rob's father Val gripped his hand and said: Connell, good man. I hear you're doing great things above in Trinity. Connell's hands were wringing wet. I'm sorry, he said in a thin voice. I'm so sorry. Val kept gripping his hand and looking in his eyes. Good lad, he said. Thanks for coming. Then it was over. Connell sat down in the first available pew, shivering all over. Helen sat down beside him, looking self-conscious, pulling at the hem of her skirt. Lorraine came over and gave him a tissue from her handbag, with which he wiped his forehead and his upper lip. She squeezed his shoulder. You're alright, she said. You've done your bit, just relax now. And Helen turned her face away, as if embarrassed.

After Mass they went to the burial, and then back to the Tavern to eat sandwiches and drink tea in the ballroom. Behind the bar a girl from the year below in school was dressed in a white shirt and waistcoat, serving pints. Connell poured Helen a cup of tea and then one for himself. They stood by the wall near the tea trays, drinking and not talking. Connell's cup rattled in its saucer. Eric came over and stood with them when he arrived. He was wearing a shiny blue tie.

How are things? Eric said. Long time no see.

I know, yeah, said Connell. It's been a fair while alright.

Who's this? Eric said, nodding at Helen.

Helen, said Connell. Helen, this is Eric.

Eric held out his hand and Helen shook it, balancing her teacup politely in her left hand, her face tensed in effort.

The girlfriend, is it? Eric said.

With a glance at Connell she nodded and replied: Yes.

Eric released her, grinning. You're a Dub anyway, he said.

She smiled nervously and said: That's right.

Must be your fault this lad never comes home anymore, Eric said.

It's not her fault, it's my fault, said Connell.

I'm only messing with you, Eric said.

For a few seconds they stood looking out at the room in silence. Helen cleared her throat and said delicately: I'm very sorry for your loss, Eric. Eric turned and gave her a kind of gallant nod. He looked back at the room again. Yeah, hard to believe, he said. Then he poured himself a cup of tea from the pot behind them. Good of Marianne to come, he remarked. I thought she was off in Sweden or someplace.

She was, said Connell. She's home for the funeral.

She's gone very thin, isn't she?

Eric took a large mouthful of tea and swallowed it, smacking his lips. Marianne, detaching herself from another conversation, made her way towards the tea tray.

Here's herself, said Eric. You're very good to come all the way back from Sweden, Marianne.

She thanked him and started to pour a cup of tea, saying it was nice to see him.

Have you met Helen here? Eric asked.

Marianne put her teacup down in her saucer. Of course I have, she said. We're in college together.

All friendly, I hope, said Eric. No rivalry, I mean.

Behave yourself now, said Marianne.

Connell watched Marianne pouring the tea, her smiling manner, 'behave yourself', and he felt in awe of her naturalness, her easy way of moving through the world. It hadn't been like that in school, quite the opposite. Back then Connell had been the one who understood how to behave, while Marianne had just aggravated everyone.

After the funeral he cried, but the crying felt like nothing. Back in fifth year when Connell had scored a goal for the school football team, Rob had leapt onto the pitch to embrace him. He screamed Connell's name, and began to kiss his head with wild exuberant kisses. It was only one-all, and there were still twenty minutes left on the clock. But that was their world then. Their feelings were suppressed so carefully in everyday life, forced into smaller and smaller spaces, until seemingly minor events took on insane and frightening significance. It was permissible to touch each other and cry during football matches. Connell still remembers the too-hard grip of his arms. And on Debs night, Rob showing them those photographs of Lisa's naked body. Nothing had meant more to Rob than the approval of others; to be thought well of, to be a person of status. He would have betrayed any confidence, any kindness, for the promise of social acceptance. Connell couldn't judge him for that. He'd been the same way himself, or worse. He had just wanted to be normal, to conceal the parts of himself that he found shameful and confusing. It was Marianne who had shown him other things were possible. Life was different after that; maybe he had never understood how different it was.

The night of the funeral he and Helen lay in his room in the dark, not sleeping. Helen asked him why he hadn't introduced her to any of his friends. She was whispering so as not to wake Lorraine.

I introduced you to Eric, didn't I? Connell said.

Only after he asked. To be honest, you didn't seem like you really wanted him to meet me.

Connell closed his eyes. It was a funeral, he said. You know, someone just died. I don't think it's really a good occasion for meeting people.

Well, if you didn't want me to come you shouldn't have asked me, she said.

He breathed in and out slowly. Okay, he said. I'm sorry I asked you, then.

She sat upright in bed beside him. What does that mean? she said. You're sorry I was there?

No, I'm saying if I gave you the wrong impression about what it was going to be like, then I'm sorry.

You didn't want me there at all, did you?

I didn't want to be there myself, to be honest, he said. I'm sorry you didn't have a good time, but like, it was a funeral. I don't know what you expected.

She breathed in quickly through her nose, he could hear it.

You weren't ignoring Marianne, she said.

I wasn't ignoring anyone.

But you seemed particularly happy to see her, wouldn't you say?

For fuck's sake, Helen, he said quietly.

What?

How does every argument come back to this? Our friend just killed himself and you want to start in with me about Marianne, seriously? Like, yeah, I was glad to see her, does that make me a monster?

When Helen spoke it was in a low hiss. I've been very sympathetic about your friend and you know that, she said. But what do you expect me to do, just pretend I don't notice that you're staring at another woman in front of me?

I was not staring at her.

You were, in the church.

Well, it wasn't intentional, he said. Believe me, it was not a very sexy atmosphere for me in the church, okay? You can trust me on that.

Why do you have to act so weird around her?

He frowned, still lying with his eyes shut, face turned to the ceiling. How I act with her is my normal personality, he said. Maybe I'm just a weird person.

Helen said nothing. Eventually she just lay back down beside him. Two weeks later it was over, they broke up. By then Connell was so exhausted and miserable he couldn't even summon up a response. Things happened to him, like the crying fits, the panic attacks, but they seemed to descend on him from outside, rather than emanating from somewhere inside himself. Internally he felt nothing. He was like a freezer item that had thawed too quickly on the outside and was melting everywhere, while the inside was still frozen solid. Somehow he was expressing more emotion than at any time in his life before, while simultaneously feeling less, feeling nothing.

Yvonne nods slowly, moving her mouth around in a sympathetic way. Do you feel you've made friends here in Dublin? she says. Anyone you're close with, that you might talk to about how you're feeling?

My friend Niall, maybe. He was the one who told me about this whole thing.

The college counselling service.

Yeah, says Connell.

Well, that's good. He's looking out for you. Niall, okay. And he's here in Trinity as well.

Connell coughs, clearing the dry feeling from his throat, and says: Yeah. I have another friend who I would be pretty close with, but she's on Erasmus this year.

A friend from college?

Well, we went to school together but she's in Trinity now as well. Marianne. She would have known Rob and everything. Our friend who died. But she's away this year, like I said.

He watches Yvonne write down the name on her notepad, the tall slopes of the capital 'M'. He talks to Marianne almost every night on Skype now, sometimes after dinner or sometimes late when she comes home from a night out. They've never talked about what happened in Italy. He's grateful that she's never brought it up. When they speak the video stream is high quality but frequently fails to match the audio, which gives him a sense of Marianne as a moving image, a thing to be looked at. People in college have been saying things about her since she went away. Connell's not sure if she knows about it or not, what people like Jamie have been saying. Connell isn't even really friends with those people and he's heard about it. Some drunk guy at a party told him that she was into weird stuff, and that there were pictures of her on the internet. Connell doesn't know if it's true about the pictures. He's searched her name online but nothing has ever come up.

Is she someone you might talk with about how you're feeling? Yvonne says.

Yeah, she's been supportive about it. She, uh . . . She's hard to describe if you don't know her. She's really smart, a lot smarter than me, but I would say we see the world in a similar way. And we've lived our whole lives in the same place, obviously, so it is a bit different being away from her.

It sounds difficult.

I just don't have a lot of people who I really click with, he says. You know, I struggle with that.

Do you think that's a new problem, or is it something familiar to you?

It's familiar, I suppose. I would say in school I sometimes had that feeling of isolation or whatever. But people liked me and everything. Here I feel like people don't like me that much.

He pauses, and Yvonne seems to recognise the pause and doesn't interrupt him.

Like with Rob, that's my friend who died, he says. I wouldn't say we clicked on this very deep level or anything, but we were friends.

Sure.

We didn't have a lot in common, like in terms of interests or whatever. And on the political side of things we probably wouldn't have had the same views. But in school, stuff like that didn't really matter as much. We were just in the same group so we were friends, you know.

I understand that, says Yvonne.

And he did do some stuff that I wasn't a big fan of. With girls his behaviour was kind of poor at times. You know, we were eighteen or whatever, we all acted like idiots. But I guess I found that stuff a bit alienating.

Connell bites on his thumbnail and then drops his hand back into his lap.

I probably thought if I moved here I would fit in better, he says. You know, I thought I might find more like-minded people or whatever. But honestly, the people here are a lot worse than the people I knew in school. I mean everyone here just goes around comparing how much money their parents make. Like I'm being literal with that, I've seen that happen.

He breathes in now, feeling that he has been talking too quickly and at too great a length, but unwilling to stop.

I just feel like I left Carricklea thinking I could have a different life, he says. But I hate it here, and now I can never go back there again. I mean, those friendships are gone. Rob is gone, I can never see him again. I can never get that life back.

Yvonne pushes the box of tissues on the table towards him. He looks at the box, patterned with green palm leaves, and then at Yvonne. He touches his own face, only to discover that he has started crying. Wordlessly he removes a tissue from the box and wipes his face.

Sorry, he says.

Yvonne is making eye contact now, but he can't tell anymore whether she's been listening to him, whether she's understood or tried to understand what he's said.

What we can do here in counselling is try to work on your feelings, and your thoughts and behaviours, she says. We can't change your circumstances, but we can change how you respond to your circumstances. Do you see what I mean?

Yeah.

At this point in the session Yvonne starts to hand him worksheets, illustrated with large cartoon arrows pointing to various text boxes. He takes them and pretends that he's intending to fill them out later. She also hands him some photocopied pages about dealing with anxiety, which he pretends he will read. She prints a note for him to take to the college health service advising them about his depression, and he says he'll come back for another session in two weeks. Then he leaves the office.

A couple of weeks ago Connell attended a reading by a writer who was visiting the college. He sat at the back of the lecture hall on his own, self-conscious because the reading was sparsely attended and everyone else was sitting in groups. It was one of the big windowless halls in the Arts Block, with fold-out tables attached to the seats. One of his lecturers gave a short and sycophantic overview of the writer's work, and then the man himself, a youngish guy around thirty, stood at the lectern and thanked the college for the invitation. By then Connell regretted his decision to attend. Everything about the event was staid and formulaic, sapped of energy. He didn't know why he had come. He had read the writer's collection and found it uneven, but sensitive in places, perceptive. Now, he thought, even that effect was spoiled by seeing the writer in this environment, hemmed off from anything spontaneous, reciting aloud from his own book to an audience who'd already read it. The stiffness of this performance made the observations in the book seem false, separating the writer from the people he wrote about, as if he'd observed them only for the benefit of talking about them to Trinity students. Connell couldn't think of any reason why these literary events took place, what they contributed to anything, what they meant. They were attended only by people who wanted to be the kind of people who attended them.

Afterwards a small wine reception had been set up outside the lecture hall. Connell went to leave but found himself trapped by a group of students talking loudly. When he tried to press his way through, one of them said: Oh, hi Connell. He recognised her, it was Sadie Darcy-O'Shea. She was in some of his English classes, and he knew she was involved in the literary society. She was the girl who'd called him 'a genius' to his face back in first year.

Hey, he said.

Did you enjoy the reading?

He shrugged. It was alright, he said. He felt anxious and wanted to leave, but she kept speaking. He rubbed his palms on his T-shirt.

You weren't blown away? she said.

I don't know, I don't really get the point of these things.

Readings?

Yeah, said Connell. You know, I don't really see what they're for.

Everyone looked away suddenly, and Connell turned to follow their gaze. The writer had emerged from the lecture hall and was approaching them. Hi there, Sadie, he said. Connell had not intuited any personal relationship between Sadie and the writer, and he felt foolish for saying what he'd said. You read so wonderfully, said Sadie. Irritated and tired, Connell moved aside to let the writer join their circle and started to edge away. Then Sadie gripped his arm and said: Connell was just telling us he doesn't see the point of literary readings. The writer looked vaguely in Connell's direction and then nodded. Yeah, same as that, he said. They're boring, aren't they? Connell noticed that the stilted quality of his reading seemed to characterise his speech and movement also, and he felt bad then for attributing such a negative view of literature to someone who was maybe just awkward.

Well, we appreciated it, said Sadie.

What's your name, Connell what? said the writer.

Connell Waldron.

The writer nodded. He picked up a glass of red wine from the table and let the others continue talking. For some reason, though the opportunity to leave had at last presented itself, Connell lingered. The writer swallowed some wine and then looked at him again.

I liked your book, said Connell.

Oh, thanks, said the writer. Are you coming on to the Stag's Head for a drink? I think that's where people are heading.

They didn't leave the Stag's Head that night until it closed. They had a good-natured argument about literary readings, and although Connell didn't say very much, the writer took his side, which pleased him. Later he asked Connell where he was from, and Connell told him Sligo, a place called Carricklea. The writer nodded.

I know it, yeah, he said. There used to be a bowling alley there, it's probably gone years now.

Yeah, Connell said too quickly. I had a birthday party there once when I was small. In the bowling alley. It is gone now, though, obviously. Like you said.

The writer took a sip of his pint and said: How do you find Trinity, do you like it?

Connell looked at Sadie across the table, her bangles knocking together on her wrist.

Bit hard to fit in, to be honest, Connell said.

The writer nodded again. That mightn't be a bad thing, he said. You could get a first collection out of it.

Connell laughed, he looked down into his lap. He knew it was just a joke, but it was a nice thought, that he might not be suffering for nothing.

He knows that a lot of the literary people in college see books primarily as a way of appearing cultured. When someone mentioned the austerity protests that night in the Stag's Head, Sadie threw her hands up and said: Not politics, please! Connell's initial assessment of the reading was not disproven. It was culture as class performance, literature fetishised for its ability to take educated people on false emotional journeys, so that they might afterwards feel superior to the uneducated people whose emotional journeys they liked to read about. Even if the writer himself was a good person, and even if his book really was insightful, all books were ultimately marketed as status symbols, and all writers participated to some degree in this marketing. Presumably this was how the industry made money. Literature, in the way it appeared at these public readings, had no potential as a form of resistance to anything. Still, Connell went home that night and read over some notes he had been making for a new story, and he felt the old beat of pleasure inside his body, like watching a perfect goal, like the rustling movement of light through leaves, a phrase of music from the window of a passing car. Life offers up these moments of joy despite everything.

Four Months Later

(JULY 2014)

Her eyes narrow until the television screen is just a green oblong, yawning light at the edges. Are you falling asleep? he says. After a pause she replies: No. He nods, not taking his eyes off the match. He takes a sip of Coke and the remaining ice clinks softly in his glass. Her limbs feel heavy on the mattress. She's lying in Connell's room in Foxfield watching the Netherlands play Costa Rica for a place in the World Cup semi-finals. His room looks the same as it did in school, although one corner of his Steven Gerrard poster has come unfixed from the wall and curled inwards on itself in the meantime. But everything else is the same: the lampshade, the green curtains, even the pillowcases with the striped trim.

I can run you home at half-time, he says.

For a second she says nothing. Her eyes flutter closed and then open up again, wider, so she can see the players moving around the pitch.

Am I in your way? she says.

No, not at all. You just seem sleepy.

Can I have some of your Coke?

He hands her the glass and she sits up to drink it, feeling like a baby. Her mouth is dry and the drink is cold and flavourless on her tongue. She takes two huge mouthfuls and then hands it back to him, wiping her lips with the back of her hand. He accepts the glass without looking away from the TV.

You're thirsty, he says. There's more downstairs in the fridge if you want some.

She shakes her head, lies back down with her hands clasped behind her neck.

Where did you disappear to last night? she says.

Oh. I don't know, I was in the smoking area for a bit.

Did you end up kissing that girl?

No, he says.

Marianne closes her eyes, fans her face with her hand. I'm really warm, she says. Do you find it hot in here?

You can open the window if you want.

She tries wriggling down the bed towards the window and reaching for the handle without actually having to sit up the whole way. She pauses, waiting to see if Connell will intervene on her behalf. He's working in the college library this summer, but he's visited Carricklea every weekend since she got home. They drive around in his car together, out to Strandhill, or up to Glencar waterfall. Connell bites his nails a lot and doesn't talk much. Last month she told him he shouldn't feel obliged to visit her if he doesn't feel like it, and he replied tonelessly: Well, it's really the only thing I have to look forward to. She sits up now and opens the window herself. The daylight is fading but the air outside feels balmy and still.

What was her name again? she says. The girl at the bar.

Niamh Keenan.

She likes you.

I don't think we really share interests, he says. Eric was looking for you last night actually, did you see him?

Marianne sits cross-legged on the bed, facing Connell. He's

propped up against the headboard, holding the glass of Coke on his chest.

Yes, I saw him, she says. It was weird.

Why, what happened?

He was really drunk. I don't know. For some reason he decided he wanted to apologise to me for the way he acted in school.

Really? says Connell. That is weird.

He looks back at the screen then, so she feels at liberty to study his face in detail. He probably notices she's doing this, but politely says nothing about it. The bedside lamp diffuses light softly over his features, the fine cheekbone, the brow in its frown of mild concentration, the faint sheen of perspiration on his upper lip. Dwelling on the sight of Connell's face always gives Marianne a certain pleasure, which can be inflected with any number of other feelings depending on the minute interplay of conversation and mood. His appearance is like a favourite piece of music to her, sounding a little different each time she hears it.

He was talking about Rob a bit, she says. He was saying Rob would have wanted to apologise. I mean, it wasn't clear if this was something Rob had actually said to him or if Eric was just doing some psychological projection.

I'm sure Rob would have wanted to apologise, to be honest.

Oh, I hate to think that. I hate to think he had that on his conscience in some way. I never held it against him, really. You know, it was nothing, we were kids.

It wasn't nothing, says Connell. He bullied you.

Marianne says nothing. It's true they did bully her. Eric called her 'flat-chested' once, in front of everyone, and Rob, laughing, scrambled to whisper something in Eric's ear, some affirmation, or some further insult too vulgar to speak out loud. At the funeral back in January everyone talked about what a great person Rob had been, full of life, a devoted son, and so on. But he was also a very insecure person, obsessed with popularity, and his desperation had made him cruel. Not for the first time Marianne thinks cruelty does not only hurt the victim, but the perpetrator also, and maybe more deeply and more permanently. You learn nothing very profound about yourself simply by being bullied; but by bullying someone else you learn something you can never forget.

After the funeral she spent evenings scrolling through Rob's Facebook page. Lots of people from school had left comments on his wall, saying they missed him. What were these people doing, Marianne thought, writing on the Facebook wall of a dead person? What did these messages, these advertisements of loss, actually mean to anyone? What was the appropriate etiquette when they appeared on the timeline: to 'like' them supportively? To scroll past in search of something better? But everything made Marianne angry then. Thinking about it now, she can't understand why it bothered her. None of those people had done anything wrong. They were just grieving. Of course it didn't make sense to write on his Facebook wall, but nothing else made sense either. If people appeared to behave pointlessly in grief, it was only because human life was pointless, and this was the truth that grief revealed. She wishes that she could have forgiven Rob, even if it meant nothing to him. When she thinks of him now it's always with his face hidden, turning away, behind his locker door, behind the rolled-up window of his car. Who were you? she thinks, now that there's no one left to answer the question.

Did you accept the apology? says Connell.

She nods, looking down at her nails. Of course I did, she says. I don't go in for grudges.

Luckily for me, he replies.

The half-time whistle blows and the players turn, heads lowered, and start their slow walk across the pitch. It's still nil-all. She wipes her nose with her fingers. Connell sits up straight and puts his glass on the bedside table. She thinks he's going to offer her a lift home again, but instead he says: Do you feel like an ice cream? She says yes. Back in a second, he says. He leaves the bedroom door open on his way out.

Marianne is living at home now for the first time since she left school. Her mother and brother are at work all day and Marianne has nothing to do but sit in the garden watching insects wriggle through soil. Inside she makes coffee, sweeps floors, wipes down surfaces. The house is never really clean anymore because Lorraine has a full-time job in the hotel now and they've never replaced her. Without Lorraine the house is not a nice place to live. Sometimes Marianne goes on day trips to Dublin, and she and Joanna wander around the Hugh Lane together with bare arms, drinking from bottles of water. Joanna's girlfriend Evelyn comes along when she's not studying or working, and she's always painstakingly kind to Marianne and interested to hear about her life. Marianne is so happy for Joanna and Evelyn that she feels lucky even to see them together, even to hear Joanna on the phone to Evelyn saying cheerfully: Okay, love you, see you later. It gives

Marianne a window onto real happiness, though a window she cannot open herself or ever climb through.

They went to a protest against the war in Gaza the other week with Connell and Niall. There were thousands of people there, carrying signs and megaphones and banners. Marianne wanted her life to mean something then, she wanted to stop all violence committed by the strong against the weak, and she remembered a time several years ago when she had felt so intelligent and young and powerful that she almost could have achieved such a thing, and now she knew she wasn't at all powerful, and she would live and die in a world of extreme violence against the innocent, and at most she could help only a few people. It was so much harder to reconcile herself to the idea of helping a few, like she would rather help no one than do something so small and feeble, but that wasn't it either. The protest was very loud and slow, lots of people were banging drums and chanting things out of unison, sound systems crackling on and off. They marched across O'Connell Bridge with the Liffey trickling under them. The weather was hot, Marianne's shoulders got sunburned.

Connell drove her back to Carricklea in the car that evening, though she said she would get the train. They were both very tired on the way home. While they were driving through Longford they had the radio on, it was playing a White Lies song that had been popular when they were in school, and without touching the dial or raising his voice to be heard over the sound of the radio Connell said: You know I love you. He didn't say anything else. She said she loved him too and he nodded and continued driving as if nothing at all had happened, which in a way it hadn't.

Marianne's brother works for the county council now. He comes home in the evening and prowls around the house looking for her. From her room she can tell it's him because he always wears his shoes inside. He knocks on her door if he can't find her in the living room or the kitchen. I just want to talk to you, he says. Why are you acting like you're scared of me? Can we talk for a second? She has to come to the door then, and he wants to go over some argument they had the night before, and she says she's tired and wants to get some sleep, but he won't leave until she says she's sorry for the previous argument, so she says she's sorry, and he says: You think I'm such a horrible person. She wonders if that's true. I try to be nice to you, he says, but you always throw it back at me. She doesn't think that's true, but she knows he probably thinks it is. It's nothing worse than this mostly, it's just this all the time, nothing but this, and long empty weekdays wiping down surfaces and wringing damp sponges into the sink.

Connell comes back upstairs now and tosses her an ice lolly wrapped in shiny plastic. She catches it in her hands and lifts it straight to her cheek, where the cold radiates outwards sweetly. He sits back against the headboard, starts unwrapping his own.

Do you ever see Peggy in Dublin? she says. Or any of those people.

He pauses, his fingers crackle on the plastic wrap. No, he says. I thought you had a falling-out with them, didn't you?

But I'm just asking if you ever hear from them.

No. I wouldn't have much to say to them if I did.

She pulls open the plastic packaging and removes the lolly

from inside, orange with vanilla cream. On her tongue, tiny flakes of clear unflavoured ice.

I did hear Jamie wasn't happy, Connell adds.

I believe he was saying some pretty unpleasant things about me.

Yeah. Well, I wasn't talking to him myself, obviously. But I got the impression he was saying some stuff, yeah.

Marianne lifts her eyebrows, as if amused. When she'd first heard the rumours that were circulating about her, she hadn't found it funny at all. She used to ask Joanna about it again and again: who was talking about it, what had they said. Joanna wouldn't tell her. She said that within a few weeks everyone would have moved on to something else anyway. People are juvenile in their attitudes to sexuality, Joanna said. Their fixation on your sex life is probably more fetishistic than anything you've done. Marianne even went back to Lukas and made him delete all his photographs of her, none of which he had ever put online anyway. Shame surrounded her like a shroud. She could hardly see through it. The cloth caught up her breath, prickled on her skin. It was as if her life was over. How long had that feeling lasted? Two weeks, or more? Then it went away, and a certain short chapter of her youth had concluded, and she had survived it, it was done.

You never said anything to me about it, she says to Connell.

Well, I heard Jamie was pissed off you broke up with him and he went around talking shit about you. But like, that's not even gossip, that's just how lads behave. I didn't know anyone really cared.

I think it's more a case of reputational damage.

And how come Jamie's reputation isn't damaged, then? says

Connell. He was the one doing all that stuff to you.

She looks up and Connell has finished his ice lolly already. He's playing with the dry wooden stick in his fingers. She has only a little left, licked down to a slick bulb of vanilla ice cream, gleaming in the light of the bedside lamp.

It's different for men, she says.

Yeah, I'm starting to get that.

Marianne licks the ice cream stick clean and examines it briefly. Connell says nothing for a few seconds, and then ventures: It's nice Eric apologised to you.

I know, she says. People from school have actually been very nice since I got back. Even though I never make any effort to see them.

Maybe you should.

Why, you think I'm being ungrateful?

No, I just mean you must be kind of lonely, he says.

She pauses, the stick between her index and middle fingers.

I'm used to it, she says. I've been lonely my whole life, really.

Connell nods, frowning. Yeah, he says. I know what you mean.

You weren't lonely with Helen, were you?

I don't know. Sometimes. I didn't feel totally myself with her all the time.

Marianne lies down flat on her back now, head on the pillow, bare legs stretched on the duvet. She stares up at the light fixture, the same lampshade from years ago, dusty green.

Connell, she says. You know when we were dancing last night?

Yeah.

For a moment she just wants to lie here prolonging the

231

intense silence and staring at the lampshade, enjoying the sensory quality of being here in this room again with him and making him talk to her, but time moves on.

What about it? he says.

Did I do something to annoy you?

No. What do you mean by that?

When you walked off and just left me there, she says. I felt kind of awkward. I thought maybe you were gone after that girl Niamh or something, that's why I asked about her. I don't know.

I didn't walk off. I asked you if you wanted to go out to the smoking area and you said no.

She sits up on her elbows and looks at him. He's flushed now, his ears are red.

You didn't ask, she says. You said, I'm going out to the smoking area, and then you walked away.

No, I said do you want to come out to the smoking area, and you shook your head.

Maybe I didn't hear you right.

You must not have, he says. I definitely remember saying it to you. But the music was very loud, to be fair.

They lapse into another silence. Marianne lies back down, looks up at the light again, feels her own face glowing.

I thought you were annoyed with me, she says.

Well, sorry. I wasn't.

After a pause he adds: I think our friendship would be a lot easier in some ways if, like . . . certain things were different.

She lifts her hand to her forehead. He doesn't continue speaking.

If what was different? she says.

I don't know.

She can hear him breathing. She feels she has cornered him into the conversation, and she's reluctant now to push any harder than she has already.

You know, I'm not going to lie, he says, I obviously do feel a certain attraction towards you. I'm not trying to make excuses for myself. I just feel like things would be less confusing if there wasn't this other element to the relationship.

She moves her hand to her ribs, feels the slow inflation of her diaphragm.

Do you think it would be better if we had never been together? she says.

I don't know. For me it's hard to imagine my life that way. Like, I don't know where I would have gone to college then or where I would be now.

She pauses, lets this thought roll around for a moment, keeps her hand flat on her abdomen.

It's funny the decisions you make because you like someone, he says, and then your whole life is different. I think we're at that weird age where life can change a lot from small decisions. But you've been a very good influence on me overall, like I definitely am a better person now, I think. Thanks to you.

She lies there breathing. Her eyes are burning but she doesn't make any move to touch them.

When we were together in first year of college, she says, were you lonely then?

No. Were you?

No. I was frustrated sometimes but not lonely. I never feel lonely when I'm with you.

Yeah, he says. That was kind of a perfect time in my life,

to be honest. I don't think I was ever really happy before then.

She holds her hand down hard on her abdomen, pressing the breath out of her body, and then inhales.

I really wanted you to kiss me last night, she says.

Oh.

Her chest inflates again and deflates slowly.

I wanted to as well, he says. I guess we misunderstood each other.

Well, that's okay.

He clears his throat.

I don't know what's the best thing for us, he says. Obviously it's nice for me hearing you say this stuff. But at the same time things have never ended well with us in the past. You know, you're my best friend, I wouldn't want to lose that for any reason.

Sure, I know what you mean.

Her eyes are wet now and she has to rub them to stop tears running.

Can I think about it? he says.

Of course.

I don't want you to think I'm not appreciative.

She nods, wiping her nose with her fingers. She wonders if she could turn over onto her side and face the window now so he couldn't look at her.

You really have been so supportive of me, he says. What with the depression and everything, not to linger on that too much, but you really helped me a lot.

You don't owe me anything.

No, I know. I didn't mean that.

She sits up, swings her feet off the bed, puts her face down in her hands.

I'm getting anxious now, he says. I hope you don't feel like I'm rejecting you.

Don't be anxious. Everything's fine. I might head home now, if that's okay.

I can drop you.

You don't want to miss the second half, she says. I'll walk, it's alright.

She starts putting her shoes on.

I forgot there was even a match on, to be honest, he says.

But he doesn't get up or look for his keys. She stands up and smooths her skirt down. He's sitting on the bed watching her, an attentive, almost nervous expression on his face.

Okay, she says. Bye.

He reaches for her hand and she gives it to him without thinking. For a second he holds it, his thumb moving over her knuckles. Then he lifts her hand to his mouth and kisses it. She feels pleasurably crushed under the weight of his power over her, the vast ecstatic depth of her will to please him. That's nice, she says. He nods. She feels a low gratifying ache inside her body, in her pelvic bone, in her back.

I'm just nervous, he says. I feel like it's pretty obvious I don't want you to leave.

In a tiny voice she says: I don't find it obvious what you want.

He gets up and stands in front of her. Like a trained animal she stays stock-still, every nerve bristling. She wants to whimper out loud. He puts his hands on her hips and she lets him kiss her open mouth. The sensation is so extreme she feels faint.

I want this so much, she says.

It's really nice to hear you say that. I'm going to switch the TV off, if that's okay.

She gets onto the bed while he switches off the television. He sits beside her and they kiss again. His touch has a narcotic effect. A pleasurable stupidity comes over her, she wants very badly to remove her clothes. She lies back against the quilt and he leans over her. It has been years now. She feels his cock pressed hard against her hip and she shudders with the punishing force of her desire.

Hm, he says. I missed you.

It's not like this with other people.

Well, I like you a lot more than other people.

He kisses her again and she feels his hands on her body. She is an abyss that he can reach into, an empty space for him to fill. Blindly, mechanically, she starts removing her clothes, and she can hear him unbuckle his belt. Time seems so elastic, stretched out by sound and motion. She lies on her front and presses her face into the mattress, and he touches the back of her thigh with his hand. Her body is just an item of property, and though it has been handed around and misused in various ways, it has somehow always belonged to him, and she feels like returning it to him now.

I actually don't have condoms, he says.

It's okay, I'm on the pill.

He touches her hair. She feels his fingertips brush the back of her neck.

Do you want it like this? he says.

However you want.

He gets on top of her, one hand planted on the mattress beside her face, the other in her hair.

I haven't done this in a while, he says.

That's okay.

When he's inside her she hears her own voice crying out again and again, strange raw cries. She wants to hold onto him but she can't, and she feels her right hand clawing uselessly at the quilt. He bends down so his face is a little closer to her ear.

Marianne? he says. Can we do this again like, next weekend and so on?

Whenever you want to.

He takes hold of her hair, not pulling it, just holding it in his hand. Whenever I want, really? he says.

You can do anything you want with me.

He makes a noise in his throat, leans into her a little harder. That's nice, he says.

Her voice sounds hoarse now. Do you like me saying that? she says.

Yeah, a lot.

Will you tell me I belong to you?

What do you mean? he says.

She says nothing, just breathes hard into the quilt and feels her own breath on her face. Connell pauses now, waiting for her to say something.

Will you hit me? she says.

For a few seconds she hears nothing, not even his breath.

No, he says. I don't think I want that. Sorry.

She says nothing.

Is that okay? he asks.

She still says nothing.

Do you want to stop? he says.

She nods her head. She feels his weight lift off her. She feels empty again and suddenly chill. He sits on the bed and pulls the quilt over himself. She lies there face down, not moving, unable to think of any acceptable movement.

Are you okay? he says. I'm sorry I didn't want to do that, I just think it would be weird. I mean, not weird, but . . . I don't know. I don't think it would be a good idea.

Her breasts ache from lying flat like this and her face prickles.

You think I'm weird? she says.

I didn't say that. I just meant, you know, I don't want things to be weird between us.

She feels terribly hot now, sour heat, all over her skin and in her eyes. She sits up, faces the window, pushes her hair out of her face.

I think I'm going to go home now, if that's okay, she says.

Yeah. If that's what you want.

She finds her clothes and puts them on. He starts getting dressed, he says he'll drive her home at least, and she says she wants to walk. It becomes a farcical competition between them, who can dress faster, and having a head start she finishes first and runs down the stairs. He's on the landing by the time she closes the front door behind her. Out on the street she feels like a petulant child, slamming the door on him like that while he raced out to the landing. Something has come over her, she doesn't know what it is. It reminds her of how she used to feel in Sweden, a kind of nothingness, like there's no life inside her. She hates the person she has become, without feeling any power to change anything about herself. She is someone even Connell finds disgusting, she has gone past what he can tolerate. In school they were both in the same place, both confused and somehow suffering, and ever since then she has believed that if they could return to that place together it would be the same. Now she knows that in the intervening years Connell has been growing slowly more adjusted to the world, a process of adjustment that has been steady if sometimes painful, while she herself has been degenerating, moving further and further from wholesomeness, becoming something unrecognisably debased, and they have nothing left in common at all.

By the time she lets herself into her own house it's after ten. Her mother's car isn't in the driveway and inside the hall is cool and sounds empty. She takes her sandals off and puts them on the rack, hangs her handbag on a coat hook, combs her fingers through her hair.

At the end of the hall, Alan comes up from the kitchen with a bottle of beer in his hand.

Where the fuck were you? he says.

Connell's house.

He moves in front of the staircase, swinging the bottle at his side.

You shouldn't be going over there, he says.

She shrugs. She knows a confrontation is coming now, and she can do nothing to stop it. It's moving towards her already from every direction, and there's no special move she can make, no evasive gesture, that can help her escape it.

I thought you liked him, says Marianne. You did when we were in school.

Yeah, how was I supposed to know he was fucked in the head? He's on medication and everything, did you know that?

He's doing pretty well at the moment, I think.

What is he hanging around you for, so? says Alan.

I suppose you'd have to ask him.

She tries to move towards the stairs but Alan puts his free hand down on the banister.

I don't want people going around town saying that knacker is riding my sister, says Alan.

Can I go upstairs now, please?

Alan is gripping his beer bottle very tightly. I don't want you to go near him again, he says. I'm warning you now. People in town are talking about you.

I can't imagine what my life would be like if I cared what people thought of me.

Before she's really aware of what's happening, Alan lifts his arm and throws the bottle at her. It smashes behind her on the tiles. On some level she knows that he can't have intended to hit her; they're only standing a few feet apart and it missed her completely. Still she runs past him, up the stairs. She feels her body racing through the cool interior air. He turns and follows her but she manages to make it into her room, pushing herself hard against the door, before he catches up. He tries the handle and she has to strain to keep it from turning. Then he kicks the outside of the door. Her body is vibrating with adrenaline.

You absolute freak! Alan says. Open the fucking door, I didn't do anything!

Forehead against the smooth grain of the wood, she calls out: Please just leave me alone. Go to bed, okay? I'll clean up downstairs, I won't tell Denise.

Open the door, he says.

Marianne leans the whole weight of her body against the door, her hands firmly grasping the handle, eyes screwed shut. From a young age her life has been abnormal, she knows that. But so much is covered over in time now, the way leaves fall and cover a piece of earth, and eventually mingle with the soil. Things that happened to her then are buried in the earth of her body. She tries to be a good person. But deep down she knows she is a bad person, corrupted, wrong, and all her efforts to be right, to have the right opinions, to say the right things, these efforts only disguise what is buried inside her, the evil part of herself.

Abruptly she feels the handle slip from underneath her hand and before she can step away from the door, it bangs open. She hears a cracking noise when it connects with her face, then a strange feeling inside her head. She steps backwards while Alan enters the room. There's a ringing, but it's not so much a sound as a physical sensation, like the friction of two imagined metal plates somewhere in her skull. Her nose is running. She's aware that Alan is inside the room. Her hand goes to her face. Her nose is running really quite badly. Lifting the hand away now, she sees that her fingers are covered in blood, warm blood, wet. Alan is saying something. The blood must be coming out of her face. Her vision swims diagonally and the sense of ringing increases.

Are you going to blame me for that now? says Alan.

She puts her hand back to her nose. Blood is streaming out of her face so fast that she can't stem it with her fingers. It runs over her mouth and down her chin, she can feel it. She sees it land in heavy drops on the blue carpet fibres below.

Five Minutes Later

(JULY 2014)

In the kitchen he takes a can of beer out of the fridge and sits at the table to open it. After a minute the front door opens and he hears Lorraine's keys. Hey, he says, loud enough for her to hear. She comes in and closes the kitchen door. On the lino her shoes sound sticky, like the wet sound of lips parting. He notices a fat moth resting on the lampshade overhead, not moving. Lorraine puts her hand softly on the top of his head.

Is Marianne gone home? says Lorraine.

Yeah.

What happened in the match?

I don't know, he says. I think it went to penalties.

Lorraine draws a chair back and sits down beside him. She starts taking the pins out of her hair and laying them out on the table. He takes a mouthful of beer and lets it get warm in his mouth before swallowing. The moth shuffles its wings overhead. The blind above the kitchen sink is pulled up, and he can see the faint black outline of trees against the sky outside.

And I had a fine time, thanks for asking, says Lorraine.

Sorry.

You're looking a bit dejected. Did something happen?

He shakes his head. When he saw Yvonne last week she told him he was 'making progress'. Mental healthcare professionals are always using this hygienic vocabulary, words wiped clean as whiteboards, free of connotation, sexless. She asked about his sense of 'belonging'. You used to say you felt trapped between two places, she said, not really belonging at home but not fitting in here either. Do you still feel that way? He just shrugged. The medication is doing its chemical work inside his brain now anyway, no matter what he does or says. He gets up and showers every morning, he turns up for work in the library, he doesn't really fantasise about jumping off a bridge. He takes the medication, life goes on.

Pins arranged on the table, Lorraine starts teasing her hair out loosely with her fingers.

Did you hear Isa Gleeson is pregnant? she says.

I did, yeah.

Your old friend.

He picks up the can of beer and weighs it in his hand. Isa was his first girlfriend, his first ex-girlfriend. She used to call the house phone at night after they broke up and Lorraine would answer. From up in his room, under the covers, he would hear Lorraine's voice saying: I'm sorry, sweetheart, he can't come to the phone right now. Maybe you can talk to him in school. She had braces when they were going out together, she probably doesn't have those anymore. Isa, yeah. He was shy around her. She used to do such stupid things to make him jealous, but she would act innocent, as if it wasn't clear to both of them what she was doing: maybe she really thought he couldn't see it, or maybe she couldn't see it herself. He hated that. He just withdrew from her further and further until finally, in a text message, he told her he didn't want to be her boyfriend anymore. He hasn't seen her in years now.

I don't know why she's keeping it, he says. Do you think she's one of these anti-abortion people?

Oh, is that the only reason women have babies, is it? Because of some backwards political view?

Well, from what I hear she's not together with the dad. I don't know does she even have a job.

I didn't have a job when I had you, says Lorraine.

He stares at the intricate white-and-red typeface on the can of beer, the crest of the 'B' looping back and inwards again towards itself.

And do you not regret it? he says. I know you're going to try and spare my feelings now, but honestly. Do you not think you could have had a better life if you didn't have a kid?

Lorraine turns to stare at him now, her face frozen.

Oh god, she says. Why? Is Marianne pregnant?

What? No.

She laughs, presses a hand to her breastbone. That's good, she says. Jesus.

I mean, I assume not, he adds. It wouldn't have anything to do with me if she was.

His mother pauses, hand still at her chest, and then says diplomatically: Well, that's none of my business.

What does that mean, you think I'm lying? There's nothing going on there, trust me.

For a few seconds Lorraine says nothing. He swallows some beer and puts the can down on the table. It is extremely irritating that his mother thinks he and Marianne are together, when the closest they have come in years to actually being together was earlier this evening, and it ended with him crying alone in his room.

You're just coming home every weekend to see your beloved mother, then, are you? she says.

He shrugs. If you don't want me to come home, I won't, he says.

Oh, come on now.

She gets up to fill the kettle. He watches her idly while she tamps her teabag down into her favourite cup, then he rubs at his eyes again. He feels like he has ruined the life of everyone who has ever even marginally liked him.

In April, Connell sent one of his short stories, the only really completed one, to Sadie Darcy-O'Shea. She emailed back within an hour:

Connell it's incredible! let us publish it please! xxx

When he read this message his pulse hammered all over his body, loud and hard like a machine. He had to lie down and stare at the white ceiling. Sadie was the editor of the college literary journal. Finally he sat up and wrote back:

I'm glad you liked it but I don't think it's good enough to be published yet, thanks though.

Instantly Sadie replied:

PLEASE? XXX

Connell's entire body was pounding like a conveyor belt. No one had ever read a word of his work before that moment. It was a wild new landscape of experience. He paced around the room massaging his neck for a while. Then he typed back:

Ok, how about this, you can publish it under a pseudonym. But you also have to promise you won't tell anyone who wrote it, even the other people who edit the magazine. Ok?

Sadie wrote back:

haha so mysterious, I love it! thank you my darling! my lips are forever sealed xxx

His story appeared, unedited, in the May issue of the magazine. He found a copy in the Arts Block the morning it was printed and flipped straight to the page where the story appeared, under the pseudonym 'Conor McCready'. That doesn't even sound like a real name, he thought. All around him in the Arts Block people were filing into morning lectures, holding coffee and talking. On the first page of the text alone Connell noticed two errors. He had to shut the magazine for a few seconds then and take deep breaths. Students and faculty members continued to walk past, heedless of his turmoil. He reopened the magazine and continued reading. Another error. He wanted to crawl under a plant and burrow into the earth. That was it, the end of the publication ordeal. Because no one knew he had written the story he could not canvass anyone's reaction, and he never heard from a single soul whether it was considered good or bad. In time he began to believe it had only been published in the first place because Sadie was lacking material for an upcoming deadline. Overall the experience had caused him far more distress than pleasure. Nonetheless he kept two copies of the magazine, one in Dublin and one under his mattress at home.

How come Marianne went home so early? says Lorraine.

I don't know.

Is that why you're in a foul mood?

What's the implication? he says. I'm pining after her, is that what you're saying?

Lorraine opens her hands as if to say she doesn't know, and then sits back down waiting for the kettle to boil. He's embarrassed now, which makes him cross. Whatever there is between him and Marianne, nothing good has ever come of it. It has only ever caused confusion and misery for everyone. He can't help Marianne, no matter what he does. There's something frightening about her, some huge emptiness in the pit of her being. It's like waiting for a lift to arrive and when the doors open nothing is there, just the terrible dark emptiness of the elevator shaft, on and on forever. She's missing some primal instinct, self-defence or self-preservation, which makes other human beings comprehensible. You lean in expecting resistance, and everything just falls away in front of you. Still, he would lie down and die for her at any minute, which is the only thing he knows about himself that makes him feel like a worthwhile person.

What happened tonight was inevitable. He knows how he could make it sound, to Yvonne, or even to Niall, or some other imagined interlocutor: Marianne is a masochist and Connell is simply too nice of a guy to hit a woman. This, after all, is the literal level on which the incident took place. She asked him to hit her and when he said he didn't want to, she wanted to stop having sex. So why, despite its factual accuracy, does this feel like a dishonest way of narrating what happened? What is the missing element, the excluded part of the story that explains

247

what upset them both? It has something to do with their history, he knows that. Ever since school he has understood his power over her. How she responds to his look or the touch of his hand. The way her face colours, and she goes still as if awaiting some spoken order. His effortless tyranny over someone who seems, to other people, so invulnerable. He has never been able to reconcile himself to the idea of losing this hold over her, like a key to an empty property, left available for future use. In fact he has cultivated it, and he knows he has.

What's left for them, then? There doesn't seem to be a halfway position anymore. Too much has passed between them for that. So it's over, and they're just nothing? What would it even mean, to be nothing to her? He could avoid her, but as soon as he saw her again, even if they only glanced at one another outside a lecture hall, the glance could not contain nothing. He could never really want it to. He has sincerely wanted to die, but he has never sincerely wanted Marianne to forget about him. That's the only part of himself he wants to protect, the part that exists inside her.

The kettle comes to the boil. Lorraine sweeps the line of hairpins into the palm of her hand, closes her fist around them and pockets them. She gets up then, fills the cup of tea, adds milk, and puts the bottle back in the fridge. He watches her.

Okay, she says. Time for bed.

Alright. Sleep well.

He hears her touch the handle of the door behind him but it doesn't open. He turns around and she's standing there, looking at him.

I don't regret it, by the way, she says. Having a baby. It was the best decision I've ever made in my life. I love you more than anything and I'm very proud that you're my son. I hope you know that.

He looks back at her. Quickly he clears his throat.

I love you too, he says.

Goodnight, then.

She closes the door behind her. He listens to her footsteps up the stairs. After a few minutes have passed he gets up, empties the dregs of his beer down the sink and puts the can quietly in the recycling bin.

On the table his phone starts ringing. It's set to vibrate so it starts shimmying around the surface of the table, catching the light. He goes to get it before it falls over the edge, and he sees it's Marianne calling. He pauses. He looks at the screen. Finally he slides the answer button.

Hey, he says.

He can hear her breath hard on the other end of the line. He asks if she's okay.

I'm really sorry about this, she says. I feel like an idiot.

Her voice in the phone sounds clouded, like she has a bad cold, or something in her mouth. Connell swallows and walks over to the kitchen window.

About earlier? he says. I've been thinking about it as well.

No, it's not that. It's really stupid. I just tripped or something and I have a small injury. I'm sorry to bother you about it. It's nothing. I just don't know what to do.

He puts his hand on the sink.

Where are you? he says.

I'm at home. It's not serious, it just hurts, that's all. I don't really know why I'm calling. I'm sorry.

Can I come get you?

She pauses. In a muffled voice she replies: Yes, please.

I'm on my way, he says. I'm getting in the car right now, okay?

Sandwiching the phone between his ear and shoulder, he fishes his left shoe out from under the table and pulls it on.

This is really nice of you, says Marianne in his ear.

I'll see you in a few minutes. I'm leaving right now. Alright? See you soon.

Outside he gets in the car and starts the engine. The radio comes on and he snaps it off with a flat hand. His breath isn't right. After only one drink he feels out of it, not alert enough, or too alert, twitchy. The car is too silent but he can't stand the idea of the radio. His hands feel damp on the steering wheel. Turning left onto Marianne's street, he can see the light in her bedroom window. He indicates and pulls into the empty driveway. When he shuts the car door behind him, the noise echoes off the stone facade of the house.

He rings the doorbell, and almost straight away the door opens. Marianne is standing there, her right hand on the door, her left hand covering her face, holding a crumpled tissue. Her eyes are puffy like she's been crying. Connell notices that her T-shirt, her skirt and part of her left wrist are stained with blood. The proportions of the visual environment around him shudder in and out of focus, like someone has picked up the world and shaken it, hard.

What happened? he says.

Footsteps come thumping down the stairs behind her. Connell, as if viewing the scene through some kind of cosmic telescope, sees her brother reach the bottom of the staircase.

Why have you got blood on you? says Connell.

I think my nose is broken, she says.

Who's that? says Alan behind her. Who's at the door?

Do you need to go to hospital? says Connell.

She shakes her head, she says it doesn't need emergency attention, she looked it up online. She can go to the doctor tomorrow if it still hurts. Connell nods.

Was it him? says Connell.

She nods. Her eyes have a frightened look.

Get in the car, Connell says.

She looks at him, not moving her hands. Her face is still covered with the tissue. He shakes the keys.

Go, he says.

She takes her hand from the door and opens her palm. He puts the keys into it and, still looking at him, she walks outside.

Where are you going? says Alan.

Connell stands just inside the front door now. A coloured haze sweeps over the driveway as he watches Marianne get into the car.

What's going on here? says Alan.

Once she's safely inside the car, Connell closes over the front door, so that he and Alan are alone together.

What are you doing? says Alan.

Connell, his sight even blurrier now, can't tell whether Alan is angry or frightened.

I need to talk to you, Connell says.

His vision is swimming so severely that he notices he has to keep a hand on the door to stay upright.

I didn't do anything, says Alan.

Connell walks towards Alan until Alan is standing with his back against the banister. He seems smaller now, and scared.

He calls for his mother, turning his head until his neck strains, but no one appears from up the stairs. Connell's face is wet with perspiration. Alan's face is visible only as a pattern of coloured dots.

If you ever touch Marianne again, I'll kill you, he says. Okay? That's all. Say one bad thing to her ever again and I'll come back here myself and kill you, that's it.

It seems to Connell, though he can't see or hear very well, that Alan is now crying.

Do you understand me? Connell says. Say yes or no.

Alan says: Yes.

Connell turns around, walks out the front door and closes it behind him.

In the car Marianne is waiting silently, one hand clutched to her face, the other lying limp in her lap. Connell sits in the driver's seat and wipes his mouth with his sleeve. They are sealed into the car's compact silence together. He looks at her. She's bent over her lap a little, as if in pain.

I'm sorry to bother you, she says. I'm sorry. I didn't know what to do.

Don't say sorry. It's good you called me. Okay? Look at me for a second. No one is going to hurt you like that again.

She looks at him above the veil of white tissue, and in a rush he feels his power over her again, the openness in her eyes.

Everything's going to be alright, he says. Trust me. I love you, I'm not going to let anything like that happen to you again.

For a second or two she holds his gaze and then finally she closes her eyes. She sits back in the passenger seat, head against the headrest, hand still clutching the tissue at her face. It seems to him an attitude of extreme weariness, or relief.

Thank you, she says.

He starts the car and pulls out of the driveway. His vision has settled, objects have solidified before his eyes again, and he can breathe. Overhead trees wave silvery individual leaves in silence.

Seven Months Later

(FEBRUARY 2015)

In the kitchen Marianne pours hot water on the coffee. The sky is low and woollen out the window, and while the coffee brews she goes and places her forehead on the glass. Gradually the mist of her breath hides the college from view: the trees turn soft, the Old Library a heavy cloud. Students crossing Front Square in winter coats, arms folded, disappear into smudges and then disappear entirely. Marianne is neither admired nor reviled anymore. People have forgotten about her. She's a normal person now. She walks by and no one looks up. She swims in the college pool, eats in the Dining Hall with damp hair, walks around the cricket pitch in the evening. Dublin is extraordinarily beautiful to her in wet weather, the way grey stone darkens to black, and rain moves over the grass and whispers on slick roof tiles. Raincoats glistening in the undersea colour of street lamps. Rain silver as loose change in the glare of traffic.

She wipes the window with her sleeve and goes to get cups from the press. She has work from ten until two today and then a seminar on modern France. At work she answers emails telling people that her boss is unavailable for meetings. It's unclear to her what he really does. He's never available to meet any of the people who want to meet him, so she concludes that he's either very busy or just permanently idle. When he appears in the office he often provocatively lights a cigarette, as if to test Marianne. But what is the nature of the test? She sits there at her desk breathing in her usual way. He likes to talk about how intelligent he is. It's boring to listen to him but not strenuous. At the end of the week he hands her an envelope full of cash. Joanna was shocked when she heard about that. What is he doing paying you in cash? she said. Is he like a drug dealer or something? Marianne said she thought he was some kind of property developer. Oh, said Joanna. Wow, that's much worse.

Marianne presses the coffee and fills two cups. In one cup: a quarter-spoon of sugar, a splash of milk. The other cup just black, no sugar. She puts them on the tray as usual, pads up the hallway and knocks the corner of the tray on the door. No response. She hefts the tray against her hip with her left hand and opens the door with her right. The room smells dense, like sweat and stale alcohol, and the yellow curtains over the sash window are still shut. She clears a space on the desk to put the tray down, and then sits on the wheelie chair to drink her coffee. It tastes slightly sour, not unlike the air around her. This is a pleasant time of day for Marianne, before work begins. When her cup is empty she reaches a hand out and lifts a corner of the curtain with her fingers. White light floods the desk.

Presently, from the bed, Connell says: I am awake actually.

How are you feeling?

Alright, yeah.

She brings him the cup of black unsweetened coffee. He rolls over in bed and addresses her with small squinting eyes. She sits down on the mattress.

Sorry about last night, he says.

Sadie has a thing for you, you know.

Do you think?

He pulls his pillow up against the headboard and takes the cup from her hands. After one large mouthful he swallows and looks at Marianne again, still squinting so that his left eye is screwed shut.

Wouldn't be remotely my type, he adds.

I never know with you.

He shakes his head, drinks another mouthful of coffee, swallows.

Yes you do, he says. You like to think of people as mysterious, but I'm really not a mysterious person.

She considers this while he finishes his cup of coffee.

I guess everyone is a mystery in a way, she says. I mean, you can never really know another person, and so on.

Yeah. Do you actually think that, though?

It's what people say.

What do I not know about you? he says.

Marianne smiles, yawns, lifts her hands in a shrug.

People are a lot more knowable than they think they are, he adds.

Can I get in the shower first or do you want to?

No, you go. Can I use your laptop to check some emails and stuff?

Yeah, go ahead, she says.

In the bathroom the light is blue and clinical. She opens the shower door and turns the handle, waits for the water to get warm. In the meantime she brushes her teeth quickly, spits white lather neatly down the drain, and takes her hair down from the knot at the back of her neck. Then she strips off her dressing gown and hangs it on the back of the bathroom door.

Back in November, when the new editor of the college literary magazine resigned, Connell offered to step in until they could find someone else. Months later no one else has come forward and Connell is still editing the magazine himself. Last night was the launch party for the new issue, and Sadie Darcy-O'Shea brought a bowl of bright-pink vodka punch with little pieces of fruit floating in it. Sadie likes to show up at these events to squeeze Connell's arm and have private discussions with him about his 'career'. Last night he drank so much punch that he fell over when attempting to stand up. Marianne felt this was in some sense Sadie's fault, although, on the other hand, it was undeniably Connell's. Later, when Marianne got him back home and into bed, he asked her for a glass of water, which he spilled all over himself and on the duvet before passing out.

Last summer she read one of Connell's stories for the first time. It gave her such a peculiar sense of him as a person to sit there with the printed pages, folded over in the top-left corner because he had no staples. In a way she felt very close to him while reading, as if she was witnessing his most private thoughts, but she also felt him turned away from her, focused on some complex task of his own, one she could never be part of. Of course, Sadie can never be part of that task either, not really, but at least she's a writer, with a hidden imaginary life of her own. Marianne's life happens strictly in the real world, populated by real individuals. She thinks of Connell saying: People are a lot more knowable than they think they are. But still he has something she lacks, an inner life that does not include the other person.

She used to wonder if he really loved her. In bed he would say lovingly: You're going to do exactly what I say now, aren't you? He knew how to give her what she wanted, to leave her open, weak, powerless, sometimes crying. He understood that it wasn't necessary to hurt her: he could let her submit willingly, without violence. This all seemed to happen on the deepest possible level of her personality. But on what level did it happen to him? Was it just a game, or a favour he was doing her? Did he feel it, the way she did? Every day, in the ordinary activity of their lives, he showed patience and consideration for her feelings. He took care of her when she was sick, he read drafts of her college essays, he sat and listened while she talked about her ideas, disagreeing with herself out loud and changing her mind. But did he love her? Sometimes she felt like saying: Would you miss me, if you didn't have me anymore? She had asked him that once on the ghost estate, when they were just kids. He had said yes then, but she'd been the only thing in his life at that time, the only thing he had to himself, and it would never be that way again.

By the start of December their friends were asking about Christmas plans. Marianne still hadn't seen her family since the summer. Her mother had never tried to contact her at all. Alan had sent some text messages saying things like: Mum is not speaking to you, she says you are a disgrace. Marianne hadn't replied. She'd rehearsed in her head what kind of conversation it would be when her mother did finally get in touch, what accusations would be made, which truths she would insist on. But it never happened. Her birthday came and went without a word from home. Then it was December and she was planning to stay in college alone for Christmas and get some work done on the dissertation she was writing on Irish carceral institutions after independence. Connell wanted her to come back to Carricklea with him. Lorraine would love to have you, he said. I'll call her, you should talk to her about it. In the end Lorraine called Marianne herself and personally invited her to stay for Christmas. Marianne, trusting that Lorraine knew what was right, accepted.

On the way home from Dublin in the car, she and Connell talked without stopping, joking and putting on funny voices to make each other laugh. Looking back now, Marianne wonders if they were nervous. When they got to Foxfield it was dark and the windows were full of coloured lights. Connell carried their bags in from the boot. In the living room Marianne sat by the fire while Lorraine made tea. The tree, packed between the television and couch, was blinking light in repetitive patterns. Connell came in carrying a cup of tea and put it on the arm of her chair. Before sitting down he stopped to rearrange a piece of tinsel. It did look much better where he put it. Marianne's face and hands were very hot by the fire. Lorraine came in and started telling Connell about which relatives had visited already, and which were visiting tomorrow, and so on. Marianne felt so relaxed then that she almost wanted to close her eyes and sleep.

The house in Foxfield was busy over Christmas. Late into the night people would be arriving and leaving, brandishing wrapped biscuit tins or bottles of whiskey. Children ran past at knee height yelling unintelligibly. Someone brought a PlayStation over one night and Connell stayed up until two in the morning playing FIFA with one of his younger cousins, their bodies greenish in the screen light, a look of almost religious intensity on Connell's face. Marianne and Lorraine were in the kitchen mostly, rinsing dirty glasses in the sink, opening chocolate boxes, endlessly refilling the kettle. Once they heard a voice exclaim from the front room: Connell has a girlfriend? And another voice replied: Yeah, she's in the kitchen. Lorraine and Marianne exchanged a look. They heard a brief thunder of footsteps, and then a teenage boy appeared in the doorway wearing a United jersey. Immediately on seeing Marianne, who was standing at the sink, the boy became shy and stared at his feet. Hi there, she said. He flicked her a nod without making eye contact, and then trudged a retreat to the living room. Lorraine thought that was really funny.

On New Year's Eve they saw Marianne's mother in the supermarket. She was wearing a dark suit with a yellow silk blouse. She always looked so 'put together'. Lorraine said hello politely and Denise just walked past, not speaking, eyes ahead. No one knew what she believed her grievance was. In the car after the supermarket Lorraine reached back from the passenger seat to squeeze Marianne's hand. Connell started the car. What do people in town think of her? Marianne said.

Who, your mother? said Lorraine.

I mean, how do people see her?

With a sympathetic expression Lorraine said gently: I suppose she'd be considered a bit odd.

It was the first time Marianne had heard that, or even thought about it. Connell didn't engage in the conversation. That night he wanted to go out to Kelleher's for New Year's. He said everyone from school was going. Marianne suggested she might just stay in and he appeared to consider this for a moment before saying: No, you should come out. She lay face down on the bed while he changed out of one shirt into another one. Far be it from me to disobey an order, she said. He looked in the mirror and caught her eye. Yeah, exactly, he said.

Kelleher's was packed that night and damp with heat. Connell was right, everyone from school was there. They kept having to wave at people from a distance and mouth greetings. Karen saw them at the bar and threw her arms around Marianne, smelling of some faint but very pleasant perfume. I'm so glad to see you, Marianne said. Come and dance with us, said Karen. Connell carried their drinks down the steps to the dance floor, where Rachel and Eric were standing, and Lisa and Jack, and Ciara Heffernan who had been in the year below. Eric gave them a mock-bow for some reason. Probably he was drunk. It was too loud to have an ordinary conversation. Connell held Marianne's drink while she took her coat off and stowed it under a table. No one was really dancing, just standing around shouting in each other's ears. Karen occasionally made a cute boxing motion, as if punching the air. Other people joined them, including some people Marianne had never seen before, and everyone embraced and yelled things.

At midnight when they all cheered Happy New Year, Connell took Marianne into his arms and kissed her. She could feel, like a physical pressure on her skin, that the others were watching them. Maybe people hadn't really believed it until then, or else a morbid fascination still lingered over something that had once been scandalous. Maybe they were just curious to observe the chemistry between two people who, over the course of several years, apparently could not leave one another alone. Marianne had to admit that she, also, probably would have glanced. When they drew apart Connell looked her in the eyes and said: I love you. She was laughing then, and her face was red. She was in his power, he had chosen to redeem her, she was redeemed. It was so unlike him to behave that way in public that he must have been doing it on purpose, to please her. How strange to feel herself so completely under the control of another person, but also how ordinary. No one can be independent of other people completely, so why not give up the attempt, she thought, go running in the other direction, depend on people for everything, allow them to depend on you, why not. She knows he loves her, she doesn't wonder about that anymore.

She climbs out of the shower now and wraps herself in the blue bath towel. The mirror is steamed over. She opens the door and from the bed Connell looks back at her. Hello, she says. The stale air in the room feels cool on her skin. He's sitting up in bed with her laptop on his lap. She goes to her chest of drawers, finds some clean underwear, starts to get dressed. He's watching her. She hangs the towel on the wardrobe door and puts her arms through the sleeves of a shirt.

Is something up? she says.

I just got this email.

Oh? From who?

He looks dumbly at the laptop and then back at her. His eyes look red and sleepy. She's doing the shirt buttons. He's sitting with his knees propped up under the duvet, the laptop glowing into his face.

Connell, from who? she says.

From this university in New York. It looks like they're offering me a place on the MFA. You know, the creative writing programme.

She stands there. Her hair is still wet, soaking slowly through the cloth of her blouse.

You didn't tell me you applied for that, she says.

He just looks at her.

I mean, congratulations, she says. I'm not surprised they would accept you, I'm just surprised you didn't mention it.

He nods, his face inexpressive, and then looks back at the laptop.

I don't know, he says. I should have told you but I honestly thought it was such a long shot.

Well, that's no reason not to tell me.

It doesn't matter, he adds. It's not like I'm going to go. I don't even know why I applied.

Marianne lifts the towel off the wardrobe door and starts using it to massage the ends of her hair slowly. She sits down at the desk chair.

Did Sadie know you were applying? she says.

What? Why do you ask that?

Did she?

Well, yeah, he says. I don't see the relevance, though.

Why did you tell her and not me?

He sighs, rubbing his eyes with his fingertips, and then shrugs.

I don't know, he says. She's the one who told me to apply. I thought it was a stupid idea honestly, hence why I didn't tell you.

Are you in love with her?

Connell stares across the room at Marianne, not moving or breaking eye contact for several seconds. It's hard to tell what his face is expressing. Eventually she looks away to rearrange the towel.

Are you joking? he says.

Why don't you answer the question?

You're getting a lot of stuff messed up here, Marianne. I don't even like Sadie as a friend, okay, frankly I find her annoying. I don't know how many times I have to say that to you. I'm sorry I didn't tell you about the application thing but like, how does that make you jump to the conclusion that I'm in love with someone else?

Marianne keeps rubbing the towel into the ends of her hair.

I don't know, she says eventually. Sometimes I feel like you want to be around people who understand you.

Yeah, which is you. If I had to make a list of people who severely don't understand me, Sadie would be right up there.

Marianne goes quiet again. Connell has closed the laptop now.

I'm sorry I didn't tell you, okay? he says. Sometimes I feel embarrassed telling you stuff like that because it just seems stupid. To be honest, I still look up to you a lot, I don't want you to think of me as, I don't know. Deluded.

She squeezes her hair through the towel, feeling the coarse, grainy texture of the individual strands.

You should go, she says. To New York, I mean. You should accept the offer, you should go.

He says nothing. She looks up. The wall behind him is yellow like a slab of butter.

No, he says.

I'm sure you could get funding.

Why are you saying this? I thought you wanted to stay here next year.

I can stay, and you can go, she says. It's just a year. I think you should do it.

He makes a strange, confused noise, almost like a laugh. He touches his neck. She puts the towel down and starts brushing the knots out of her hair slowly.

That's ridiculous, he says. I'm not going to New York without you. I wouldn't even be here if it wasn't for you.

It's true, she thinks, he wouldn't be. He would be somewhere else entirely, living a different kind of life. He would be different with women even, and his aspirations for love would be different. And Marianne herself, she would be another person completely. Would she ever have been happy? And what kind of happiness might it have been? All these years they've been like two little plants sharing the same plot of soil, growing around one another, contorting to make room, taking certain unlikely positions. But in the end she has done something for him, she's made a new life possible, and she can always feel good about that.

I'd miss you too much, he says. I'd be sick, honestly.

At first. But it would get better.

They sit in silence now, Marianne moving the brush methodically through her hair, feeling for knots and slowly, patiently untangling them. There's no point in being impatient anymore.

You know I love you, says Connell. I'm never going to feel the same way for someone else.

She nods, okay. He's telling the truth.

To be honest, I don't know what to do, he says. Say you want me to stay and I will.

She closes her eyes. He probably won't come back, she

thinks. Or he will, differently. What they have now they can never have back again. But for her the pain of loneliness will be nothing to the pain that she used to feel, of being unworthy. He brought her goodness like a gift and now it belongs to her. Meanwhile his life opens out before him in all directions at once. They've done a lot of good for each other. Really, she thinks, really. People can really change one another.

You should go, she says. I'll always be here. You know that.

Acknowledgements

Thanks: firstly to John Patrick McHugh, who was with this novel long before I had finished writing it, and whose conversation and guidance contributed so substantially to its development; to Thomas Morris for his thoughtful, detailed feedback on the manuscript; to David Hartery and Tim MacGabhann for reading early drafts of the novel's opening chapters and offering wise advice; to Ken Armstrong, Iarla Mongey and all the members of the Castlebar writers' group for their early support of my writing; to Tracy Bohan for doing pretty much everything other than actually writing the book; to Mitzi Angel, who has made this a better novel and me a better writer; to John's family; to my own family, and particularly to my parents; to Kate Oliver and Aoife Comey, as ever, for their friendship; and to John, for everything.